I0760915

# Hidden Gem

ENNI AMANDA

2nd edition, 2023



ISBN 978-0-473-58772-7 (paperback)
ISBN 978-1-99-116507-7 (hardcover)
ISBN 978-0-473-58773-4 (EPUB)
ISBN 978-0-473-58774-1 (Kindle)
Designed by Yummy Book Covers
Typeset in PT Serif, 10pt

*To James, who shared his knowledge,*
*and to Fraser, who shared his pain.*

# Hidden Gem

# Chapter 1

Marnie snapped her fingers, waiting for her 15-year-old daughter to look up from her phone. "Can you please pay attention? I won't be here to do this for you."

Tanya had spent the last half-hour filming herself and was busy posting something on TikTok. She expelled a disdainful huff and dropped the phone two inches. "I was just about to post." Her gaze landed on the row of sealed plastic containers. "Is that all the same stuff?"

Marnie took a calming breath, reminding herself that she was dealing with a developing brain, not a fully formed human. "Half of these are cannelloni, half lasagne. They didn't have a lot of choice, and I don't have time to cook right now. You can mix it up, make a different salad every day. I'll be gone a week, and this should last you four or five days. You'll have to cook something at least a couple of times, okay?"

Tanya's carefully pencilled eyebrows shot up. "Like what?"

Marnie opened the pantry and rummaged through the contents. Why hadn't she stocked up on noodles? She'd practically run through the supermarket, desperate to organise herself so she could get on the road. The sooner she could convince herself that her teenage daughter wouldn't starve or burn down the house, the sooner she'd be out of town, taking calming breaths and achieving clarity. That was the plan, anyway.

Tuna. Pasta. Cheese. That would do. Marnie pulled the ingredients from the fridge and pantry and slammed them on the kitchen counter. "This is easy. Just cook the pasta, throw in some tuna and grate the cheese. It'll be great."

Tanya wrinkled her nose. "Why do you have to go so far away? Can't you write at home?"

"I need peace and quiet." Marnie scribbled the week's menu on the notepad and found enough magnets to fasten it on the refrigerator. "Here you go. Just follow this as a guide. You can't live on toast."

"Or you could give me enough money to order food?"

Marnie rubbed her forehead. This was her own fault. She'd been the housekeeper, the chauffeur, the ATM. With her firstborn, Tom, she'd somehow succeeded. He'd grown into an independent, functioning adult. An artist. Maybe she'd worked harder. She'd been freshly divorced, trying to prove something to her ex-husband. With Tanya, she'd cruised on autopilot and evidently created a human incapable of the simplest household chores.

Stacking the food back in storage, Marnie found her wallet and placed five twenty-dollar notes in her daughter's hand. Yes, she'd messed up, but now was not the time to fix this. She'd try again upon her return.

"No McDonald's!" she called as Tanya turned and headed to her bedroom. "Try to find something with nutritional value, please!"

Tanya stopped at her bedroom doorway, throwing a glance at her mother. "Like ginger kisses? Blueberry muffins?"

Marnie lifted her eyes heavenward, counting to ten. She'd been good lately, following her workout regimen and a decent diet, but Tanya knew her weaknesses. Still, it was pointless to argue with 15-year-olds; they dragged you down to their level. Swallowing the comebacks, Marnie located her cardigan and sneakers by the door.

Tanya's icy voice cut through the room as she watched her getting dressed. "Are you really going out in public like that?"

"What? It's cold." Marnie examined her outfit in the full-length mirror by the front door. Okay, her trusted cardigan resembled a worn-out sheep costume, but it kept her warm.

"Yeah, that thing's hideous, but I'm talking about your

hair."

Without even looking, Marnie could hear the eye-roll in Tanya's voice. She had a point. The perpetually wet autumn weather had turned her chestnut curls into a matted, furry mess that matched the texture of her cardigan.

"It's fine."

She combed her fingers through the damp tangles, disregarding the teenage snipes. She was driving to a remote cabin in Paraparaumu, a sleepy seaside village on the West Coast, the cheapest last-minute booking she could find. A bit farther away than she'd have liked, but the six-hour drive would give her time to think.

Tanya's face appeared in the mirror, two perfectly lined eyes peering over Marnie's shoulder. She cocked her head, lips puckered. "You've lost weight."

"Five kilos," Marnie confirmed, pride flushing her cheeks. She'd worked hard, and finally, her clothes felt a little loose.

Tanya frowned. "Then why do you dress like that? It looks like you're covering up rolls of fat, but you're not even fat anymore. Not like... properly fat."

Marnie wondered what constituted 'properly fat' but didn't ask. "I'm not going out in public. No one will see me."

"You still don't have to look like a wet dog wrapped in a blanket." Tanya turned on her heels and headed for the stairs again.

"Love you, too!" Marnie flashed her daughter a pained smile. "Remember, you have to leave for school in half an hour."

Marnie picked up her suitcase and rolled her blanket-adorned self out the door, letting out a long sigh as the lock clicked behind her. Tanya would be fine. What she lacked in domestic skills, she made up for in sass.

Marnie hoisted her suitcase into her station wagon and climbed behind the wheel. Before starting the car, she sent a text to Shasa, her best friend and next-door neighbour.

*Leaving now. Tanya should be sorted for food. If you can check in every night to see that she's eaten and done her homework, that would be amazing.*

Shasa was at work, but she'd promised to check in with Tanya.

Marnie dropped her phone on the passenger seat. Tanya would be fine, but what about her? As she turned the key in the ignition, pain shot through her fingers. Panic fluttered around her stomach like a deranged moth searching for light. This is why she had to get on the road and just drive.

Three hours later, she stared at the motorway stretching ahead of her. The long drive had rendered her bottom numb, but her mind remained restless. Her phone buzzed to life on the front seat. She glanced at it, deciding it was time for a break. Spotting a rest stop ahead, she pulled over.

Stretching her aching fingers, she picked up the phone. Tom. As she read the text, her breath caught in her throat.

**Tom:** Cancel everything, Mum!!! You're my plus one for a gala at the Beehive! This Saturday, 8pm. They chose my painting!!! Please tell me you can make it. Tanya said you're driving this way.

Marnie stared at the words, her chest swelling. She didn't notice her tears until one fell on the screen, blurring the words. Her 20-year-old son's artwork had been chosen among hundreds to be displayed at an event in the parliament building, known by locals as the Beehive.

This Saturday? The timing couldn't be worse. Technically, the cabin she'd booked was only an hour's drive from Wellington, and the Beehive. She was driving in the right direction, but for the wrong reason. She'd planned to hole up in the cabin in her sweatpants for a week to work on her next book. She could hardly wait to light up the fireplace and curl up on what, based on the photos, looked like a very comfortable couch. She wasn't prepared for a gala. She wasn't even prepared for an upmarket mall.

Marnie stared at the rain-soaked vista of grass and powerlines along the main road. She'd already passed the higher ground of Tongariro National Park. No more mountain tops in the horizon, only endless, rain-beaten grass dotted by large trees, with cows grazing in the distance. The late summer mugginess had shifted to autumn's constant wind and rain. Unseasonably cold, they said. Miserable. It suited her mood.

The swelling and pain in her fingers each morning wasn't just the result of too much keyboard time. She'd been diagnosed with early onset arthritis, and she was only 39. Her doctor had reassured her it was treatable, and she was lucky to get diagnosed early, but so far, the drugs hadn't made any difference to the constant pain and swelling in her fingers, elbows and ankles. She felt jealous of the ladies in her writing group dealing with the far more common and more easily manageable osteoarthritis. If it had to happen, why couldn't she get that in her sixties like everyone else? Why did she have to get the rare, aggressive disease? And why this early?

Since the divorce, she'd wasted five years hibernating, gathering courage to join the dating scene. With relatively smooth skin, she looked younger than her years. She had a bit of extra padding, but nothing truly drooped yet. She'd been on a diet, planning to reinvent herself. Once she worked up the courage, she'd wear something a bit more eye-catching, and put herself out there. She'd even joined the gym and done whatever Sergei, her ex-army Serbian trainer with a wonderful talent for barking orders, told her to do, surprising herself by sticking to the routine for months.

Now she had a rather nice waistline and a thigh gap – if she wore special tights and stuck her bum out, which probably didn't count as a true thigh gap. Why did a grown woman need such a thing anyway? To let flies through without circling your bottom? Either way, toning her thighs felt like a waste of time. How could she keep up her exercise routine with aching joints? She wasn't a masochist. If the pain forced her to permanently curl up under a blanket, she'd lose all the progress.

Marnie sighed, trying to shake off the dark thoughts. Nobody could avoid aging, but she didn't want to do this alone. You were meant to find your soulmate in your vital youth, right? Like the way she'd been when she'd found Steve – two rosy-cheeked high school students. If only that had worked out.

Marnie dropped the phone in her lap and massaged her aching fingers, trying to warm them up. She tilted her hands in the cool daylight. Did they look swollen? Was it getting worse? She'd stopped at a pharmacy on the way and picked up her prescription and a pile of supplements the lovely pharmacist had recommended. Anti-aging. Anti-something-else. Despite the recurring waves of desperation, she wasn't giving up. Not yet.

Shasa, her best friend was six years younger, still high on the new love she'd found with Mac, happily planning a wedding. Marnie was her maid of honour. She planned to tell everyone about her diagnosis later, when she'd had a chance to digest the news. There was no need to spread the anti-joy just yet. Shasa deserved another week of happy wedding preparations without worrying about whether her maid-of-honour could stand in heels.

Marnie sank into the driver's seat, tucking her unruly curls behind her ears. They'd dried on the way, fluffing into a soft cloud around her face, like a clown who'd missed a haircut. The phone slipped between her thighs, and she fished it out, staring at the text.

She had to reply to Tom. His lovely gesture reminded her of the big-hearted boy he'd been all those years ago, sharing his lunchbox with schoolmates, sometimes to the point that he came home hungry. Sweet and handsome, he could have his pick of potential dates, but he wanted to take his mother. Marnie shook her head in disbelief, re-reading the message. If she said no, he'd be free to ask someone else, someone his own age who looked good in a cocktail dress and could hold a champagne glass without joint paint.

But before she could form her reply, her phone pinged again.

> **Tom:** I know you'll be worried about what to wear, so I booked a stylist. It's all paid for, including the clothes. Non-refundable. So, get here by 10am Saturday. I'm counting on you.

Tom had done well with commissions lately, but how could he afford this? How much did a stylist cost?

Marnie took a deep breath and considered her options. It was Friday. She could go to the cabin, stay for one night, then make her way to Wellington on Saturday morning. Maybe she could do this. Tom only needed her for one night. She'd get dolled up, bound with whale-bone corsets or whatever they needed to do to make her presentable, and the next day she'd return to her remote cabin for almost a week of uninterrupted hiding, just as she'd planned.

This was such a big deal for Tom. She had to put her troubles aside and enjoy it. Which meant she had to make some arrangements. Step one – book a hotel room in the city for Saturday night. She couldn't drive back to the cabin in the middle of the night, possibly tipsy. Step two – comfortable shoes. Maybe the stylist Tom had found could help her with that.

The idea of being dressed up by someone else made her stomach lurch but she fixed her mind on the positive. This could be her last hurrah, her one glamorous night before she shifted her focus on getting well. A tiny flicker of excitement entered her mind, like a pinprick of light that gradually grew brighter. She'd find a way forward and enjoy what she could.

Marnie wiped another tear off her phone screen and typed,

**Marnie:** So proud of you!!! I'm on my way.

# Chapter 2

Jason turned over on the crispy white sheets and flipped his pillow. The alarm clock on the nightstand read 01:35 a.m. Traffic noise from the street below competed with the whirring air-con. He should have chosen a place farther from the city centre, although it probably wouldn't have helped. Since starting his second term as Associate Minister of Housing, he'd struggled to sleep. His government allowance paid for the serviced apartment across the road from the Beehive, but he'd tried various other hotels and Airbnbs in and around Wellington. He would have paid anything for a good night's sleep, but it didn't matter where he stayed – he could no longer sleep.

As soon as he returned to his cottage by Lake Rotoroa in Hamilton, he slept a little better. Still not great but putting distance between himself and the capital city seemed to calm his mind a notch. If only he could make it home every weekend, but with his new high-profile role, it was hard to get away for a proper break.

Life had been much easier in his junior MP days, working on members' bills, writing articles and giving the occasional speech. He'd been excited about everything, sitting on committees, pushing through petitions. In his first term, Jason had been unknown, able to come and go as he pleased. But after the last election, things had changed. With a few well-timed interviews and events, he'd risen to semi-stardom that put him under the microscope. Now it was time to make good on his election promises: to address the chronic housing shortage, which had created inflated prices and massive inequality; and to fix the runaway market with unsustainable price growth.

Everyone was watching and waiting. But the housing market was out of control, making it look like everything the government did only exacerbated the problem. Maybe it did. Nobody seemed to have any answers. Still, Jason couldn't shake the weight of responsibility. He was here to fix things, not to make them worse. The countless angry emails didn't help, or the members of the public who now recognised him in the street and hurled abuse. His high profile was supposed to help him create real change but instead it made him a target.

He had to stop thinking about all that. Another wave of exhaustion flooded his head, making him sink into the pillow. The moment of bliss before drifting off. If only. Within a couple of minutes, he woke again, heart pounding in his chest, sweat forming on his brow.

*Everything's fine. There's no reason to panic.*

Gradually, his pulse settled, and his earlier fatigue crept back. But he knew better than to trust it. Jason pushed himself up on the bed and reached for his laptop. His fingers flew over the keyboard, inputting his own name in Google. He browsed the latest search results – a list of articles, blog posts and online discussions. He sensed the anger and frustration about the housing market, but there was nothing untoward, nothing too personal. Nobody knew his secret. Jason blew out a breath, trying to settle his heartbeat. He was safe, for now.

Distraction. That's what he needed. Jason opened a new tab and logged into his wallet in the crypto exchange, lowering the screen brightness to its absolute minimum, just enough to see the green and red candles climbing up and down, always in motion. Over the past six months, he'd learnt to read the patterns, figuring out what his favourite coins would do next. His strategy wasn't fool proof, but he only invested what he could afford to lose, and since he couldn't sleep... well, what else was there to do? It had become a bit of a game – a way to prove to himself that buying houses wasn't the only way to set yourself up for the future.

Jason flicked through his wallet. Most of his coins were moving sideways. Some would bottom out soon before rising again. He was waiting for the right moment to buy more. Buy low, sell high. In the end, it was simple, even for a sleep-deprived wreck like him.

It would take until three a.m. before he could fall asleep again, he could feel it in his bones. Tomorrow night, as the head of an arts committee, he was expected to make an appearance at some pompous gala for emerging New Zealand artists. A local trust had invited the artists to listen to the Minister of Arts, Culture and Heritage boasting about how much the country valued their talent. All for show, of course. The government had already cut some of the arts funding and would likely do it again through some kind of obscure reshuffle where a couple of entities received bigger grants and others lost out.

Jason didn't mind turning up for the event. He was vocal about trying to improve the housing for the next generation instead of protecting the interest of the wealthy, which made him popular with the younger voters. He only wished it wasn't on a Saturday night, which meant he had to give up his trip back home. The compounding lack of sleep would kill him.

Jason closed the laptop, unable to focus on the charts. Worry churned his stomach and brought a rancid taste into his mouth. He'd made it to parliament as an underdog candidate, a young, small-town schoolteacher with little political experience. It was a dream come true; one he'd worked towards for years. He should have been charged, ready for anything, enjoying every minute of it, not staring at the ceiling questioning his life choices and, worst of all, popping pills. They never gave him a good sleep, only a momentary blackout, followed by a metallic-tasting, fuzzy-headed hangover he couldn't afford. Not when he had to be ready with the perfect one-liner for any question, radiating self-confidence and smarts.

Oh, how he hated these sleepless nights, dominated by the baseless feeling of impending doom. He hated them as much as the loneliness that engulfed him whenever he looked out the window to the busy capital. Right now, behind the heavy mauve drapes, the streets no doubt buzzed with the Friday night crowd – young professionals leaving restaurants, entering bars and vaping on Lambton Quay. Between the tall buildings, the restless black ocean reflected the orange glow of the city lights. He should have been out there, building relationships, being seen, maybe even hooking up with someone. But he lived in the perpetual twilight of sleep deprivation, the mere thought of taking the lift down to the ground level filled him with dread.

Jason got up, made himself a cup of peppermint tea and took it to a small armchair. He preferred it to the bed – the chair didn't make empty promises. Since he was up, he might as well read about the young artists and wow everyone with his knowledge and personal interest. First up was Tom Browne, a 20-year-old from Hamilton. The other artists had only one small photo each, but his Executive Assistant, Tracy, had added three photos of this guy, including one in a fitted suit with two buttons of his collar shirt open. His paintings were abstract and strong, but Jason wondered if he'd been chosen for his looks. A guy like that made for enticing media coverage.

After ten minutes of reading, Jason dropped the folder in his lap and rested his head on the back of the chair. The sweet sleepiness had turned into a wired buzz. Sleep wouldn't find him tonight. He'd have to take another pill to get through the night, and he'd be woolly-headed in the morning. He always did this – got his hopes up at the first wave of tiredness, thinking things might be different and that maybe tonight, he'd fall asleep naturally. Without the wishful thinking, he could have drugged himself to sleep at a decent hour and avoided a lot of pain. But he couldn't lose hope, could he?

He pulled a small bottle from his toiletry bag and washed the tiny white pill down with the rest of his tea, sighing with relief. In half an hour, his brain would turn off. Tomorrow, he would find a way to sleep without drugs, to stop the downward spiral. Somehow, he would turn things around.

Jason crawled back on the crumpled sheets, breathing in the smell of industrial strength laundry powder, breathing out a quiet prayer for help.

# Chapter 3

Marnie blinked at the sight of her name on a small backboard held by a terrifyingly gorgeous woman. She reminded her of Nigella Lawson, all luscious curves in a terracotta wrap dress. Even under the yellow fluorescent lighting of the Wellington train terminal, she looked like she'd just set down her spatula and stepped off the TV set.

Marnie gave a shy wave, pointing at the blackboard. "That's me."

Afraid of exorbitant parking costs, she'd left her car outside of town and taken the train. The stylist, Luna Bella, had agreed to meet her at the station. Marnie had winced when she'd heard the name, wondering what kind of social media personality she was dealing with.

"Marnie! Welcome to Wellington!" Luna wiggled the blackboard into her leather handbag and hooked arms with Marnie like they were besties. "I take it's not your first time in Wellington. Tom told me a bit about you, but you can fill me in on the rest as we walk."

"Okay. What do you want to know? Like … measurements?" How hard was it to find one dress? It was ten in the morning, exactly ten hours until the event.

Luna's laugh echoed in the tunnel. "Ha! I measure with my eyes!" She nodded graciously at a young man who held the door for them as they stepped out of the station. "First things first. Have you had breakfast? If not, I know a great place."

"I'm fine." Marnie had gobbled a sandwich on the train to make sure she didn't faint during the shopping trip. As soon as she had the dress, she'd check into the hotel and lie in bed watching TV until it was gala time. She didn't want to extend the stylist experience with any unnecessary cafe trips. She had to save her strength for tonight.

The sun hid behind a light layer of clouds, but Luna covered her face with oversized sunglasses. "Fine isn't good enough. Let's get some champagne." She looked like a movie star. A movie star escorting an elderly relative.

Marnie glanced at her wrinkled tunic and stretchy jeans paired with comfortable walking sandals. When had she become like this? It was easy to forget about appearances when you lived in Hamilton. If New Zealand was laid back, Hamilton was a pyjama party of 165,000 largely overweight people. No wonder she felt out of her depth in Wellington where lithe, stylish young people roamed the streets on electric scooters. She couldn't hide behind the wheel of her station wagon. The tree-lined square outside the station stretched out like a catwalk.

Submitting to Luna's lead, Marnie followed, hoping the champagne was somewhere close. Her feet ached and she longed to hide away, preferably in a corner of a dimly lit restaurant.

To Marnie's relief, Luna led her to a historic stone building and opened a heavy oak door into a restaurant with moody lighting. The place had been restored to its early settler glory with an abundance of kauri wood and chandeliers. The smell of burnt oregano lingered in the air, and Billy Joel crooned softly in the background. Marnie took a seat and relaxed, happy to tuck her unfashionable footwear under the table.

She smiled at Luna. "I do need help. I haven't really paid attention to myself. Not for a while. Maybe ever. I married young and stayed home with the kids. Steve travelled, so he needed a wardrobe. I didn't. Even after the divorce... anyway, I don't want to embarrass Tom, this is so important to him. And I think there might be someone taking photos."

"There will be," Luna confirmed, gesturing at the waiter. "Two glasses of Dom Pérignon, please."

The young waiter nodded and swirled around to fill the

order. There was a look of recognition on his face, a hint of caution.

Luna squared herself to face Marnie, her perfectly made-up green eyes studying her latest client. "How would you describe yourself?"

Marnie's mouth fell open as her brain searched for words. "I'm ... Marnie. I work at a community centre in Hamilton. I have two kids. I ... I ... write books, as a hobby. I—"

"No! I mean your style, looks, essence. What vibe are you going for? Sexy? Quirky? Cosy?"

Marnie looked down her loose top. Surely the stylist could see she wasn't going for sexy. There was nothing intentional about the way she dressed, other than her desire for comfort and reluctance to spend money on clothing.

"Cosy," she finally whispered. "If those are the choices."

Luna laughed. "The choices are unlimited. But you need to know what you want to communicate to be able to say it, right?"

"You mean with my clothes?"

"And your hair, accessories, how you carry yourself. Everything you present to the world before you open your mouth and speak. It all tells a story, whether you do it intentionally or not."

Marnie shuddered. "So, what am I saying?" She looked down at her outfit again, then raised her eyes to Luna, bracing herself.

Luna peered into her eyes, refusing to even glance at her

clothing. "What do you think?"

"That I'm a sad, middle-aged woman who gave up a long time ago?" She tried to smile, fiddling with the sugar container.

Luna shot her an icy look. "That's harsh, Marnie. You may think you're joking, but anything you think or say about yourself becomes part of you. That's why I never say something like that, even as a joke. I control the narrative. I am fabulous, savvy, sexy. That's my story, and when I tell it consistently to everyone, they start telling it too. You can feed people lines you want them to repeat. Just like politicians do. You just slip it in there, have the media absorb it, pass it on, and voila! It becomes the truth."

The champagne arrived, and Marnie gulped a mouthful, her eyes watering from the smooth fizz rising to her nose. Fake Nigella had a point, but she wasn't here to work on her self-esteem. She just needed a dress for one night. If Tom hadn't booked this lady, she'd already be in a changing room somewhere, squeezing herself into something uncomfortable.

"Look. I just need help choosing a dress, or I don't know, maybe I can do it myself. I've lost weight, so it should be a bit easier to find something that fits. I know Tom really wanted to gift me this... experience"—she made a hapless hand gesture at Luna—"but you shouldn't waste time on trying to fix me. If it's at all possible, could you just bill me for the time you've spent so far and refund Tom? I think he went a bit overboard with all this..." She flashed the stylist an apologetic smile, gathered her saggy canvas handbag and got up. Her legs felt like pool noodles.

"Sit down." Luna's low voice froze Marnie in mid-motion, and she dropped back to her seat, perfectly in sync with the firm downward gesture Luna made with her hand.

The stylist eyed her for a moment, then slid her champagne glass aside and leaned forward. "I see where you're coming from. Most of my clients have a goal like getting someone's attention, advancing their career, making someone jealous. You just want to get through this one night, right?"

Marnie nodded, her cheeks suddenly hot. She hated sounding like such a sad sack, but this was the best she could do. Her body had failed her, making her push pause on any dream she'd had of reinventing herself. This perfectly made-up, sexy woman would never understand.

Luna placed her hands against the table. "I can work with that. One dress, make-up and hair, and I'll make sure you feel nice and presentable for that gala. Tom told me about it. There are some very interesting people there, it's quite an opportunity to mingle, if you were looking for that. But I can see that you're not."

Marnie caught a glimpse of disappointment, as if her invitation to this party constituted a terrible waste, an opportunity someone else might have used to great advantage. She was probably right.

They finished the champagne, left the restaurant and

walked towards the city centre. The bubbly lightness of the drink carried Marnie to the first shop, a small boutique off Lambton Quay. Presented like a gallery, it was one of those retailers that regarded price tags as distasteful.

"We're working to Tom's budget," Luna assured, noticing Marnie's alarmed face. "Don't worry about the price. I'll let you know if anything is out of our range."

Marnie's eyes widened. "What's the budget?" She couldn't let her boy pay some exorbitant amount for a dress she'd only wear once. Despite his success, he paid ridiculously high rent for his inner city flat. Wellington's rental market was out of control.

Luna pushed her towards a private fitting room with luscious couches and a disturbing number of mirrors. "I agreed not to discuss the budget with you. Now, I usually like to start by taking a 'before' shot, but I have feeling you'll fight me on this?" Her voice carried a tinge of tired resignation as she held up her phone.

Marnie cringed. "Is it going to end up on social media or something?"

Luna gave her a condescending smile. "That's kind of the point."

"I ... I..." Marnie searched for the nicest way to shut this down, a heavy feeling in her stomach. She detected the flicker of exasperation on Luna's face, and it amplified her guilt. But she couldn't.

"It's okay." Luna sighed, guiding her to a gold-and-purple armchair. Marnie sat, sneaking a peek of herself in the massive mirror on her side. She looked smaller than she remembered, but utterly lost, like a stray cat they'd dragged in from the street.

Luna disappeared and was immediately replaced by a young, impossibly skinny shop attendant carrying a tray of cold drinks. Marnie picked one of the organic sodas and twisted it open, wincing at the pain that shot through her finger joints.

An hour later, her whole body vibrated with exhaustion. She'd been in and out of a dozen dresses. There was nothing wrong with most of them – the beautiful, shiny materials and figure-hugging cuts suited her new shape – but she couldn't imagine wearing any of them in public.

Masking her apparent impatience with a professional smile, Luna handed her yet another dress – a shiny, champagne-coloured number with a low-cut cleavage. Dutifully, Marnie wiggled herself into it and stepped out from behind the curtain.

"Absolutely gorgeous! That chest is going to steal the show!"

Marnie blushed, hovering her hand over her chest like a palm leaf.

Noticing her discomfort, Luna grabbed another piece off the rack. "It comes with this little bolero, but I'm not sure..."

Marnie slipped on the little velvety jacket and breathed a sigh of relief. Ah! Something dark and soft to hide under.

Luna pursed her lips. "Too bulky. You can take it to shield you from the wind, I know it's a bit chilly out there, but promise me you'll take it off when you get inside. Let that dress shine."

Marnie nodded obligingly. She'd never take it off. "I think this is it."

She changed back into her tunic and jeans while Luna organised the purchase.

Back on the street, Marnie turned to the stylist. "Thank you so much for your help. I don't want to keep you any longer. If you just let me know where you think I should get my hair done, I can take it from here."

Luna smiled, hooking arms with her again. "I'll take you there. I've booked you in for some treatments, hairdo and makeup. But I need to discuss the details with the team."

She led Marnie around the corner and a couple of blocks down a side street. "Don't worry. The Beehive's just around the corner, so your hair won't get undone by the wind. And did you say your hotel was close, too?"

"On Ballance street."

"Perfect! You can rest up before the party. Put your feet up."

"And my head on the pillow?"

"No!" Luna laughed. "You're a hoot."

Worth a try.

They stepped into a busy salon, and Marnie plonked herself into the appointed chair. She listened as Luna spoke to the hairdresser, lifting Marnie's lumpy curls and planning how to tame them. The hairdresser had a remarkably similar style to Luna herself. Maybe she had an army of Nigella-lookalikes dotted around the city. Marnie wondered if Tom had chosen the stylist because she was closer to her age. With Luna's flawless skin, it was hard to estimate her exact age, but she had to be in her forties. There wasn't a hint of uncertainty in her, that tell-tale sign of actual youth.

Leaving the ladies to worry about her hair and makeup, Marnie dug up her phone. She had two missed calls from Shasa. With everything else going on, Marnie hadn't been in touch with anyone back home like she'd promised. Swallowing a lump of guilt, she called back.

Shasa answered on the second ring, a little out of breath. "Hey! How's the writing retreat going?"

"Good. Except I'm not writing. I'm actually in Wellington."

"Wellington?"

"Yes. Tom has this art thing at the Beehive. They're displaying one of his paintings, and he invited me. I'm getting my hair done and everything. It's so weird."

"Go Tom! That's amazing. I hope you're enjoying the glitz and glamour?" Her voice carried a dose of doubt.

"I'll try."

"The reason I called ... you know how Lando is doing your garden?"

"Right." Marnie pictured the tall guy who lived in cycling shorts and hung around the community house. He ran a landscaping business and had just finished working on the shared garden of their small co-housing community. Shasa and Mac had overseen the work, and the area had turned out well, but Marnie could tell Lando craved more creative freedom. When she'd agreed for him to design her private backyard, she'd fought hard to dismiss her own concerns, along with the burning look in his eyes. And now she wasn't even there to oversee the work. She had to stop agreeing to things just to be nice.

"Did you okay a massive fountain with ceramic dolphins?"

"Massive what?"

"I told him I'd call you, and he got all weird, said it was a gift and you don't have to pay, that you two have an understanding. Is it true you agreed to go out with him when you come back?"

Marnie grimaced. "I ... can see why he'd think that. He talked a lot, and I was a bit distracted, so I just nodded. I nodded a lot."

Shasa laughed, albeit good-naturedly. "I love you Marnie, but you can't do that with Lando! He needs boundaries. When he was working on the shared gardens, I had to talk him out of two tacky water features, a koi pond and other weird shit that kids would either drown in or fall off."

"That's the thing. I don't have young children, so I have no excuse."

"How about 'I don't like it?' It's your backyard."

Marnie winced. "How bad is it?"

"Hang on, I'll send you a photo."

Marnie waited until a photo popped up on screen. Holy cow! Her tiny backyard was overtaken by a rainbow-coloured ceramic bowl with huge dolphins cavorting in and out of it. They were covered in tiny glistening tiles that must have been made of mirrors. One of them had caught the evening light, turning it into a starburst on the camera lens. Marnie felt sick. She'd go blind looking at the shiny mammals. Or worse, they'd start a wildfire.

"Are you still there?" Shasa asked.

Marnie brought the phone back to her ear. "It's... big. But don't worry about it. I'll sort it out when I get back. I have to get ready for the party now."

"Okay. Have fun!"

Marnie dropped her phone in her handbag and settled back in the chair. Luna handed her a magazine and pointed at a picture of a gorgeous woman in an evening dress, her loose curls partly gathered up, diamond earrings shining. "We're thinking something like this."

"Wow. I never wear my hair up."

Luna's melodic laugh filled the room. "What if, for one night, you did something new? You're not from around here, nobody knows how you usually dress or wear your hair. Think of this as an opportunity to be whoever you want to be!"

"Sure. It just feels... fake."

Luna narrowed her eyes, her smile curling into a cheeky

grin. "I'll let you in on a secret. Everything about me is fake, as you say. Luna Bella's not my real name. My hair's not this colour. I've had two mini facelifts this year and microdermabrasion. All this"—she swept a hand down her body—"is just material to work with. You're free to do whatever you want with it. I don't think of it as fake or natural. Rather, original or upgraded. It's like renovating a house. You can replace a lot of stuff and increase its value. You can do it badly or well, but you have no responsibility to stick to the original. It's in no way better. It's just the starting point."

"S ... sure."

"Look, I have to love you and leave you. But just think about it. Allow yourself to be someone else tonight, just for fun. You deserve it."

Marnie nodded. "Thank you."

Luna kissed the hairdresser goodbye, waved her hand at Marnie and made for the door. Marnie stared at the picture of the magazine woman, wondering if she could pull it off. The hairdresser appeared behind her and guided her to the washing station. Leaning her neck against the cold rim of the basin, she closed her eyes. It would be nice to be someone else for one night. Someone gorgeous, carefree, and healthy. Someone like Luna. And maybe if she could take a small part of that new self home with her... maybe she could be someone else for a little bit longer.

# Chapter 4

Up close, the Beehive really did look like a beehive. Marnie circled the round grey construction on foot, wincing with pain every time her strapped heels hit the pavement. And these were supposed to be the comfortable shoes! Clearly she and Luna had very different ideas about comfort. The icy Wellington wind made her shiver, and she secured the bolero tighter around herself.

Finally, she spotted the function signs and simultaneously, Tom. Thank goodness! Marnie picked up speed, ignoring the pain, and waved to get her eldest child's attention. A gust of wind tried to steal her bolero, and she grabbed it with her free hand, desperately pulling the inadequate pieces of fabric to meet in the middle. They did not.

Tom looked handsome in a Sherlock-style overcoat. The dress code was smart casual, possibly to allow room for the young artists and their dates to express their personalities. They'd gathered on the steps, splashing more colour around the government buildings than Marnie had ever seen before. Browsing the statement sideburns, overlong bangs, oversized blazers, loud T-shirts and shin-length pleated skirts, Marnie felt overdressed and old-fashioned. Her figure-hugging dress harked from a different era. To these edgy youngsters, she must have looked like a wannabe fifties movie star.

Marnie approached Tom's group. "Hi there!"

"Oh, my God, Mum!"

Tom's appreciation gave Marnie a warm glow and she smiled, smoothing the fabric of her dress. "You found a very fancy stylist. She insisted on… this."

"Yeah, I follow her on TikTok. I always thought she'd be perfect to work with you. That dress looks amazing!"

Luna was on TikTok?

"Shall we?" Tom asked, taking her arm.

He led them up the stairs to the double doors that an usher had just opened. They were guided through security, into a huge foyer. Marnie tried to follow the crowd to the wide staircase, but Tom escorted her to the coat check. He peeled off his overcoat, handed it to the redhead in charge and turned to Marnie.

She tightened the bolero around herself, panic constricting her throat. "It's part of the dress."

Tom narrowed his eyes. "I feel like I should check with Luna. It doesn't look like something she'd pick..."

Marnie sighed. Why was everyone ganging up on her? They were here to admire Tom's art, not her cleavage.

The redhead extended her arm, huffing impatiently. Someone in the queue behind Marnie cleared their throat – a middle-aged lady with purple hair, her pink jacket already in her hand, loose skin hanging under her arm. Well, if she was letting it all hang out... Marnie removed the bolero and passed it to the coat check girl, muttering apologies and thank-yous.

"That looks way better. Trust me. This way, Mum. Wroom..." Tom grabbed her shoulders and manoeuvred her up the stairs. It was their running joke. Teenage Tom, eager to get his mother out the door to whatever activity he needed a ride for, had taken to driving her around the house like a little vehicle, complete with engine sounds and a warning beep as they reversed to pick up forgotten keys or her handbag.

The curved banquet hall had moody lighting and spotlights on the paintings. Marnie immediately recognised Tom's trademark explosion of colour. She had one of his works in her living room, looking oversized and out-of-place in the small space. Here, it belonged.

"It looks incredible." She squeezed her son's arm.

To Marnie's relief, the room was well heated. She tried to loosen her shoulders, enjoying the feel of Tom's hands. She had such an easy relationship with him, much more relaxed than with Tanya.

The crowd settled around the curved room, huddling around the paintings. Waiters weaved between the people, distributing champagne. Tom grabbed two from a by-passing tray, and they raised glasses.

"I'm so proud of you!" Marnie gushed. "Are they going to introduce you, or your work... I mean, is there a programme?"

Tom shrugged. "Not that I know of. A couple of politicians will talk about how much they love the arts or whatever. We prance around, trying to get our picture taken by the press, that kind of thing. It's pretty boring. But I'm so glad you're here!"

"Me, too! Now, I know I'm not the press, but can I take a picture of you? With your painting, obviously."

Tom moved closer to his artwork and grinned for Marnie's camera. "I should take a picture of you as well! Tanya needs to see this!"

Marnie laughed. "She told me I looked like a wet dog when I left Hamilton."

Tom frowned and took out his phone. "Why do you let her talk to you like that?"

Marnie frowned, thinking of a way to change the subject. Thankfully, Tom turned his attention to photographing Marnie in her dress and she conjured up a smile. When he showed her the result, she gasped. The woman in the photo was unrecognisable. Someone else. She'd have to ask Shasa to use this picture on the community house website. Her friend had been urging her to get a new one taken for two years. In the current photo, she had a deer-in-the-headlights look that resembled the kind of mugshots you saw in the news about missing persons.

They wandered around the hall admiring the other paintings. Tom filled her in on what he knew about the artists. Most had Māori names. Even the names of the paintings were written in Te Reo. "How did you get in? You're not Māori," Marnie whispered.

Tom grinned. "Token white guy?"

"Maybe it means you're just that good that they were willing to overlook your ancestry?"

"Maybe. I'm not going to question it. You have to take every opportunity..." The words died on his lips as he caught the sight of something over her shoulder.

Marnie turned to look. The hall buzzed with roaming people, yet she instantly knew who Tom was staring at – Hana, his first girlfriend, who'd moved overseas two years ago. What was she doing here?

Tom's eyes glistened with pain and longing.

"It's okay," she said softly, squeezing his arm. "Go talk to her. I'll be fine."

Tom's eyebrows knitted in regret. "A bunch of us were going to slip out after the speeches to a private party. You're invited, of course. It's on a rooftop!"

Marnie's feet protested the idea with a stab of pain. Climbing stairs would be the end of her. "That's okay. I'm happy to eat nibbles and listen to the speeches and then Uber myself to the hotel. Go talk to your girl!"

"I'll come and find you later, okay?" Tom shot her a grateful look and sauntered away, leaving her with two champagne glasses.

Marnie smiled, suddenly lost and lonely. Would she see him again before the night was over? With the swarming crowd, it would be easy to lose sight of each other. She drank the champagne to shake off her melancholy and tried to ignore the pain shooting up from her feet. There were no seats. She couldn't stand all evening in these shoes. Maybe she could sit on the toilet for a bit? After one more champagne, she'd have to pee anyway. This wasn't quite the last hurrah she'd envisioned, but she could always buy one of those cinnamon crepes from a street kitchen for a late-night snack and retreat to her hotel room. Better yet, she could have something delivered.

With her plan formulated, Marnie moved towards the drinks table. If she lowered her expectations, everything would be okay.

# Chapter 5

Jason cast one last glance at the restroom mirror. Apart from the dark circles under his eyes, he looked as put together as the situation demanded. His suit had arrived from the dry cleaner's just in time. Reporters were covering the exhibition, and they loved catching him on camera. Most of the other male politicians sported bald spots and beer guts, so they went after the younger ones, the single ones. Every photo with an unmarried female would end up on the gossip sites with speculations about a relationship.

It was all part of the deal. His career depended on the publicity, yet it felt wrong. As a high school teacher, he'd never benefited from his looks. He'd been happy to live a quiet life under the radar, but that was no longer an option.

Jason shook his head. He was here on a mission. To accomplish that, he'd smile at the camera and flirt with every other fool out there. Eventually, his hard work would pay off. Maybe sooner rather than later.

He had an inkling the Minister of Housing, Kathleen Rush, was hiding an illness. Jason had noticed the slight tremor in her hand, mood swings and moments when she seemed to lose track of the conversation. She covered it well, too well for strangers to take notice, but Jason knew Kathleen, and this wasn't normal. So far, his only evidence came from his observations, but he couldn't help wondering. Not that he rejoiced over anyone's illness, but the idea of Kathleen stepping down provided an opportunity he couldn't dismiss. As Associate Minister, he was primed to take over Kathleen's housing portfolio, and if he did, he could finally push through the changes he'd promised his voters. Every sacrifice he'd made on the way would finally be worth it. He was young, but so was the Prime Minister. And housing was one of those hot topics nobody had real expertise on, only passion. Kathleen didn't even have that. With her out of the way, Jason could tighten the belt on Kiwis' love of property investing. Kathleen was driven, but biased. A housing minister with a portfolio of twenty-five investment properties couldn't stay impartial. As a renter, Jason could at least look at the situation objectively. Most of the sitting government had a vested interest in the unstable housing market and its skyrocketing asset prices.

Jason stepped out of the bathroom and scanned the hall for Kathleen. She must have been still in the ladies' room. Rumour had it she was able to nap on the toilet, leaning against the cubicle wall. An impressive skill, he had to admit. He would have given anything to be able to fall asleep on cue.

As he walked into the hall, Jason admired the artwork. Five large paintings hung on the banquet hall's wall, illuminated by spotlights. The vivid strokes and colours reminded him of Khayden, the awkward preteen at a low decile school where he'd taught. Jason couldn't remember who'd thought to give him a canvas and some paints, but they'd all been blown away by his raw talent. After that, Jason had wondered how many other gifted youngsters they'd missed. How many kids were never given a chance and went on thinking they were good at nothing?

Jason glanced at his watch. It was past eight p.m. As Minister of Culture and Heritage – one of Kathleen's many hats – she should have been up at the podium already, to open the evening. Where was she? Was she really napping?

Jason texted her number and waited. No answer.

"Where's Kathleen?" Malcolm made Jason jump. The middle-aged, long-term South Auckland representative stood right behind Jason. A rotund man with an appetite for anything deep fried, he should have been the one with health issues, not Kathleen.

"I think she's still in the loo." Jason gestured at the bathroom sign.

"Well, go get her." Malcolm waddled away, shaking his head.

Jason huffed. He was an Associate Minister, not an assistant. But he couldn't be too angry; Malcolm was on his side. When Jason first started as a junior MP, Malcolm had shown extraordinary patience with him, guiding him through his first weeks on duty. The big guy was probably the closest thing to a friend he had in Parliament.

Where was Kathleen's actual assistant? That boy seemed more interested in posting on social media than assisting his minister.

Jason hurried down a side corridor to the bathrooms, wondering what to do. He couldn't sneak into the ladies' room with reporters roaming about. As he looked around for a solution, he noticed a woman in a figure-hugging dress. Oh God, those shiny curves. Jason quickly lifted his gaze to her eye level. Focus. He couldn't be seen leering over anyone, especially not in a dark corridor. He'd seen what happened to those who let their guard down, thinking they were safe. There was always someone watching with a camera, and rumours spread like wildfire.

He offered a friendly smile. "Excuse me. I could use a little help."

"Help?" The woman raised a pair of delicate eyebrows. She looked a bit lost, like she'd been dropped in front of him by a fairy godmother, dressed by the sparkly spin of a magic wand. Despite the glamour, her eyes were sincere, free of the assessing and calculating undercurrents he was used to.

Jason glanced over his shoulder, making sure they had no audience, and dropped his voice. "Do you know Minister Kathleen Rush? She's in there, I think." He gestured at the ladies' room. "I can't get hold of her, and she might not remember she's the first speaker. Could you go in and check on her for me? Just say Jason's outside, asking for her."

The woman gave him an apologetic smile. "I don't really follow politics. What does she look like?"

Jason blinked, taking in the lightly pursed lips and earnest hazel eyes. Kathleen Rush had been in the news only yesterday and her face was plastered over the news sites on a weekly basis. How could this woman not know the high-profile minister holding two major portfolios? "She's got short, blonde hair and..." Jason thought back to when Kathleen had walked in. "She's wearing a pantsuit." It was an educated guess. She mostly wore pantsuits in black, or red – the official Labour Party colour.

The curvy woman gave him a slow nod and cracked the bathroom door. After peeking in, she tiptoed through the doorway as if on a secret mission. Jason couldn't help smiling. He also couldn't help staring at her shapely bottom moving beneath the glossy fabric. How fortunate that one dress could highlight both an incredible pair of breasts and a backside like that. His hands twitched, longing to trace the body he couldn't tear his eyes away from.

Thankfully, the soft-closing bathroom door finally shut, leaving him to gather his wits. What was happening to him? He hadn't been this flustered in weeks. In his sleep deprived state, he could barely find energy for tying his shoelaces, but the pulsing in his trousers told him this was a special occasion.

Jason leaned on the wall, letting the delicious distraction fade into the background. He had to stay on track. This could be the turning point he'd been waiting for – the moment the great Kathleen Rush fell.

The silence in the hallway told him Kathleen hadn't hit the panic button, which would have issued the white-shirted Parliament staff. They'd come running. So, she'd either lost track of time, or she was unconscious. Or she'd decided *not* to raise the alarm. Hiding a health condition was a serious breach, one that could cost her position.

Jason shifted closer to the door, but the buzz of the crowd in the banquet hall drowned any softer sounds. He hoped nobody else happened upon them. Not that he minded having witnesses on Kathleen – they were necessary – but he desperately wanted to steal a private moment with the woman whose mere presence had distracted him for a moment. Who was she?

# Chapter 6

Marnie stepped into the disabled bathroom, her pulse skyrocketing. She wasn't the right woman for this mission, but how could anyone say no to a face like that? He'd peered into her eyes like no one else existed. She'd embarrassed herself by not knowing the minister he was talking about – she didn't follow politics, beyond watching a couple of debates around election time – but he hadn't displayed a hint of annoyance. Those steely eyes had only softened, letting her imagine a connection that probably wasn't there. He must have been a politician. Someone famous. The name Jason didn't ring a bell, but there'd been something familiar about him.

The door leading to the toilet was closed, but not locked. It must have been empty. Who would go into the toilet and leave the door unlocked? What a relief. She could just tell Mr Gorgeous that nobody was here and get on with her night.

But that's when Marnie's bladder reminded her why she'd come here in the first place. She might as well quickly pee before returning to the corridor.

She opened the door and yelped. A woman lay on the floor, her shoulder against the back wall, eyes open, her breath coming in short gasps. Blond hair, pantsuit. Kathleen Rush?

"Oh, my God! Are you okay?"

The woman moaned.

Marnie sprang into action. She hoisted the minister off the floor and propped her on the covered toilet seat.

Kathleen supported herself against the handrails, attempting to focus on Marnie, a hint of clarity flickering behind her blurry gaze. "Who're you?"

"Marnie ... Browne."

"Who do you work for?"

Marnie stared back at her, eyes wide. Surely her part-time job at the community house had nothing to do with this. "I'm ... nobody," she whispered. "Are you Kathleen Rush?"

"You're not from around here?" The woman's expression softened, and she tried to straighten her back, planting her sensible heels against the floor.

"No, I'm from Hamilton."

Kathleen smiled. "Bless you, Marnie Browne from

Hamilton. Is there any way you could keep this between us?"

"Are you sure you don't need help? What happened?"

Kathleen shook her head. "I slipped and fell. Could happen to anyone. But in my position, people like to read into things. Do you understand what I mean?"

Marnie nodded. "I won't tell anyone."

"Promises aren't worth the paper they're written on in this building, but I have no choice. I have to trust you, Marnie Browne."

The way she repeated her name made Marnie shiver. Why on earth had she volunteered her full name to this lady? What if word got out somehow? Would she track her down and take revenge?

"You can trust me," Marnie said in a small voice, backing out of the toilet. She still needed to pee, but she could do that later, maybe in another toilet somewhere far away from here. Or in her pants.

Kathleen struggled to her feet, refusing Marnie's help. As she got to the sink, she glanced in the mirror and smoothed her hair.

"I'll go first?" Marnie nodded at the door. "There's a man out there asking for you. Jason. He said you're needed out there to give a speech or something?"

Kathleen blinked, a vacant look falling over her eyes. "Who're you?"

Marnie looked around, confused. "I'm ... Marnie."

After a few seconds, Kathleen's eyes lit up again and she

smiled. "Yes, of course. Marnie. It was great to meet you. Now, off you go." The smiled fixed on her face, she shooed Marnie off with a sinewy hand.

Marnie stepped back into the corridor. Whatever was going on with the minister, at least she was now on her feet and seemed to require no further assistance.

Jason appeared beside her and leaned in to whisper. "Is she there?"

The sensation of his warm breath in her ear sent a tremor down her body and she fought hard to ignore it.

"She's there. She's just ... freshening up. She'll come out in a minute." Marnie straightened her shoulders and turned to face those steel grey eyes – Jason. Oh, dear. So perfect. In a fitted jacket over a crisp white shirt and no tie, his jawline defined by a five o'clock shadow with a tinge of silvery grey. He had blue-tinted shadows under his eyes and a look of subtle defiance that stood out against the rigid tradition of the Parliament. A rebel. In a different life, if she'd been ten years younger, and a lot braver, she would have flirted with him. It would have been so much fun, like a scene from a movie, or one she would write in a book.

Marnie sighed. This was as much excitement as she was going to have tonight, and probably as much as she could handle. Her last hurrah involved a 60-year-old woman collapsed in the toilet – perhaps a terrifying sneak peek into her own future.

"Thank you." Jason flashed her a smile and hurried down

the dark corridor, back into the banquet hall.

She allowed herself one more look at his broad shoulders, until her bladder signalled a more pressing need. She still needed to pee. To her relief, Kathleen stepped out of the ladies' room and followed Jason, brushing past her without a second look. Marnie caught the closing door and snuck back in.

Sitting down on the toilet felt heavenly. Marnie relaxed her posture, stretching her feet. How long could she hide out here?

A faint crackle of the loudspeakers alerted her that the official programme was starting. She couldn't miss Tom's moment. Marnie washed up and hurried back to the hall.

Kathleen Rush smiled under a bright spotlight as her commanding voice filled the room. There was no sign of the previous wobble as she waxed lyrical about the government's commitment to arts and education.

After her short speech, another politician – a fat, balding man with rattling breath – stepped behind the microphone, introduced himself as Malcolm something and continued in the same vein.

Marnie made her way to the drinks table to get another glass of champagne. It was probably unwise, but she wanted something to hold. The bubbles tickled her chest, lightening her mood. As soon as the official programme finished, she could make her way back to the hotel. She wouldn't even bother with the cinnamon crepes; it was too much of a walk.

All she wanted was to take off the shoes and lie down.

The formalities ended and the crowd dispersed, the people likely rushing to better parties. Marnie looked around for Tom and smiled as he approached.

"There you are! I was looking for you earlier." His eyes held a subtle concern.

"I must have been in the bathroom, sorry. Are you leaving now?"

"Yes. Are you sure you don't want to join us?"

Marnie waved her hand. "It's fine. I'm dying to go back to the hotel and take off my shoes, if you don't mind."

Tom flashed her a knowing smile. "Okay. I didn't have high hopes, to be honest. But I'm glad I got you to come out for this." He gestured at the hall. "I wish they'd done a sit-down dinner or something, but—"

"No! This has been perfect!" Marnie shut him up with a vigorous head shake. "I am one proud mama. This day has been so special. You have no idea. Thank you for everything." She glanced at her dress, eyes wide with wonder. She still couldn't believe she was dressed like this in public.

"Totally worth it," Tom said, flashing her a victorious grin.

He gave her a tight hug before disappearing down the grand staircase leading to the exit. He didn't get very far, as the simultaneous departure of a hundred people created a long queue by the security doors, which only let one person through at a time.

Marnie had no desire to stand in line, so she wandered in

the opposite direction, hoping to find a seat where she could wait it out. At the back of the banquet hall, she spotted two chairs, perhaps set up for the elderly. Perfect. She lowered herself onto one in the far corner, removed her shoes and tucked her feet under the seat. An involuntary moan escaped her lips as she stretched her aching feet.

"That good?"

She flushed when she looked up and saw Jason standing next to her. His Adam's apple moved up and down as he swallowed.

Marnie dropped her head to hide from his eyes and caught a glimpse of her own cleavage. Goodness. She'd forgotten how revealing her dress was. From where Jason was standing, he could have dropped a coin down there, like a slutty slot machine.

She grasped her greenstone necklace to cover his view. "I'm just waiting for that queue at the door to clear. Didn't feel like standing."

Jason grabbed the other vacant chair. "Great idea. Do you mind if I wait with you?"

Marnie shrugged, her heartbeat climbing to triple digits. "You're a politician, right?"

He offered his hand, along with a campaign grin. "MP Jason Hallett, Labour."

Marnie's breath caught at the firm handshake as her brain searched for a fake name to offer. She'd learnt her lesson in the bathroom and wouldn't make the same mistake again.

Jason's hand squeezed hers. This shouldn't be hard. She made up names for fictional characters all the time. In fact...

"I'm ... Beatrice." The name of her last heroine, a fictional woman much braver and more adventurous than she was. "I voted for Labour. I mean, you have my vote. No need to ... you know. You can relax."

Jason's mouth dropped open for a second, and he burst out laughing. "Thank you. But I'm not here to win your vote. I wanted to discuss something else." His smile turned pained, and a hint of uncertainty clouded his eyes. He shifted closer, his voice turning so quiet she could barely hear it. "I just wanted to ask about what you witnessed in the bathroom earlier and whether you'd told anyone about it."

Marnie's fingers gripped the edge of her seat like it was about to take flight. "It's none of my business. I haven't talked to anyone. I won't."

His gaze dipped to her chest, heating her skin, and she brought both her hands to her necklace again.

"It's okay. Tell anyone you like. Nothing like that will ever stay a secret. If it's something the public should know, for the good of the country, better that it's out, right?" He studied her face as if it had the bathroom saga written on it.

Marnie swallowed the lump in her throat. Was a lady slipping and falling in the loo a matter of national security? She'd promised Kathleen to keep it to herself. She couldn't go back on her word. Marnie shook her head, trying to look as casual as possible. "I don't think there's anything worth sharing."

"Are you sure?"

The intensity of his gaze made Marnie's cheeks flood with warmth. She thought back to the moment by the wash basin, that little stumble, a memory lapse of a few seconds. What if the minister was losing her mental faculties? Could it possibly be that serious? Would Marnie get into more trouble by revealing the secret, or by keeping it? Dammit, why did life have to be this difficult? All she wanted was to run off to the hotel room and put her head under a pillow.

Beatrice would know what to do. Her fictional leading lady was fearless and fascinating. She'd have played this game and enjoyed every minute of it. How was it that she could write these characters but not impersonate them? Or could she?

"Please, Beatrice?" Jason's eyes pleaded, searching for the truth.

A strange feeling stirred in Marnie's gut, getting stronger by the second. Maybe this was her last hurrah, this moment right here. She had a chance to truly be someone else for one night. What happened if she took it? Marnie removed her hand from her necklace, letting the cool stone rest against her skin.

His eyes followed it as if hypnotised. He blinked twice, eventually meeting her eyes.

"I don't want to discuss it here," she whispered, her voice disappearing into her throat. "Can we go somewhere private?"

Jason's eyes lit up. "I know the perfect place. Follow me."

# Chapter 7

The banquet hall had nearly emptied and the queue at the door had dwindled, but instead of the stairs, Jason led them to the lifts. He swiped his key card and the doors opened. Smiling, he gestured for Marnie to step in. She did, her heart drumming a steady beat. The confined space forced her closer to him, and she caught a whiff of his aftershave. Something spicy. The lift shot up, and her stomach lurched. She took a half-step away, leaning against the wall, searching for something to say. The moment she'd introduced herself as Beatrice, her insides had turned into liquid and stayed that way, excitement chasing nausea, everything swirling and spinning. Or maybe it was the champagne. Either way, she couldn't stop now. She had to stick to this bid.

"Do you have access to all the floors?"

"Pretty much."

"You must spend a lot of time here."

"In Wellington? Or Beehive? Yeah, I suppose. We're required to be on site Tuesday to Thursday, from nine a.m. to ten p.m. But there's a lot of other work that falls over the long weekend. I don't have a family, so it's hard to even argue for work-life balance. I don't really have a life outside." His hollow laugh echoed in the small space.

Marnie cocked her head and studied him. "Sounds... lonely."

The doors pinged, and they stepped into a round hall.

"The middle of the Beehive," Jason announced, pointing at the spherical arrangement of marble tiles.

"Wow."

He led her through another door, down a red-carpeted hallway, then a green-carpeted one. Not another soul was in sight. The walls were lined with endless black-and-white group portraits. White men in dark suits. The inside of the building had a regal feel you would have never guessed from its ugly Sixties exterior. Their steps fell softly on the patterned carpet.

Jason led her to a heavy door which opened onto a footbridge between two buildings covered by a glass ceiling. Underneath, a luscious indoor garden grew on either side of a winding path. On the other side of the bridge, another heavy door opened to what looked like a dimly lit country club with leather couches and oversized snooker tables, empty and quiet as a mausoleum.

Jason flashed her a conspiratorial smile. “Welcome to the Members Lounge.”

Marnie looked around. “No members?”

“I’ve never seen anyone use it. Back in the day, when you were allowed to smoke here, it was quite popular. Scotch and cigars, that kind of thing. But not anymore.”

Marnie meandered deeper into the room, tracing her hand along the huge snooker tables. What a waste of space.

Jason led them to a two-seater along the wall, not directly visible from the entrance.

He took off his jacket and they sat, his sleeve brushing against her bare arm. “Is this okay? There are no cameras here.”

“It’s fine,” Marnie whispered, trying to ignore his proximity.

It was impossible. His broad shoulders encroached into her space, and she found herself leaning sideways to avoid physical contact. Did being in the public eye give people a presence like this? It was hard to breathe around this guy. Or maybe all the sideways leaning was engaging her core a bit too much. She wasn’t great at Russian twists. Marnie sucked in her stomach, worried that her tight dress would display a roll around her waist.

Jason’s smile broadened, his eyes boring into hers, warm

and encouraging. "Look, Beatrice. I want to be honest with you. There's so much at stake here. But first I have to ask you something." His eyes wrinkled at the corners as he studied her face. "Are you a property investor?"

Marnie blinked twice, trying to understand the direction of the conversation. "No, I only have one house... an apartment, really. I don't make a lot of money." She had a unit in a small co-housing development she'd built with Shasa and two other friends. Quite miraculous that they'd managed it, really.

Jason's face split into a delighted grin that made her chest flutter. "Great! We're working on ways to cool down the housing market. It's out of control and so many people are struggling – renters, first home buyers, low-income families. We have some tools to use, existing laws that could be enforced, but they'll anger a lot of people, particularly investors. Kathleen isn't ready for that. She has a lot to lose."

"You mean her career?"

"And investments. Most of the sitting MPs are property investors. They don't want to shoot themselves in the foot. And most voters own property. If the value of their investment goes down, they turn on the government. That's why I'm here. I'm a renter. I choose not to invest in housing. My money's in start-up businesses, gold and the crypto market. I'm able to make decisions without worrying about my housing portfolio, or even my political career. I don't care if this is my last term. I want to push for the changes we need. I want to free up land for development. I want a punishing tax on empty homes and land banking." He raked his fingers through his dirty blond hair, freshly cut but longer on the top than the standard MP haircut. His voice turned darker. "If Kathleen had to step down, I know I'd have a shot at the housing portfolio. I'm telling you this in confidence. This might be the biggest mistake I've ever made, but I need your help, Beatrice."

Marnie stared at him. "How could I possibly help you?"

"If there's any chance that Kathleen is not okay, that she might not be fit and healthy, I'd really appreciate it if word of that got out. That could lead to an investigation."

Marnie's eyes widened in horror. "You want everyone to know about her health issues... I mean if she had health issues. Isn't that her private business?" Her fingers curled into tight fists, causing a soft ache in her joints. She felt for Kathleen, as abrupt as the lady had been. It wasn't easy to be a sick woman, especially in the public eye.

Jason's voice tinged with regret. "It's not, actually. The health and wellbeing of MPs is matter of national security. We have a duty to disclose any condition that may affect our work. If anything happens, we have a panic button. You push that, and staff in white shirts will come running."

The image of Kathleen lying on the bathroom floor flashed behind Marnie's eyes. There had been no white-shirted staff, which meant she hadn't sounded the alarm. Was she hiding something?

Marnie rubbed her throat, trying to loosen the tightness squeezing her windpipe. "I don't want to betray her trust or get in trouble."

Jason's eyes sharpened. He reached for her hands, squeezing them for emphasis. "That's very honourable, Beatrice, but she should have never asked you to keep a secret. That's not right!" His indignant voice resonated down her spine, making her shiver.

She wanted to believe him. She wanted to trust him. After all, she knew nothing about this Kathleen woman, and the New Zealand housing market was a hot mess. Jason kept his eyes on hers, searching for answers.

Marnie took a deep breath. Despite her gut-wrenching discomfort, there was something electrifying about this moment. She had his full attention. Nobody had paid attention to her in a long time, not like this. She felt like a dried-up plant that someone had accidentally watered, maybe over-watered, but she would drink it all up. Who knew how long she would have to survive on this? As soon as she spilled the beans, he would lose interest.

"Please, Beatrice. I beg you to reconsider your loyalties. You don't know me, and I get that you're a person with integrity, which is very rare. Honestly, if it had been anyone else, with anything newsworthy"—he searched her eyes again, a hint of a smile on his lips—"the press would already know about this. The fact that they don't is remarkable."

"You wish you'd asked someone else to go into that

bathroom?" Marnie attempted a playful smile, but her mouth tugged downward in disappointment.

"No! I don't." Jason seemed surprised, giving her another long look. "I'm so glad I met you, circumstances aside."

She caught a hint of embarrassment in his eyes. In better lighting, she might have been able to confirm the colour of his cheeks.

Marnie's pulse whooshed in her ears. She was probably being played, but she was willing to take the risk. Maybe she couldn't reveal her real name, but she could give him what he was after. Some deep part of her wanted to make him happy.

Shivering, she launched in. "She said she slipped and fell, but I think she'd been lying there for a while. She had that look, the way she was splayed on the floor... and there was a moment afterwards when she couldn't remember something I'd just said, as if her mind went blank. But she recovered quickly."

Jason stared at her, his mouth ajar. She could almost hear the engine purring behind those cool, grey eyes.

"You want me to tell someone about that? Like one of those staff members in white shirts?" she asked.

Jason rubbed his chin, his nails scraping the stubble. Marnie had a sudden urge to touch him. When was the last time she'd touched a man's face? Or any other part for that matter. Her fingertips tingled at the thought.

"It would be better if the press got wind of it."

"You want me to go to the media?" Marnie's chest flooded with panic. She really didn't want to get involved in this. What if Kathleen found out? She was a minister with a lot of influence. What if she wasn't sick? They had no solid evidence. She could be sued for slander.

Reading the alarm in her eyes, Jason shook his head. "No, we have to be smart about this. I don't want you caught in the middle. It could blow up big time, and that's not fair. But if the right people heard about this, it would get to the media. If it's true, there will be other supporting evidence."

Marnie shuddered. "It would destroy her. I mean her career."

Jason pinned her with his gaze, sucking in a deep breath. "Trust me, if there was any other way, if I could get her onboard with the changes we need... This might look malicious, but we could actually be saving thousands, maybe hundreds of thousands of people from perpetual poverty, help lift them out of these situations, living in unhealthy and crowded rentals."

Marnie nodded. Despite the fear tightening her gut, she felt an overwhelming desire to help him. Please him. Touch him. Goodness, she really needed to reel in these thoughts. "Okay. Just let me know who I need to tell. Point me to the right person."

She placed her shoes on the floor, ready to get up. Okay. She'd caved and agreed to give him exactly what he wanted. It was over – her moment in the sun, feeling borderline young again, even a little bit important. She hoped it was worth a potential lawsuit.

Jason didn't get up. He sank deeper into the couch, dropping his head against the black leather. "I'm sorry," he mumbled. "I'm just so tired."

"You must have a full schedule." Marnie watched his eyelids dip lower and close for a moment. His thick, gold-tipped lashes cast shadows across his cheeks. Such a beautiful, sculpted face. Oh, how she wanted to trace her fingers along the hollows of those stubbled cheeks, along the blue-tinted circles under his eyes. He looked spent. Passion laced with exhaustion. She recognised the latter, but her world was so much smaller, her activities insignificant. Nothing she did affected hundreds of thousands of people. She liked her work at the community house, helping people. She enjoyed looking after her friend's four-year-old. She was used to dealing with her teenage daughter, and the frantic calls from her ex-husband's demented mother. She couldn't even imagine what it was like trying to fix a broken country. Another shiver ran down her spine and she adjusted herself on the couch.

Poor Jason. Nobody was worse equipped to help this guy. What was she doing frolicking in the parliament building in a skimpy dress and heels, her face painted to look like someone else? Marnie wove her fingers into her carefully styled up-do.

*Remember, you're Beatrice. Act like it.*

Watching Jason's rising and falling chest, Marnie removed her heels and curled her feet under her body, her head swimming. She'd had too much champagne in a short amount of time. Since sitting down, she'd felt the effect of those drinks more keenly, like she'd been drugged. The sensation both thrilled and terrified her. The powerful tug of intoxication pulled her into a swirl she couldn't fight. Maybe it was better to just ride the wave. Her head would clear soon enough, and she'd be back to her boring existence.

Marnie relaxed against the couch, anchoring her hot body against the cool leather. Better. She needed to enjoy this; she'd likely never experience anything like it for the rest of her life.

"I'm sorry," Jason mumbled, leaning forward and dropping his head into his hands. "I ... I don't get much sleep. I can't fall asleep. Ever since I started as Associate Minister, I just can't turn off my brain, even when I'm exhausted."

The raw desperation in his voice stirred her, like she was peering into the core of him through a deep surface crack. Associate Minister. That was a bigger deal than an MP. Despite the exhaustion, he looked young, maybe still in his thirties. He'd done well for himself.

"But you can't survive without sleep." Without thinking, she placed her fingers on his shoulder, feeling the tight muscles under his shirt. She kneaded the muscle, willing it to relax.

Jason groaned. "I just have to survive long enough. I have

to make these things happen. Otherwise, it will have been all for nothing."

Marnie kept massaging his shoulder. He let out another groan that made her heart ache.

"I'm not a great masseuse, but I can try give you a proper shoulder rub if you'd like?"

Jason smiled. "That's okay. This sounds weird, but I feel more relaxed right now than I've felt in months. Just sitting here with you. I don't know why." He glanced at her over his shoulder, his gaze roaming down to her cleavage.

Marnie burst into uncontrollable laughter. "Is it the boobs?" She was certainly drunk, those sneaky champagnes loosening her tongue. She tried to stop, but the giggles bubbled up, making her hiccup.

Jason hung his head, trying to look away. There was a smile in his voice as it cracked from embarrassment. "I can't *not* look at them. I'm only human. Although I haven't really had energy for that stuff lately, so I guess it's good that... I'm not totally dead from lack of sleep, you know? Not that I should be leering. Apologies."

"It's okay. My boobs are blushing, honestly. They're not used to being outdoors. I don't normally dress up like this. It feels really weird, like I'm trying to lure sailors or catch small objects falling from the sky."

"Well, I appreciate the view." His voice thicker, he turned and shamelessly stared at her cleavage, a silly grin splitting his face.

Marnie fought another bout of giggles. That bloody champagne was messing with her head, but she couldn't help enjoying the moment. Her whole body buzzed with giddiness, her heart thumping in her chest. If he made a move, she'd play along. She'd be Beatrice all the way.

Before she thought better of it, she lifted his index finger to study a dark ink stain. She couldn't stop touching him. Oh, no. She was in trouble. Encouraged by the clouded look in his eyes, she traced her hand along his sleeve, feeling the veins on his forearm under the smooth fabric. If only he'd lift the hand to touch her… but Jason let out another long sigh, slumping back against the couch.

"I'm sorry. You deserve better than this. I'm just… so… dead."

"It's okay." Marnie lifted her hand off his and turned to put her shoes back on. This guy was not well. He needed a good night's or a week's sleep. "Maybe you should take me to the right person, whoever you think should know about Kathleen? I'll tell them what happened, then you can go home and at least try to get some sleep."

He opened his eyes and sat up. "Yes, let's."

# Chapter 8

Marnie followed Jason through the maze of hallways, sneaking glimpses of the framed black-and-white portraits covering the walls. They arrived at another lift, and Jason led her in, holding his swipe card on the reader.

"We'll just pop into the upstairs office. There might be someone burning the midnight oil. Although it's hardly midnight, yet."

"Who are you looking for?"

"There are a few people who'd love to see Kathleen gone..." They exited the lift, and he stopped to swipe his key tag by another heavy door. "Follow my lead. We'll try to make it sound as casual as possible. Just tell them what you told me."

Marnie nodded, the knot in her stomach tightening. She wasn't an actress like Shasa, but then again, he wasn't asking her to lie.

Jason opened the door into a large open plan office, surrounded by glass-fronted rooms with MPs' names printed on them. Marnie surveyed the space, and her shoulders dropped. It was empty. She followed Jason as he traipsed across the geometrically patterned carpet, peering into various rooms and behind privacy screens. After a moment, he stopped and turned to her with a pained smile. "I'm sorry. I guess I was wrong. There must be a few good parties or something else going on tonight."

."It's okay. We can try again another time"

"Would you?" His eyes shone with relief.

Marnie gave him a vague nod. She still felt uncomfortable about his plan. Maybe the empty office was a sign, her last chance to back away. "You need to get some rest," she said, edging towards the door.

Jason nodded and led them out of the office.

Moments later, they stepped out of the lifts and descended the stairs to a deserted lobby. A friendly guard helped Marnie locate her jacket from the locked coat check. He raised his hand in greeting as they made their way through the security doors. Outside, darkness had fallen over the huge, paved square, streetlamps burning in the distance.

Marnie checked her phone, 9:45 p.m. This was it. They

would go their separate ways. It had been a wild ride, much wilder than she'd expected. That's what she wanted to focus on, not the overwhelming sense of loss that overtook her when she thought about walking away from him – a man she hardly knew. A man who lived in a world she could barely comprehend.

"Can I please get your phone number, to call you tomorrow?" he said. "We could meet here."

Marnie bit her lip. If she gave him her number, she'd risk him finding out her real name. As much as she wanted to, she couldn't. The anonymity made her feel safe, it was the only way she could give him what he was asking. "Could we just meet here, say nine a.m.?"

She gestured at the emblem-adorned glass doors, pleading for him to understand.

Jason gave her a sad smile. "Let's do that. Thank you, Beatrice. I appreciate your help." He offered his hand.

The handshake went on for seconds, neither of them willing to let go. Why he wasn't running away, she had no idea. But she liked it.

"No problem. It's been an exciting night." She smiled at him, finally letting go of his hand.

He shifted his weight from one foot to the other. "Where are you off to?"

"Back to the hotel, I think. Or maybe I'll get one of those crepes from the street kitchen. Although it's a bit of a walk." She gave him a quick wave and turned around. No point in prolonging the agony.

She made it three steps down the pavement, when he reappeared in front of her, forcing her to stop. His face radiated desperation that made her throat tight. "I know this will sound nuts but... stay with me? Just for one night. I mean – evening. Nothing you're uncomfortable with. Just hang out with me. I'm so tired, and I feel better with you. Is that crazy?" He grabbed her hands in his.

Marnie forced an awkward smile, her heart beating out of control. "It is a little crazy." She couldn't pull her hands away. His touch had arrested her whole body. She would stay here for as long as he held her. Her hands were officially his, while the rest of her cells argued over short-term rental options. Maybe she could extend this strange, magical night. This could be something to write about later. What would Beatrice do?

Jason gestured at the tall buildings in the distance, on the other side of the road. "I live over there. It's only a short walk."

"You want me to stay with you?"

"Yes. Just... be there."

"You don't want ... anything else?" Marnie couldn't hide her disappointment. He may have liked her breasts, but he wasn't interested in her. Not like that. He was just lonely, or worried that she wouldn't show up in the morning.

Jason bowed his head, his face contorting in regret. "I do. But I don't think I can. Not until I get some sleep. I'm so sorry."

Marnie couldn't stop her heart going out to him. "You poor thing. Do you really think I can help? That I can make you sleep?"

Jason shook his head with a sad smile. "I don't know. Probably not. But I'm so tired. I'm so tired of lying there by myself, staring at the ceiling. Or taking drugs that leave my head all muddled the next day. If I could break the cycle, to have someone there... I'm not making sense."

Marnie took his arm, and they walked silently across the square. He was making enough sense to her. She heard the genuine pain behind his words, could see it in his eyes, in the darkness that circled them. She'd caught a piece of his broken soul, and it called out to her. Guilt hit her for not giving him her real name. Still, she could try to help him, give him what he needed.

"Just promise not to ask me too many questions, okay? I'll go with you. I'll stay with you. In the morning, if you still think it's a good idea, we'll think of a way to alert the right people about the minister. Then we'll go our separate ways. Is that okay?"

A shadow fell over his smile. "You're not married, are you? Unavailable?"

"No. I'm just in town for one night and whatever this is... has no future. Trust me. But we have tonight."

Reaching the other side of the square, they descended a flight of stairs and crossed the street in companionable silence, approaching an old apartment building.

A bright female voice gave them both a start. "Well, hello there!"

Marnie turned, her heart jumping into her throat. She recognized that jaunty tone. Luna wore a glittery silver dress, and her impossibly high heels clicked against the pavement as she shuffled in front of them.

"Hi, Luna! Lovely to see you! This is—"

"I know Jason Hallett!" Luna offered him a toothy smile. "Wonderful to meet you!" She pulled him into a long handshake, her gaze lingering on him.

Marnie felt hot and cold, watching for Jason's reaction. Then she remembered her lie. Would Luna call her by her real name?

Jason wriggled out of the handshake, looking around. "Excuse us. We're on our way to get some crepes. It's quite a long walk." He gestured down the road, away from his apartment building.

Marnie nodded, feeling a little sick. Clearly, he didn't want the stylist to know he was taking Marnie home with him. She stared straight ahead, holding her breath, waiting for Luna to leave.

Jason slipped his hand around her, pulling her closer. "Should we get an Uber? Beatrice?"

"Beatrice?" Luna repeated, raising an eyebrow. "That sounds nice."

"Yes," Marnie said, a panicky smile on her face. "We

should go. Thank you for the makeover. I really feel like a different person. It's been so much fun."

Luna gave her a meaningful look. "It can be very liberating. Good to meet you, Jason. Hope you and... Beatrice have a lovely night." She flashed him a brilliant smile and walked on, her hips swaying seductively, night lights reflecting off the sequinned fabric. Like a mermaid.

Marnie wished she could walk like that.

Jason glanced after her as well, no doubt equally transfixed by her figure. "Who was that?"

"Um, Luna Bella. She's a stylist. She helped me choose this dress and get my hair done for the event. Otherwise, I would have looked ... it would have been bad."

Jason laughed. "I'm sure that's not true. But she did a good job."

He turned to the apartment building, which had Roman numerals carved in stone above its entrance. "Okay. We're here. Sorry, I didn't want to lead her to my place." He cast another glance at Luna's retreating figure. "She seemed like... one of those people."

Marnie nodded. She hated making assumptions about anyone, but something about Luna bothered her, and she was relieved that Jason sensed it too.

He took her hand and guided her to the building, punched in a security code to unlock the doors and used a key card to activate the lift. Gold-tinted mirrors lined the inside of the lift, forcing Marnie to look at herself. She hardly recognised the woman staring back at her – polished, with flushed cheeks. That professional makeup had some staying power! Her disguise was perfect, almost like she belonged in this world. The thought made her feel bolder, hungry for more. She couldn't be like Luna, but Jason was still with her, wasn't he? He hadn't abandoned her on the footpath to run after the shiny mermaid. That had to count for something.

# Chapter 9

Jason steadied himself against the back wall of the lift, his body heavy with fatigue. He could barely focus his eyes on the beguiling woman with him. What a waste. She was so delicious, someone to be savoured, worshipped. The things he wanted to do to her... if only his body wasn't run to the ground.

"It's a gorgeous building," she said softly.

He met her eyes in the mirror. "It is now." He could at least flirt back, make her feel special. What he was about to ask her was wrong, weird...

Jason sighed, trying to expel the shame.

They stepped out on the fifth floor and moved to the

far end of the carpeted hallway. Jason unlocked his door, revealing a small apartment dominated by a large tidily made bed. Room service had been there, keeping everything sterile and hotel-like.

Jason touched Beatrice's elbow, guiding her through the doorway, suddenly scared she would run away. "Would you like a drink? A cup of tea?"

She shrugged. "I'm good. So, you want to get some sleep?"

Jason forced himself to look her in the eye. "I'm sorry. This is the worst booty-call ever."

To his surprise, she blushed. "I wouldn't know. I've never really... anyway. Don't be sorry. You need sleep. If I can help, I will." She nudged him towards the bed, removing her heels. Her soft but firm tone calmed him further, flooding his veins with overwhelming drowsiness.

He kicked off his shoes and undressed, sliding between the sheets in his underwear. The bed felt heavenly, and a wave of exhaustion ran through his body, reminding him of home, the deep rest he'd once experienced in his cottage with the breeze from the lake blowing through his bedroom window. Beatrice lowered herself on the bed next to him, laying her hand on his hair, stroking it softly. She spoke in a voice too low for him to hear. The old urge stirred at the back of Jason's mind, his arm reaching for a laptop that was just out of reach. What if his secret was out there, in the depths of the internet? He should have checked, just quickly... But with every stroke of those gentle fingers, the urge dampened, turning into a distant echo. Before long, another wave of sleepiness engulfed him, a blanket of black and blue swallowing his busy mind, forcing him to surrender.

Jason opened his eyes to a faint light peeking through a gap in the curtains. Was it morning? The digital alarm on his nightstand blinked at 6:30 a.m. He'd slept through! He remembered waking a couple of times with his heart pounding and listening to Beatrice's breathing. But it hadn't lasted long. Her presence must have lulled him back to sleep. His head felt groggy and disoriented, which he recognised as the sign of true rest after a period of insomnia. For the first time in weeks, he felt functional, with fresh energy brewing under the surface. What absolute magic. If he shut his eyes, he could drift off again, catch a couple more hours. It felt unreal, like someone had saved him.

Beatrice.

He turned around and caught the tangle of chestnut curls on the pillow, her hand resting next to it, her peaceful, sleeping face peeking through the gap. He watched her curves, her shoulder rising and falling with her breathing. That dress she'd worn last night. He'd dreamed about it. In his dream, he'd made love to this woman, over and over again. He'd been the man he was supposed to be, full of life and energy.

Jason pulled on the sheet, hoping to catch a glimpse of her dress and her cleavage. But Beatrice wasn't wearing the dress. Her full breasts rested against her curled-up arm, dark nipples staring at him, cherries on white icing. Unable to help himself, Jason pulled the sheet a little lower and caught a glimpse of her underwear. Thank goodness. It was too early in the morning to spontaneously self-combust from excitement. He lay in silence, staring at her soft, smooth curves sinking into the mattress. Okay. He was officially not responsible for his bodily reactions. Actions, yes. But his hard-on was an uncontrollable fact of life. She'd magicked him into sleeping all night and woken his libido, like jumpstarting a car. A sorceress. Or an angel sent from heaven. Either way, he couldn't allow her to leave. He needed her like he needed air to breathe.

Beatrice shifted. Maybe she could feel his hungry gaze burning her skin. Jason pulled the sheet up a little, hoping she wasn't too cold.

He should let her sleep, but before he closed his eyes, she cracked hers, staring at him in confusion.

"Sorry I woke you," he whispered.

She seemed to take a moment to get her bearings. Then her face morphed into the most adorable, hopeful smile, eyes wrinkling in the corners. "Did you sleep?"

"I slept," Jason croaked. "Thank you. You have no idea what this means to me."

"What time is it?"

"Only six-thirty."

"Do you want to sleep some more?"

"I do. But..." Heat rose up his chest, burning his neck. "I was looking at you. You're... you're gorgeous. Sorry. Go back to sleep."

Her cheeks reddened as she pulled the sheet up to her chin. "I... I didn't have any pyjamas and couldn't risk sleeping in that fancy dress. I want to be able to sell it later."

He grinned. "I really don't mind. But do you want to borrow a T-shirt?"

"Yes, please."

Jason shifted to get up and fetch one, but Marnie stopped him. "It's okay. Stay in bed, you might get back to sleep. Just look the other way, okay?"

He laughed but turned around and found his laptop on the nightstand. He googled himself and scrolled through the results. Nothing new. His eyes hurt and he lowered the screen brightness. The sun wasn't up yet. There was only enough light to make out the shape of the room, corners swallowed by darkness. He heard the drawer opening and couldn't help himself. Moving as softly and quietly as he could, Jason turned his head. His tongue stuck to the roof of his mouth. She held up one of his white T-shirts, her hourglass figure illuminated against the shadows. Soft. Feminine. Perfect. She glanced into the mirror hanging over the dresser and pulled the shirt over her head. As she shifted sideways, he caught a glimpse of her breast before it disappeared inside the white cotton.

Without warning, she whipped around and caught him looking.

Shit. Jason raised his hands in surrender. "I'm so sorry. I couldn't resist."

Marnie tugged at the T-shirt, which reached her mid-thigh. "You promised."

"I know." Jason grimaced, trying to communicate his remorse across the room. "It's just that you're stunning. I couldn't control my eyes!"

"I don't..."

"Please come back to bed. It's really early."

She shuffled for a moment but joined him under the sheets. "Were you looking the whole time? When I dropped that other shirt on the floor and had to pick it up?" Her words brimmed with nervousness.

"Damn! I missed that!" He couldn't help the disappointment in his voice.

Marnie disappeared behind the sheets, but he heard a quiet giggle. "My ass is really not that hard to miss."

"What are you talking about? You're not big. You're sexy, though. That ass of yours is all I can think about."

She peeked at him from behind the sheets. "Really?" She seemed to light up from his words and he felt the urge to pour more on her, to open the window and shout out to the streets.

"Honestly, you're perfect. I can't stop staring. I know my

body needs more sleep, but I don't want to close my eyes."

She blushed, burying her face in the pillow. "You're making fun of me, aren't you?"

"What do you mean?" Confused, Jason lifted the curls off her face, but she wouldn't turn her head. He gently pushed her shoulder to roll her onto her back. She didn't fight him hard but brought her hand over her face. He hovered over her, brushed away the hair and saw tears spilling out of the corners of her eyes.

"I'm not what you think." She squeezed her hands into tight fists and more tears rolled down her cheeks. "But thank you."

"For what?" He laughed a little, attempting at lightness that wasn't available.

"For saying those things. I can't believe that someone like you… you have no idea what it means. Even if it's not real."

"What's not real?"

"That you'd really want me." She lowered her fists to peek at him.

Jason stared into her hazel eyes, trying to uncover the truth she'd hidden in there. She'd told him she wasn't married or unavailable. He had to trust her word. If only she'd do the same.

"Why would I say it if I didn't mean it?" He held his hand on her face, desperate to trace it down her body. But she wasn't ready for it, so he couldn't.

"I don't know." She smiled through the tears. "Politics."

"This has nothing to do with politics! For me, this is just a ... miracle. And there are no miracles in politics, trust me."

"What's a miracle?"

"The way I feel right here, next to you. I've thought of nothing but work for months. Night or day. But when I look at you, my mind goes blank. That's how hot you are! You shut down my brain."

Her eyes widened and she gestured at her face. "It's all this styling, and hair and makeup. I don't know what they painted my face with, but it's like... permanent."

Jason took a breath, his gaze drawn towards the shape of her hips under the sheet. "Can I please kiss you? You're talking nonsense and I don't know how to shut you up."

"Okay," she rasped, and that was all the invitation he needed.

Jason closed his mouth on hers, his body waking up in excitement as she parted her lips, inviting him in. He'd slept. He was alive. Nothing else mattered. He deepened the kiss, sneaking a taste of her tongue. She whimpered into his mouth, intensifying his hunger. Tracing his lips down her body, he searched for those cherry nipples, capturing on in his mouth. His hand landed on her round stomach, and she moaned softly. He glanced up at her face and saw her eyes closed, mouth ajar. So perfect.

She arched her back, guiding his hand lower.

"Are you sure?" he asked, his voice so thick it nearly caught in his throat.

"If you are?" she gasped breathlessly.

He'd never been surer of anything.

Jason slid his fingers between her legs, shivering as he they reached a pool of wetness. He could barely think. How had he been living without this?

"Do you have a condom?" she gasped as his fingers circled her.

Did he? He'd never had any visitors here. He'd never even contemplated bringing anyone up here. Life had been about survival, about not falling over. He was pitifully ill-prepared.

"Sorry, I don't." He groaned, falling back on his back, trying to ignore the painful ache in his groin. "Do you?"

Beatrice sat up, shaking her head. "I'm willing to risk it if you are? I haven't been with anyone in ... years." Her face reddened with embarrassment.

His chest fluttered and his hard-on stood up in renewed excitement. "I had a pretty thorough physical a few months ago and haven't been with anyone since. But... what about pregnancy?"

"You don't have to worry about that," she whispered, her tone even.

Jason thought about asking why but staring at the ample pair of breasts dangling within his reach, the words got lost. The only thing he cared about was that she stayed with him. He cupped one breast in his hand, revelling in the weight of it. He wanted these breasts in his bed every night, without fail. He'd do anything to make that happen.

"How do you like it?" he asked.

Her eyes rounded in surprise, like nobody had ever asked, like she'd never had to put this into words. "I want to try everything," she said, biting her lip. "That sounds stupid. But I just want everything."

"Let's." His voice choked up and he rolled her over on the bed.

If only he'd been fully awake. His fuzzy brain was still fighting his urges, wooing his head back towards the pillow. He wanted to be better than this. He wanted to want everything, but this wasn't going to be one of those tantric sessions; there wasn't enough in his tank for that.

As if sensing his inner struggle, Marnie spread her legs, pulling him in. He traced his hand up her thigh, but she reached for him, and her eyes grew wide as her fingers wrapped around his hard-on. Jason held his breath, sliding his fingers between her legs. Marnie pushed against his hand, whimpering. He circled her opening, enjoying the slick feeling on his fingers. "You feel so good. Tell me what you like..."

He increased his pace, but his eyes dipped slightly from a wave of exhaustion, his supporting arm shaking a little. Maybe one night of sleep wasn't enough to fully restore him. Jason sucked in a breath, trying to focus.

Marnie traced his stubble with her index finger. "It's okay. Just take me," she whispered. "I'm ready."

Coaxed by her hands, Jason drove into her. The perfection

of it. She moaned under him, digging her fingernails into his arms, making him forget everything else. With every thrust, he cared less, worried less, wanted more.

He kept going, propelled by the soft moans of the woman under him, until a violent release shook his body, emptying him into the perfect, soft body of a stranger.

"I'm sorry," he mumbled, falling back on his side of the bed, still twitching from the aftershocks.

Too fast, he accosted himself. Selfish. But satisfied. Utterly empty and satisfied. He should have looked after her, made sure she came first. He should have done everything differently.

"Why are you sorry?" she asked.

"I couldn't hold any longer. I should have..." an exasperated sigh escaped his lips and he let his head sink into the pillow. "You deserve so much better. Do you want me to..." He reached for her, but she gently patted his hand away.

He felt her fingertips on his face, stroking his stubble. "Shh. It's all good. Get some more sleep."

Jason moaned, shame washing over him. But each soft stroke of her hand showed she wasn't angry with him. He'd sleep some more and do better. He'd control himself and look after her, make amends for the rest of his life. But first, he'd sleep and gather his strength.

He closed his eyes, and sparkly darkness took over, little stars bursting and twinkling behind his eyelids, his brain sinking into the sweet relief of sleep.

Jason woke again, his eyes puffy and swollen but his mind cleansed. He'd slept. He'd slept solidly until late morning. His alarm shone: 9:05 a.m. Holy shit! He turned over on the crisp sheets, revelling at the way his body felt. Ready for battle. Top of the world. Every other cliché in the book. Today was going to be a good day. And it was all thanks to...

Where was she?

Jason's arm fell on the crumpled sheets. The bed was empty. Cold. As cold as the sweat prickling between his shoulder blades when he sat up, scanning the room. No dress. No shoes. No handbag. Jason leapt up and raced into the bathroom. Empty. She'd snuck out. He'd been a hideous, selfish lover, and she'd taken her exit.

Jason rushed to the window and cranked it open to peer down the street. A handful of pedestrians moved like ants along their path, an occasional car cruised past. No one resembled Beatrice. Jason held back a growl. A rustling sound caught his attention and he turned around. The breeze from the window had sent the papers on his nightstand flying. It didn't matter. He'd pick them up later.

What could he do? If he rushed out now, would he find her still walking somewhere? He felt the sheets for any sign of warmth. No. She'd left a long time ago.

This couldn't be happening. It was worse than a nightmare.

He'd found a cure, and it had been snatched away. He'd let her slip through his fingers.

Why had he gone back to sleep? If only he'd held onto her, tried a little harder. He could have slept more the following night. If he had Beatrice, he'd sleep anytime, anywhere. Except that made no sense. She was just a woman. She wasn't magic. Maybe last night had been a fluke, a one-off. Or maybe...

Adrenaline flooded Jason's veins. If there was any chance this woman was the cure, he'd find her. He'd apologise on his knees. He'd show her he could be better.

He didn't know much about her, but he knew enough. She'd been at the gala last night and her name was Beatrice. She couldn't hide from him.

Jason took out his phone and brought up his assistant's number. The perky lady who'd boasted about her research skills would get to prove herself.

# Chapter 10

Marnie ran down the footpath, wincing every time her swollen feet hit the pavement. She'd never done the walk of shame. They made fun of it in the movies, but she'd never realised how apt the name really was. She felt everyone's eyes on her as she navigated down the city centre, towards her hotel.

Her cheeks burned, yet a silly grin broke through every now and then. She'd slept with a gorgeous politician. A tortured man, sure, but so sexy. So sweet. Did that make her a loose woman? She hadn't done anything with anyone in more than five years. She was practically a virgin again, lost and confused about every detail, yet shocked by how her body had responded to his touch. She'd craved him so desperately she'd forgotten everything else. Maybe it had been a mistake, but she now had an experience nobody could take away. She could die knowing that she'd been desired for one glorious night.

Her heel hit an uneven tile on the pavement, and she yelped in pain. The hotel entrance loomed ahead, big block letters above sliding glass doors. To get to her room, she'd have to make it past the judgmental eyes of the concierge. Then she'd lay low for a while, order room service, pack up her things and leave.

Keeping her head low, Marnie snuck in. The desk was unmanned. Small mercies. She rushed to the lifts. Ascending to her floor, she felt a tingle at the bottom of her belly. Memories of last night flooded her body with endorphins. She'd finished herself off after he'd fallen back to sleep. After being so close, she'd had to give herself the release her body was screaming for. It's what Beatrice would have done, for sure. Her heroine might have asked for a bit more from her lover, but she'd felt bad about keeping him awake. The poor man needed more sleep.

Flashing her key card in front of the electric lock, she let herself into the room. It would look odd if she left the bed completely unused, so she undressed, peeled off the covers and slid under the cool sheet.

Her plan had been solid. He didn't know her name or anything about her. He had no way of contacting her.

Except... she'd already failed the plan. She'd left a note.

Marnie smiled, her heart drumming against her breastbone. She took out her phone and propped it on the pillow. She hadn't been able to resist the temptation and now she was playing a game she couldn't win. He was young and gorgeous. Once he got over the sleep issues, he'd want someone young and gorgeous to match his style.

How old was he? Ever since she'd left his apartment, Marnie had been dying to google Jason. She'd noticed a list of search results on his laptop screen. He'd typed his own name into the search engine. She'd wondered why, but her fingers had also itched to click on those links, to find out more about him. Holding her breath, Marnie picked up her phone. It took her a couple of clicks to find out his age: 35. He was younger, but not as young as she'd feared. He was accomplished though, with a Master's in both education and legal studies. And he was famous. Properly famous, with thousands of search results. Marnie's heart pounded in her ears as she browsed the endless list of links to articles, gossip sites and conversations on Jason's politics and love life. They lived in completely different worlds.

She knew they had no future, but her heart hadn't listened to reason. She'd taken a sticky note off his desk and left her phone number on his nightstand. If he was as desperate to find her as her foolish heart hoped, he'd call.

# Chapter 11

"What do you mean there's no Beatrice?" Jason tried to keep his tone calm, but an unmistakable edge crept in.

His assistant Tracy, a 25-year-old history major with bleached hair and a fidgety manner, clutched a folder in slight panic. "I've checked the guest list twice. There's a Bridget. Could it be Bridget?"

"No. What about middle names? Check middle names."

Jason paced the short distance between his desk and bookshelf in his office, rubbing his temples. It was Monday. He'd barely slept last night, and the effects of that one amazing night were fading by the minute. He had to find her, bring her back, fix this.

Tracy blinked, her eyes glistening. "There are no middle names on this list."

"That's why it's called research!" Jason growled. He saw the girl's hands shaking. This wasn't right. He needed her on his side. He had to be honest with her.

"I'm sorry, Trace." Jason guided his assistant to a chair and sat down next to her. "I'm not trying to be a dick. I'm just desperate. I met this woman at the arts gala and she… she spent the night. You know how I've had trouble sleeping?" Tracy nodded, a flicker of compassion lighting up her eyes. Jason lowered his voice. "She's got something. I swear to you. It makes no sense, but when I was with her, I just relaxed. I slept 12 hours. It was amazing."

Tracy's mouth hung open as she studied his face. Jason tried to hear his own words as she must have heard them – he sounded like he'd completely lost it. Heart thumping in his chest, he waited.

"She made you fall asleep?"

"I know how it sounds, and I might be completely wrong, but I can't afford to get any worse. I have to get my sleep under control, keep my brain ticking. So, if there's any chance she's the answer, I have to find her. Do you understand?"

He considered telling Tracy what Beatrice had witnessed with Kathleen, but if they ever went through with the plan, it was best his assistant knew nothing about it. The fewer people he dragged down with him, the better.

"Can't you just take sleeping pills like everyone else?"

"I do, but they don't really work. They addle my brain. I'm functioning, but I'm not fighting fit. I need to be fighting fit! Wait... who else is taking pills?" Jason narrowed his eyes. In her job application, the girl had described herself a people person, and boy was that accurate. She seemed to be constantly in conversation with someone at the office.

Tracy looked up, her lips pursed, calculating. "At least five people I've spoken to."

Jason wanted to ask for their names but stopped himself. Tracy seemed uncomfortable sharing private details, which was perfect. He needed that discretion more than anyone. If he couldn't trust his closest team, everything would fall apart.

Tracy got up and glanced through the glass door into the hallway. Her eyes flashed with alarm. "Incoming."

It was her code word for Kathleen. On Mondays, the MPs were not required to be in the building, so only the most dedicated showed up. People like Kathleen. Jason instinctively straightened his back and rolled his chair behind the large desk, partially hiding behind his computer screen.

"I'll get back to my... research," Tracy concluded, passing Kathleen's burly figure at the doorway.

"Jason, you have a minute?" Not waiting for an answer, Kathleen bulldozed into his office and sat across the desk from him. She slipped her hands in her lap, away from view. If they were shaking, nothing on her face gave it away as she fixed her steely gaze on him.

"This empty homes tax. We've been investigating it for three months now, and it's time to publish some conclusions. Obviously, it isn't happening. But we have to make it sound like we looked into it, long and hard. Since you're passionate about it, I think you should make the announcement on behalf of the group."

Jason swallowed a hard lump in his throat. Currently, the working group was evenly split between those for and against the tax. Jason had tried to hide his true passion for the subject, fearing he would be seen as biased.

He met Kathleen's gaze, keeping his tone casual. "Are we sure it won't make a difference? Vancouver is collecting 40 million per year and investing it in affordable housing. It won't fix the housing crisis, but it's not *nothing* either. We could recommend one for big cities only. No one would have to pay tax for an empty holiday home in Coromandel."

"What about Waiheke Island? Piha? Muriwai? There are plenty of remote holiday spots in Auckland. You know how the media will twist this, don't you? They'll say we're forcing hard working Aucklanders to rent out their holiday homes to meth-cooking gang members."

Jason gritted his teeth. The deep-seated prejudice in Kathleen's words made his skin prickle. He lowered his voice, determined to keep his cool. "No, they'd just pay the tax to help support fellow Aucklanders into healthy homes."

A condescending smile hovered on Kathleen's fuchsia

lips. She'd made up her mind and could easily torpedo their suggestions. But if Jason could get the working group to recommend the tax, she'd have to shoot them down in public. It would make her look bad. Plenty of people who didn't own empty properties were willing to support the tax. And if there was a chance Kathleen was on her way out… Jason couldn't help daydreaming. He had to believe it was possible. Then everything he'd done to get here would be justified.

"That's the kind of passion the public wants to see. You should definitely make the announcement." Kathleen's words rang with a finality Jason recognised from earlier encounters. Play ball or get out of the way.

Kathleen got up and sailed to the door, turning to give him one last look. A warning. "Unless you're not feeling well, of course. You look tired."

The nerve! She was the one who'd passed out in a public bathroom and hadn't reported it.

"I'm feeling great." Jason bounced out of his chair. Head rush. He slung his arm on the tall cabinet for support. "Never better."

He had to find Beatrice. Now.

Half an hour later, Jason made it out of the parliament building. He crossed the square and stopped at the edge of the vast lawn, filling his lungs with cool evening air. In the distance, streetlights flickered on as Wellington transitioned into Monday night. Time marched on, carrying him towards yet another sleepless night. Was there any hope? Even if Beatrice was the answer, she likely lived at the other end of the island, possibly a nine-hour drive away. How could he ever make it work?

Setting his sights on the apartment building across the street, Jason descended the wide stairs, weaving between occasional pedestrians on his way down. He didn't notice the woman until she tapped him on the shoulder at the traffic lights.

Jason turned, drawing a sharp breath. He'd only met her in passing on Saturday night, but recognised her immediately. The stylist. She wore a similar figure-hugging dress, albeit with less sparkle, and teetered expertly on stilettos. How could she balance those curves with such little ground contact?

A warm smile lit her features as she caught his attention. "You might not remember me, but we met briefly on Saturday night."

"I remember. Luna, right?" Jason cleared his throat. "Actually, I'm glad I ran into you. I could use your help."

The light turned green, and she fell into step with him as they crossed the road. Once on the other side, she curled her long-nailed fingers around his arm. "What can I do for you, Jason?"

He dropped his arm to break contact. "You remember the woman I was with on Saturday night? Beatrice? She said you helped her find a dress. Would you have her contact details? I'm trying to get in touch."

Luna narrowed her eyes. A flicker of annoyance tugged at her mouth before she turned on her megawatt smile. "Absolutely. Let me just..."

Jason's heart leapt as she pulled a business card and a pen from her purse, wrote something on the card and passed it to him with a meaningful look.

"Here you go. My number's on the other side. We could have some fun together." She held his gaze for a moment, then spun on her heels and disappeared into the evening crowd, hips swaying with purpose like a trout swimming upstream.

Having caught the last glimpse of her round buttocks, Jason studied the business card, desperate for Beatrice's phone number. Where was it? One side displayed the woman's name, Luna Bella, stylist and influencer. On the other side, she'd written 'Call me, sexy, and I'll tell you everything'. Jason tightened his fist, overwhelmed by the desire to punch something. He wanted to rip the card to shreds, but something held him back – this woman knew Beatrice. She held the answer to his problems, and she was playing with him.

Jason stepped into his apartment, his mind reeling. Outside the window, night had fallen, the streets below dotted by thousands of lights. Familiar uncertainty tightened his throat as he approached bedtime. The time of relaxing, if only he could bring himself to let go, to reach the peace that allowed sleep. But he couldn't relax. Not here. Not by himself. And every night he stayed awake added one more bad experience to his frame of reference, convincing him of the opposite.

Jason made a cup of chamomile tea and settled in the armchair to work on press releases. He resisted the urge to call Malcolm. The big guy had talked Jason off the ledge more than once, insisting that they had no need to feel guilty, they'd merely played the game like everyone else and won. There was no other way to achieve political goals, Malcolm maintained, and it would all be worth it in the end.

Jason inhaled the steam rising from his cup, squeezing his eyes shut. He'd write those press releases, take his pills, bide his time and crawl under the covers when the nausea-like blackness closed in, narrowing his vision.

After the second press release was done, Jason's eyes jumped to the business card he'd placed on the side table. Luna's number. What would happen if he contacted her? He picked up the card, a cold sensation travelling down his spine. What kind of web was this woman weaving for him? Could he extract Beatrice's phone number from her without getting tangled in it? And what if Beatrice wanted nothing to do with him? She'd snuck away in the middle of the night without leaving her phone number. It probably wasn't every woman's dream to lull a grown man to sleep and then experience such a lame effort in bed. He longed for a do-over.

Damn it! He could handle one social media influencer. He would flirt, pretend to open up and spin some tale that got him what he wanted. Beatrice. Sleep. Kathleen's downfall. Which one was he after? Or was it all three?

Jason drained his teacup, sighing out loud. Exhaustion spun his brain in an endless loop of what-ifs. What if the magic wore off? What if it had nothing to do with Beatrice? Maybe he just needed a woman, any woman, by his side. What if Luna could help him sleep, just like Beatrice? She was here, available, contactable. He didn't feel the same primal pull to her he'd felt with Beatrice, quite the opposite, but did it matter? Lightning didn't strike twice, but maybe he could manufacture his own magic.

Darkness compressing his lungs, Jason took his phone and composed a short, simple text.

*You forgot to write down Beatrice's details. Maybe you can send them via text? Jason.*

The reply came almost instantly.

*Maybe we can meet for drinks tomorrow? I promise to give you what you need ;)*

Jason recoiled. What was he doing? Surely there was another way to find Beatrice without getting sucked into this woman's games. Tracy had promised to doublecheck the guest list. Beatrice had been at the party. She existed. More than that, she did something funny to him. It wasn't just about the sleep. For a moment, he'd been happy. At peace. What if she was the one? When had he stopped believing in love at first sight and settling for whoever gave him a phone number? Pathetic. Sure, he was lonely, bone-tired and desperate. But still, pathetic.

Jason stared at the phone screen, trying to breathe away the invasive thoughts. Focus on the present. Calm down. If merely texting with this woman gave him nausea, he'd be wise to steer clear of her.

*Sorry, can't make it tomorrow.*

It had a vague ring of avoidance. Seeing he wasn't that keen, Luna might move on and forget all about it.

After a moment, his phone beeped again.

*I don't mind waiting.*

Jason placed his phone on the table, cold sweat chilling his neck. She probably meant to sound flirtatious, but her words came off as ominous.

Jason got up to make another cup of tea, knowing that no amount of chamomile would make a dent on the swell of anxiety in his chest.

Why had he sent that text, when all he wanted was to curl up next to Beatrice, or whatever her real name was, and inhale her sweet scent while his pulse settled to a normal rhythm? Just thinking about her helped, he noted. The memory of Beatrice soothed him like a weighted blanket.

# Chapter 12

Marnie approached her own front door with trepidation. Early afternoon light made her shield her eyes, but there was a nip in the air. The drive from her hideaway in Paraparaumu had felt endless, yet she wasn't ready for this. She'd meant to come back from her trip with a new perspective, acceptance, or at least a smidgen of clarity. Instead, her head ached with confusion.

After the dream-like Wellington experience, she'd returned to her remote Airbnb and worked on her novel for the rest of the week, checking her phone every fifteen minutes. It never rang. Shasa had texted her a couple of times to check how she was doing, and Tanya once, begging for McDonalds from Uber Eats. Fighting the urge to submit, Marnie had sent her daughter the healthiest McSalad she could find and later received a string of angry emojis. But that was it. Not a word from Jason. By the time she'd checked out, the heavy realisation finally sank in: he didn't want to see her again.

At least the experience had fuelled her writing. The hero of her next novel was getting more and more like a certain politician she couldn't stop googling about. He might not have been interested in her, but she had pored over stories about him – every interview, video clip and photo she could find. If she called it book research, it sounded better in her head.

"You're home!"

Shasa's voice made her turn around and she lost her balance as little Lilla flung her arms around her legs. She clutched the suitcase she was wheeling, stumbled backwards and eventually hit her back on the door.

"Oh, I missed you, too!" She gave them both a tight hug. It was good to be missed.

"Are you ready to go in and... see the backyard?"

The backyard! Marnie had completely forgotten about the fountain. She shook her head. "I've seen the photo. How much worse can it be? You're welcome to stay for a drink if there's anything left in the house. Tanya's still at school."

She opened the door, and Shasa and Lilla followed her inside.

Lilla ran to pull the curtains covering the sliding doors leading to her backyard. "Ta-daa!"

Oh, dear God.

Her back garden basked in the bright afternoon sun, making the dolphin feature glisten like a massive jewel. It was so much bigger than she'd thought, taking over most of her little yard. Marnie looked away, colourful floaters crowding her vision.

Shasa pulled a sympathetic face. "Lando called in yesterday to ask if you're back. He was dropping these hints about… courting you. You should talk to him."

Marnie nodded, cold sweat prickling her neck. As tacky as the water feature was, it must have been expensive. "Do you think he's done that to impress me?"

Shasa cocked her head, her eyebrows knitted. "You let him design your garden. I think he saw that as an opening and decided to… go big or go home. He actually said that."

Marnie rubbed her temples. The swoosh of her sliding door drew her attention. Lilla had flipped the lock and managed to pull it open. With a delighted squeal, she ran to the fountain.

Thank goodness it wasn't running with water, yet.

"Dolphins!" the girl enthused, trying to climb up the side, but failing.

Satisfied that the child wouldn't be able to get up on it and fall, Marnie joined Shasa in the kitchen.

"How was the trip? Did you get a lot of writing done?"

Shasa asked, filling the jug to boil some water.

Marnie leaned her elbows on the kitchen counter, eyeing the shrivelled apples and kiwifruit she'd left for Tanya. "I did. The story's changing though."

"How?"

Marnie smiled to herself. "This hero's a bit different. More of a tortured soul. How are you and Mac? How are the wedding plans?"

Shasa's eyes lit up, and she launched into details about their wedding preparations. Good. Marnie needed a moment to regroup. Was she ready to tell Shasa about what had happened in Wellington?

"Mac's parents want to invite all the cousins, everyone from the street and half the town. Sue hates excluding anyone, so the list keeps growing. But we can't afford it, and I can't let them pay for it. Honestly, neither of us want such a big party. It's just too grand. I don't know what to do."

Shasa made herself a cup of tea, then another one for Marnie. "You don't drink coffee this late, do you?"

"No, this is perfect. Have you thought about having two weddings? One for just the two of you and the other for John and Sue with everyone else? With the second one, you could skip the ceremony and just have a low-key party. Might be cheaper."

Shasa sipped her tea, looking out the deck door where her daughter was throwing small rocks at the dolphins. "You mean like eloping? I admit I'm fantasising about that right now. Maybe we can just travel to South Island and ... all you need is two people to testify or sign something, right? We could just ask two random people in the street and get it over with."

"I didn't mean that! I don't want to miss your wedding and have some random strangers standing there! Promise me you won't do that."

Shasa smiled. "Fine." She studied Marnie's face for a beat. "You look different."

She cocked her head, her dark bob falling over a pair of concerned eyes. Marnie's chest swelled with emotion. Why hadn't she shared everything with her from the start? Dealing with her issues by driving away had been the stupidest idea, a panic solution that had only brought her more pain.

"I have early onset arthritis," she blurted, wincing at the pain that shot through her fingers as if her body had just remembered it was supposed to be hurting. "It's not far along yet, but it might get worse. It's more aggressive than osteoarthritis that older people get. And I guess I wasn't ready for it, any of it, so that's kind of why I went away for a bit, to digest the news. I'm sorry, I should have told you."

Shasa pulled her friend into a tight hug. "Oh, Marnie. That's rough. And so unfair. You're so young." She released Marnie's to look her in the eye. "Oh, my God! You've been doing all that packing and boxing at work! You can't do that anymore! I won't let you."

Words stuck in Marnie's throat. This is what she'd been afraid of, unwilling to even consider. If you took away everything that hurt, she couldn't do her job at all. She'd have to retire and write books. Except, typing hurt too. She'd have to dictate. Great. She'd be home alone all day, every day, talking to herself, with no way to pay her mortgage.

"There's treatment for it, right?" Shasa studied her face.

"Sure. And a diet."

"What kind?"

Marnie winced. "I've been to scared to check. It'll be all carrots and celery juice."

Shasa was already on her phone. "Avoid sugar, dairy, processed foods, alcohol..."

Of course. Unwilling to hear the rest, Marnie snuck outside to check on Lilla.

When she came back, Shasa jumped up, holding her phone. "Look! I found this article about fasting. A 48-hour fast might reset your body and make the symptoms go away completely."

Marnie grabbed the phone and scrolled through the article, a hope igniting. She'd never fasted in her life, but maybe she could do it. The idea of resetting her body sounded amazing. If she could start over, be okay for a little bit longer, then maybe she wouldn't end up alone. She could find someone like Jason. Or, more likely, someone like Lando. Despite his propensity for fanny packs and bicycle shorts, he wasn't a bad guy. All that cycling had made his calves really pop.

Marnie looked out the glass doors. The sun had dropped behind the neighbouring house, leaving the dolphins in the shadow. Lilla had lost interest in the fountain and was exploring the decorative pebbles outside the door. "It doesn't look too bad in the shade."

Shasa narrowed her eyes. "I know that look! You're not keeping it."

"Lando will be crushed if I say I don't like it. He must have spent a lot of money on it."

"Then he can sell it and get his money back!"

Marnie shook her head. "Who would buy it though?"

Shasa cast her a stern look. "Listen to yourself! You're dealing with an illness, you need to look after yourself, not worry about some middle-aged man-child's feelings! He never asked for your opinion. It's all on him!"

Marnie bit her lip. Shasa was right, but she couldn't help how she was wired.

"Fine." Marnie patted Shasa's arm and guided them onto the couches, away from the direct view of the backyard.

"So, how was the gala? Do you have any photos?" Shasa asked.

"Yes!" Marnie looked around for her phone. Where was it? Oh, right. Charging on the kitchen counter.

As she picked it up, she noticed a missed call. A blocked number. Could it be...? Before the she made it back to the couch, the phone rang. Again, a blocked number. Her hands shaking, Marnie glanced at Shasa. "Sorry, I should take this."

She skipped across the floor and hid in Tanya's bedroom, cringing at the pile of clothes covering her daughter's bed.

"Hello?"

"Is this Marnie Browne?"

Marnie immediately recognised Kathleen's voice. Her entire body froze, and she had to remind herself to breathe. "Yes."

"Oh, I'm so glad I reached you! I just wanted to follow up on our little conversation."

"Okay." Marnie swallowed air. Why couldn't she think of a complete sentence?

"Look, Marnie. I saw you talking to Jason Hallett at the end of the evening, and I just wanted to offer some words of advice, woman to woman."

"Advice?" Marnie parroted. The air around her felt freezing, and she glanced to see whether Tanya had left her window open. No, the chill was coming through the phone.

"I know he's a charming fellow and a gifted orator. But he has an agenda." She drew a breath, as if for dramatic effect. "He's after my housing portfolio, Marnie. Jason wants me gone. There's nothing wrong with ambition, of course. But he's digging for dirt."

"How do you know?"

"I'm not stupid, Marnie. Despite what some suggest, I haven't lost my mental faculties. There's nothing wrong with me!" The strain in her voice broke through the controlled veneer. She didn't sound okay.

"That's good," Marnie replied, keeping her tone calm. "Then why did you call me?"

The line went quiet for a moment. Marnie checked to make sure the call hadn't ended.

"Marnie? Is this Marnie Browne?"

"Yes, it's still Marnie Browne." Had Kathleen forgotten the previous two minutes?

"Yes, of course it is!" Kathleen spat back. "I called to warn you about Jason. You should know who you're dealing with. What his motives might be."

"That's okay. I'm not worried. Is that all, or..."

"Well, obviously, I want to make sure I can trust your discretion, Marnie. Especially around people like Jason. Even the most innocuous conversation might reveal far more than you intended. What exactly did you talk about with him?"

Marnie's stomach tensed. "Oh... election issues. I think he just wanted my vote." As the lie left her lips, the knot in her stomach tightened. Jason had promised not to drag her in the middle of this. She had to trust him, even if he didn't want to see her again. It had only been a week. Politicians were busy people. Maybe he'd still call. Even if he didn't, telling Kathleen about the night she'd spent with Jason would hurt them both.

"Wonderful, Marnie. My assistant will send you something nice as a little thank you. Do you enjoy spas?"

"No, no! There's absolutely no need—"

"You don't like spas? How about artisan chocolate? I know

a lovely chocolatier."

Marnie shuffled her feet. If she fought too hard, Kathleen would get suspicious. "Yes, chocolate sounds great, thank you!"

"Very well, I'll make sure that gets to you. Must run now, thank you for your time."

She ended the call, leaving Marnie squeezing the phone. Kathleen hadn't even asked for her address, but Marnie had no doubt she'd find it as easily as she'd found her phone number. Marnie rarely picked up a call from an unknown number, scared of scam artists, but this time she'd taken the risk, desperate to hear from Jason. And now she was terrified of a chocolate delivery.

Marnie sat on the pile of clothes, hoping to settle her pulse before joining Shasa in the lounge. Was Jason as ruthless as Kathleen made out? Was his interest in her only for her help in bringing down Kathleen? Why had he invited her back to his place, then? Why had he slept with her? As much as her gut twisted at the thought, she still felt the powerful pull for him. She wanted to talk to him, now more than ever. She wanted to ask him what he thought of all this.

Kathleen had seen her sitting with Jason at the end of the gala, but she didn't seem to know about the night they'd spent together. Nothing about her health issues had reached the news – Marnie had checked regularly, wondering if Jason would go to the media. Now, she could only hope things stayed that way. Or maybe she could get in touch with him?

She wanted to see him again, desperately. Could she use her anxiety over Kathleen's phone call as an excuse? Could she stomach the regret on his face if it turned out he really didn't want to see her again? If he wasn't just busy, but had decided to blow her off? The thought made her shiver.

Marnie gathered her wits. She had to tell Shasa. Maybe she couldn't talk about Kathleen, but she could tell her friend about Jason. Given she could think about nothing else, it seemed the only way forward.

She found Shasa on the couch, dodging Lilla's acrobatics as she tried to somersault across the length of the seat. "Who was that? Are you okay?"

Marnie caught Lilla in mid-jump and secured the child in her lap. She squirmed and giggled, but finally settled.

"I want to tell you about something else. Something that happened in Wellington. I just need to think of a kid-friendly way to word it." Marnie gave her friend a meaningful look.

Despite the icy aftertaste of Kathleen's phone call, the corners of her mouth tugged upwards. Thinking about Jason did that to her, every time. Momentarily, the aches disappeared, and her chest filled with warmth. In her mind, those moments she'd spent with him were coated in fairy dust. Even if she never saw him again, which was probably safest, he'd given her the greatest gift – an escape from reality.

Shasa's eyebrows sailed up in surprise. "Oh, seriously? Spill!"

# Chapter 13

Tracy caught Jason at his office door, her eyes shining with excitement. "I have something for you."

She handed him two printouts. Jason glanced at the Facebook profiles of two women, pulled his assistant into the office and closed the door, his palm sweaty on the doorknob. He'd taken two sleeping tablets the night before. In the morning he'd washed off the metallic aftertaste with two strong coffees, which probably explained his palpitations.

Tracy waited as he studied the profile pages. Both women had made good use of Facebook's privacy settings. Neither was recognisable from their photo – a coastal scenery and a shadowy figure against a sunset. Why didn't people upload proper photos?

Tracy pointed at the page in his left hand. "This one's the closest match. Sara Mitchell. She's from Auckland, single, 30 years old, her middle name is Beatrice and she obviously likes sunsets..."

"Can you friend them on Facebook to see their full profile?"

Tracy shook her head. "I tried, but they haven't accepted me."

"Google image search?"

"Nothing. Sorry. Neither of them has a high profile."

Jason shook his head, wondering how it was possible for anyone to avoid Google's invasive reach. Every time he googled his own name, the list of results was as endless as it was demoralising.

He shifted his focus on the other page. "Who's this?"

"Marnie Browne, from Hamilton. Thirty-nine, and ... well, she's even more private, couldn't get anything on her. I only included her because I haven't been able to rule her out. Most people went to one of three other parties afterwards, so if they were seen somewhere else that night, I was able to cross them off the list."

Jason nodded, impressed with Tracy's thinking. He thought about Beatrice, how she'd felt against his chest, her supple skin under his fingertips. She couldn't be thirty-nine, and the middle name felt like a good sign. "No. It's got to be this one." He lifted the Auckland woman's profile. "Can you find out where she lives?"

Tracy smiled and handed him a sticky note. "I have her address right here. Found it through IRD. She's listed as a business owner – a one-person operation that sells trinkets, earrings and such."

"Good work! She said she didn't make a lot of money."

"Yeah, this wouldn't."

"Jason, my boy!" Malcolm hollered, simultaneously knocking on the door and bursting in.

Tracy caught the swinging door and slipped out past him. She couldn't stand Malcolm's weekend stories.

"Hi! How's it going?" Jason asked, folding the printouts in his hand.

"Can't complain. Bought a new barbecue on sale. The best time to upgrade the equipment. Off season!" Malcolm launched into a detailed account about meats he'd cured and prepared. Jason nodded along, feigning enthusiasm over Hoisin sauce. Tracy had a point.

Malcolm's tone turned serious. "How're you doing? Got those sleep issues sorted?"

"I'm working on it."

Jason tried to smile, uncomfortable under Malcolm's discerning gaze.

"For what it's worth, I don't think the degree made much of a difference. You'd have been selected regardless. You have support, and you're doing a great job. So, it doesn't really matter."

Jason's heartbeat kicked up a notch and he looked over his shoulder. A nervous tick. There was nobody else in the office. His voice came out low and strained. "I have a fake Master's degree in my CV and you're saying it doesn't matter? What if someone finds out?"

Malcolm tilted his head. "Who reads resumes anyway? I'm just saying, nobody else cares. They only care about the policy changes. They care about getting on the property ladder. So don't let that keep you up at night. Not worth thinking about.

Jason's nails dug into the printouts he was holding and tried to control his breathing. He recognised the logic in Malcolm's words. Why couldn't he get past this? Why couldn't he just forget and move on?

Malcolm turned his attention to the crumbled papers in Jason's hand. "Whatcha got there?"

Jason shrugged as casually as possible. "Research."

Not satisfied, Malcolm snatched the papers, unfolded them and read. Jason should have known better than to try to mislead the guy. Despite his slow waddle and boring stories, Malcolm missed nothing.

"Two mystery ladies," he mused. "Someone from Saturday night?"

"Yes. Did you happen to see the lady I was talking to?"

"The one with the curls and curves?"

"That's the one," Jason croaked and quickly cleared his throat. Great. Now he sounded like he was sporting a partial at work.

Malcolm belted out a hearty laugh, his belly shaking from the vibration. "Good to see you looking alive, my man! I've been worried about you."

"Thanks."

"She was a fine-looking woman," Malcolm concluded, slapping him on the back like he'd announced an engagement. "Having trouble locating her?"

"Yes. Do you know who she came with?"

"No, sorry. I only noticed her at the end of the night. She was by herself, until you stepped in, of course. I directed Kathleen elsewhere, though. She had her eye on you two and I thought you might appreciate a bit of privacy."

"Thank you."

Jason smiled. Malcolm was on his side, personally and professionally, a rare guy willing to push for changes which could hurt his personal investments. For the next generation, he often said – the man had four children and twelve grandchildren.

After making loose plans to go fishing one weekend, Malcolm made for the door. "Hope you find her!"

As the door closed behind him, Jason opened his calendar app. Could he make it to Auckland this weekend?

In answer to his question, his email pinged, signalling a Priority one message from the Prime Minister. Jason waded through the formalities to get to the crux of the message. There it was. 'Jason, could you please go to Hamilton this weekend and take over the Peacocke development visit? Kathleen is required at an urgent press conference on the media sector support.'

An urgent press conference? Jason read on, trying to figure out what had happened. It wasn't on the page, but he guessed someone had leaked details of the proposed arts funding cuts to the media, sending local media outlets – the ones losing out – on a warpath. Kathleen would have to diffuse the situation and put any rumours to rest. Jason felt for her but couldn't help the surge of adrenaline. Peacocke was an unbeatable media opportunity – a chance to pose in front of New Zealand's first 3D printed family homes. Fast and affordable, the new technology offered a glimpse of a brighter future. Kathleen must have been kicking herself for the schedule clash.

Jason stared at the sticky note with the Auckland address. His desire to find Beatrice had only intensified in the last two weeks, but he had to be patient.

Jason took a deep breath and typed his reply. 'I'm on it. Will fly out tomorrow.'

With his weekend now written off, he had one day to write three press releases. He decided return to his apartment to get the rest of the work done in peace. Then he could try to catch some sleep. Double dose on the pills or something. He was running on fumes of fumes. He gathered his laptop and phone into his carry-on and pulled on his coat.

As he entered the lift, his phone buzzed. A text message.

*Been thinking of you. Let's grab a coffee? I know ur busy, but don't worry I'm flexible :) – Luna*

The phone buzzed again, this time with a photo of the stylist. Naked. That was the first thing he noticed. It took him a moment to process the rest – she was upside down in a ridiculous yoga pose, balancing on her hands with her legs hooked around her arms. Her head was turned towards the camera, smiling.

The lift pinged as it arrived on the second floor, and Jason scrambled to hide the phone like it was burning his hands. The image was etched in his mind, haunting him all the way out of the building. Why, oh why had he given this woman his phone number?

# Chapter 14

A wave of dizziness hit Marnie as she glanced at the digital clock on her car dashboard. It was getting late. She'd told Shasa she was going to check on her demented ex-mother-in-law. A solid cover. Nanette needed checking on, so much so that Marnie felt guilty for not going. Instead, she was driving in an opposite direction, around the lake. The sunset behind the stadium had painted the sky in all the shades of peach. Marnie's hands shook against the steering wheel. This was not good. She was back to lying to her best friend, sneaking around at night.

Maybe the fasting was messing with her head. She was 35 hours into her 48-hour fast and feeling spaced out. The hunger pangs had subsided after the first day, but not eating or preparing food, and trying not to think about food, left a lot of time for other activities. When it came to distractions, googling Jason was the best one. Back home with a fibre connection and limitless data, it was far too easy. During her search, she'd come across an old interview of Jason at his lakeside villa, explaining why he chose to rent instead of buying a house. But Marnie could hardly pay attention to his principles on home ownership and property investment. She was transfixed by the street view behind him, a street she recognised on the south side of the lake. Jason's Hamilton home was within walking distance from her house!

Since her discovery, Marnie hadn't missed one evening walk. Many times, she went with Shasa, sometimes Mac's mother Sue, or their friend Elsie who also lived on the other side of the lake, close to Jason's cottage. Marnie knew Jason was in Wellington, but she couldn't help slowing down to peer into his garden, imagining him there. No harm in looking, right?

Tonight was different. Tonight, she wanted to go alone. She'd read on the government website that Jason was visiting Hamilton on the weekend. With Saturday morning commitments, she hoped he would spend the night at his house by the lake. The press release had stated Jason would stand in for the housing minister Kathleen Rush. Marnie wondered if it had anything to do with Kathleen's health. She hadn't heard from the minister again, apart from the huge basket of chocolates that had arrived the day before. Marnie had taken the artisan treats to the community house to add to their afterschool snack supplies, hoping the school kids appreciated gold-leaf-adorned raspberry chocolate bark as much as Weetbix and toast. Giving away the chocolates had eased her guilt and she hoped Kathleen had no reason to ever contact her again. If only she could stay away from Jason.

Marnie crawled down Lake Crescent, her spine tingling. She didn't have a plan, only his address. She had no reason to knock on his door, but she could walk around the lake, like everyone else who lived in his neighbourhood. Passing his house, she could slow down and have a quick peek. If by some miracle she ran into him, she'd gracefully let him off the hook. No hard feelings. It was such a stupid phrase. So untrue. But she'd coached herself to say the right words, for his sake. She didn't want Jason to feel bad because she couldn't stop pining for him. She had to let him walk free, love him from afar.

Parking behind the yacht club, Marnie checked her face in the rear-view mirror. She'd made herself presentable, even smoothed her curls with an iron. They'd refused to straighten, but at least they weren't a furry, tangled mess.

Marnie shook her head at the wide hazel eyes staring back at her in the mirror. She'd spent the last couple of weeks hyper aware of her own body, its appearance, aches and pains. After years on auto pilot, she now faced crisis.

It felt unfair. She'd seen middle-aged women on those makeover TV shows, suddenly walking proud, looking and acting like someone brand new had slipped into their skin. Why couldn't it be that simple? Thanks to Luna, she'd experienced a glimpse of what was possible. Thanks to Jason, she'd felt desired, alive, if only for a moment. Now, that flickering hope refused to die. She couldn't go back to her old life. She wasn't the same anymore. Yet, her makeover was incomplete. After the trip, she'd emptied her wardrobe of everything unflattering and ended up with empty shelves. How had she never noticed it before? Everything she owned made her look fat and frumpy. Marnie smoothed down her loose sweater. It had a scooped neckline and gathered around her waist, accentuating her figure. It was the best thing she owned, an outfit her trainer had called a 'winner', wanting to take 'before' and 'after' photos of her for the club wall – an offer Marnie had firmly declined.

Marnie gathered her phone and keys and scrambled out of the car, her pulse racing. The lakeside path buzzed with evening walkers. She approached the familiar path leading to the pedestrian bridge that wound through subtropical bush then past the beautiful backyards of multimillion-dollar properties backing up to the lake. Most of the gardens were hibernating through the winter, the rose bushes gathering strength for the new season.

Marnie looked over her shoulder to check she wasn't being closely followed by anyone. All clear. She rounded a corner, and Jason's backyard came into view. She'd seen the low, wooden gate countless times and wondered how easy it would be to open it, to slip through. The trick was looking like you belonged, right?

Marnie slowed, staring at Jason's house. No lights or movement. After all the anticipation, an empty house? Her lungs deflated. If she kept walking, that was it. The path momentarily empty, Marnie veered towards the gate and stood there, wondering what to do. The stunning backyard had fruit trees and evergreens planted in formation. Raised flowerbeds framed the house.

Without warning, her vision went black and her ears buzzed. A headrush. She grabbed the gate for support. What kind of idiot went on a walk without a water bottle during a two-day fast? Marnie dropped her head between her knees, waiting for her vision to return.

Forcing herself upright, she noticed a lemon tree, its branches hanging over the fence, bursting with produce. Desperate for sugar, she picked one, dug her nails into the flesh and squeezed every drop into her mouth and onto her top. The citrus was tart, making her eyes water, but she sucked it dry, and it worked. After hanging her head for another long moment, she felt a flicker of energy return. Maybe, she could make it out of here.

Marnie hid the peels in the native grass and returned to the path. Grateful no one had seen her, she rushed down the footbridge. If she kept moving, she could get around the lake before darkness fell and drive home, with a bit of Jason's lemon in her. As stupid as it sounded, the thought soothed her.

The path disappeared back into the bush, with glimpses of the darkening lake peeking between the giant flax and kākābeak trees. Finally, she emerged from the bush onto a huge playground, which was under construction. A temporary chain link fence cut off the footpath. Marnie looked for a way around, the orange signs barely visible in the dim light.

And that's when she saw him.

# Chapter 15

Jason stared through the fence, his jaw slack. It was her. The woman. Beatrice – although he now suspected that wasn't her real name. But it was definitely her, those chestnut curls framing her face, huge eyes reflecting the orange evening light. She hugged herself like she was cold or afraid of falling. Just a few steps away, she stood frozen like a statue behind two layers of fencing that guided walkers around a path that was being resurfaced.

Jason found his voice. "Hey."

The woman stepped back. Was she going to run? Jason's limbs flooded with adrenaline. Could he catch her? He shouldn't be seen chasing a woman through a public playground. A group of teenagers lounged on the nearby park bench, vaping, their faces lit by their phones. They'd recognise him. Going after the youth vote, he'd given interviews to countless YouTubers. He'd taught at an inner-city high school. He had zero anonymity. Still, he couldn't lose sight of her.

"Beatrice?" Jason tried again, like talking to a flighty cat. "Can I talk to you? Please?" He had to raise his voice more than he'd hoped. Pleading with his eyes, he gestured at the far end of the fence, the ridiculous detour the contractors had set out on the wet grass. He'd question the city council on this stupid setup. He'd shut it down.

She took a tentative step forward, hooking her fingers on the fence, peering at him through the gaps in the metal grid. "There's no need. Don't worry about it. You've been busy." It was almost a whisper, but he heard the hurt in her voice.

"I'm sorry about—"

"I understand," she cut him off with forced ebullience. "No hard feelings." With a flicker of a smile, she turned and walked away.

On the brink of nausea, Marnie retreated from the fence. She'd done it. She'd let him go like she'd intended to, released him from any guilt or awkwardness over how things had ended.

His voice cut through her thoughts like a knife. "Wait!"

Marnie halted, her heart beating out of control. She turned to look over her shoulder. The teenagers on the bench looked up from their phones, their heads whipping back and forth between them.

"If you run, I will catch you!" His commanding tone held a touch of desperation.

Marnie shivered. How long would it take for him to run around the fence to reach her? In track pants and sneakers, he'd be fast. He must have been out for a run. She had a head start, but her legs felt heavy as lead, as if someone had amped up gravity itself. What on earth did he want from her? She was the obsessed one, the one who'd been stalking him.

Jason's voice carried across the distance. "I know why you ran away."

Marnie shook her head. "I don't think you do."

The teenagers lifted their phones. Were they taking photos of him?

"It's Jason Hallett," one of them gasped, shifting closer to him.

Jason voice crept up. "I do know. Do I have to say it?"

Marnie bit her lip. Could he possibly know about her health issues? It didn't seem likely. Still, she was curious. "Go ahead. Say it." If he knew about her condition, so be it. She wouldn't apologise for it.

"Okay. I was selfish. I was a terrible lover! But I can do

better, if you give me chance. I've been looking for you all over the place. I can't sleep... I need you, Beatrice. Please."

Marnie forgot to breathe; her eyes fixed on the young guy who'd edged closer with his phone. He was recording video! His face alight with glee, he filmed the scene like he'd stumbled upon a plane crash. Didn't Jason see what was happening?

Jason raised his voice even louder. "I'm desperate! Please..."

"Stop!" Marnie raised her hand. "For the love of God, shut up!"

She grabbed one of the idle teens, a younger boy, and whispered, "Can you run to him and tell him I'll meet him at his house? Tell him to just... stop talking, okay?"

The boy nodded and sprinted off, his sneakers squishing against the damp grass. Marnie took off in the opposite direction, running as fast as she could. She didn't stop to look over her shoulder, simply pounded the pavement with her heart beating in her throat.

With a woozy head and low blood sugar, she barely made it to his house. By the time she reached the gate, darkness had fallen. She'd swallowed a mouthful of flying bugs – protein, she told herself. Out of breath and seeing stars, the figurative kind, she missed a step and fell.

Just before she hit the ground, he caught her.

Jason scooped her into his arms. All the uncertainty and awkwardness washed away like a thick layer of dirt as she collapsed against his solid chest, inhaling the scent of laundry powder and sweat and lemon – no, wait, that was her fingers. His heart pounded fast under his shirt. He must have been running right behind her. Marnie curled her aching hands around the fabric of his T-shirt, hanging on as the world spun.

"I'm sorry. I haven't eaten in two days," she rasped into the white cotton, trying to regain balance.

"Why?"

"Can we go inside? I need to tell you something." She felt his breath slow down in sync with hers as his arms propped her up, kept her from falling.

She followed Jason through his garden, up the steps to his back porch. He unlocked the sliding door and led her into the lounge. She sank into the leather couch as he turned on a set of frosted-glass wall lights, transforming the room into a cosy haven. Private. Safe.

Marnie spotted the kitchen at the other end of the space and asked for a glass of water.

Jason circled the kitchen island to reach the tap. "It sounds like you need some food."

She shook her head. "I can't. I'm fasting."

He filled a glass from the tap and brought it over, his forehead wrinkling in confusion.

She grabbed the glass and downed half of it, burrowing her fidgety heels against the plush grey carpet, gathering courage. She had to tell him, before anything else happened.

Marnie squeezed her eyes shut, surprised by the big fat tears that escaped. "I have arthritis, the aggressive kind, so I'm fasting to reset my body or something like that. I don't know if it'll help. I'm sorry. I should have told you."

Silence fell between them. Marnie opened her eyes but kept her gaze on the water glass, afraid of his reaction.

He sat next to her, slid his arm around her lower back and nuzzled her hair. "I can't believe you're here. I found you." His words, full of bliss and wonder, flowed down her back like a cascade of bright light. Too bright to look at.

"Did you hear what I said? About arthritis..."

He sat up and cleared his throat. "Yes, sorry. That sucks. But you'll get through it. Don't worry. I can help you find the best doctors and..."

"No, you don't get through it! There's no cure."

His eyes widened with compassion. "Are you in pain?"

Marnie swallowed a lump. "Not right now." She could only feel the hot sensation of his hand resting on the small of her back. "Those guys were filming us. They were filming you."

Jason stiffened. "I know. I didn't notice until it was too late. It'll be in the Herald tomorrow."

Marnie shifted on the couch, every nerve misfiring at the thought of it. "What you said... It's not true. I never thought that. I never thought you were selfish. I wish you hadn't said it."

Jason shrugged. "I wasn't great. I've been so tired, so messed up. But I want to be better, for you."

"You look tired. Do you want to go to sleep right now?" She studied his face in the moody lighting. The darkness under his eyes was even more pronounced.

"Sleep"—he yawned—"that's not what you do when you finally find the woman you've been looking for."

Marnie raised her brow. "Looking for? I gave you my phone number."

"No, you didn't." He shook his head. "Don't you think I'd have called, instead of having my assistant track down every woman at that party?"

"I left my number on a sticky note on your nightstand."

Jason stared at her, his brow knitted. "There was no note on my nightstand."

Marnie's heart fluttered. "That's strange. I assumed you didn't want to see me again."

"Oh, my God! I'm officially never buying sticky notes again! I'm banning them from my life. The only way people are allowed to leave notes is by magic marker, on my forearm."

Marnie smiled, but she couldn't relax. Her insides swirled like she was on a carousel. Maybe she needed to eat something. She was finally with him, in his house, and felt like her poor brain couldn't keep up with what was happening and what he was saying. She could try fasting again later.

"You might be right about the food. Do you have any?" Marnie straightened her spine, looking across the room at the very tidy, very bare kitchen.

"No, sorry. I don't really cook. I was going to just order something. I kind of live on takeaway, to be honest."

Marnie shuddered at the thought, her chest filling with a sudden desire to cook for him. The man needed real sustenance.

She got up and wandered into the kitchen. He was right. There was nothing there, not even a piece of fruit in the bowl on the counter. "Maybe I should order something. I might have to break my fast just so that I can make it back home without falling over."

"You're not going home." Jason appeared behind her, his hand slipping around her just as the alarm in his words shot through her. "I'm sorry. I didn't mean it to sound so serial-killerish. But I can't let you go."

Marnie chuckled, gripping the edge of the kitchen counter for support. She had to get out of here. Part of her melted at his every word, her heart lighting up at every joke. But it wasn't real. He was a young, single, unmarried man. He needed to find a young, single, healthy woman. Someone he could start a family with.

"What's wrong?" Jason brushed the hanging curl off her face.

"I'm older than you."

"Yeah, I can't believe it. You don't look thirty-nine. That's why I was going to Auckland to look for you. I had two leads, and the other one was thirty, with the middle name Beatrice so I thought that must be you. I was supposed to go there this weekend, but something else came up, and I had to come home instead."

He'd really been looking for her. Marnie's chest glowed, but her fuddled brain piped up with nagging doubts. "You want me to tell someone about Kathleen, right?"

Jason shook his head. "No. I never should have asked you to do that in the first place. That's not why I was looking for you." He shifted his hips, pinning her against the kitchen island.

Warmth flooded through Marnie, pooling at the bottom of her belly. Danger zone. "You don't know me. I'm not what you're looking for. I'm divorced. I have two grownup kids..." Marnie buried her face in her hands.

"That's great! Not the divorce, obviously. But I'm happy you're single."

"You don't get it."

"You're right, I don't. Are you saying I'm not old enough to be with you?"

Why was he twisting her words? Marnie slumped against the kitchen island, hiding her face in her hands. "You know what I mean. You should find someone young, someone ... not like me."

"Would you like some ashes to sprinkle on yourself?"

"What?" She looked up at his grinning face.

"I mean, let me quickly burn something. I'll try to find you a sack to wear with it."

"You're making fun of me?" She raised her head and blinked at him, incredulous, but couldn't help the amusement bubbling up in her chest, ruining the perfectly good glare she was about to give him. "I'm serious!"

"So am I! I'll take up smoking to provide the ashes. I'll sacrifice my lungs for you."

She playfully punched his side.

Jason pretended to the take the hit, doubling over the kitchen counter. "I'm just trying to join your pity party, you thirty-nine-year-old, ancient woman."

Marnie's face blazed but laughing with him felt so good it didn't matter. "You shouldn't mock the elderly."

"I would never! It's an important part of my voter base. The old ladies think I'm cute." He flashed her a shit-eating grin that turned her heart into a puddle. She couldn't stick to her bid, no matter what her head told her.

Sensing the weakening of her defences, Jason drew her closer. "I'm sorry. I can't change how I feel. I want you, Marnie Browne. Please stay with me tonight." He pronounced her name slowly, with meaning. His voice didn't hold the thinly veiled threat Kathleen's had but served as an apt reminder.

"Kathleen called me about that bathroom incident," she whispered into his chest. "She saw us talking at the gala and she... warned me about you."

Jason grabbed her by the shoulders, his eyes wide. "She *warned* you?"

"Yeah. She said you're digging for dirt, that you're after her portfolio. She must have been worried I'd tell you about her."

Jason let go of her and slammed the kitchen counter, the muscles in his neck twitching. "She has no right to go after you like that. Fuck! That is too far." His volume dropped and his eyes filled with regret. "I'm so sorry, Marnie. I never wanted to put you in the middle of this, dealing with her—"

"Don't worry, I didn't say anything. I just let her believe that her secret was safe. It is, isn't it? You haven't told anyone?"

"No, I haven't. But that's not the point. Kathleen has no business going after you. blackmailing you—"

Marnie's eyebrows shot up. "She didn't blackmail me."

"Did she offer you money? Gifts?

"Chocolates." Marnie winced. "I gave them away."

Jason fixed his dark gaze on her, his forehead wrinkling with concern. "You know why she did that, right?"

"To show gratitude?"

He shook his head, a rueful look in his eyes. "No. To make you feel like you owe her. So, you'd be more likely to do what she asks."

Marnie shuddered. "Do people really think like that?"

Jason turned away, a grim look in his eyes. "I can see that you don't and that's great. But Kathleen's not like you. She'll lie and deceive you if it serves her purpose."

"She's right though, isn't she? You want the housing

portfolio."

Jason smiled. "That's no secret. Anyone in my position would be after her job. That's how it works. Nobody goes into politics to become an associate minister. I know she'd like to paint me as the snake here, but..." He averted his eyes. "Everyone does what they have to do to get ahead. You just have to have good motives."

Marnie didn't want to ask, but she had to know. "Have you done anything like this?"

Jason grimaced, rubbing his forehead. "I'm not perfect, but I don't go around blackmailing members of the public. I'm not protecting multi-million-dollar property investments, either." He released a deep sigh, still avoiding eye contact. "But no, I'm not perfect."

Marnie sensed there was more to it, but she didn't want to push him. She waited for him to look at her. He smiled, and the pain in his eyes filled her with compassion. Even when smiling, he looked so tired, like something was eating him. Maybe she could give him what he needed tonight.

"You need sleep." She walked them to what she thought might be the door to his bedroom. Score. They both collapsed on the perfectly made king bed.

Working together as if they had a well-established routine, she helped him out of his sneakers and trackpants and under the covers. "Wait," Jason mumbled, reaching for the laptop on his nightstand. He opened it and typed his own name in the search field, filtering the results by time.

"What are you looking for?" she asked.

"Just... checking." He closed the lid and dropped the laptop on the floor.

"You think that video will be in the news?"

"Yeah. Or... something else."

He looked so tense, even when lying in bed. Unable to look away, Marnie rested her cheek against the feather down pillow, letting the room whirl as much as it liked. She stroked his temple, tracing down his golden stubble. Minutes ticked by, unhurried. Eventually, his breathing slowed, settling into a deep rhythm. It was like witnessing a miracle.

Confident he'd fallen asleep, Marnie got up and tiptoed to the kitchen. The clock on the wall showed it was 8:30 p.m. Soon, Tanya would come home from the movies. If she found her mum not home, she'd call. What could she tell her? She hardly knew what was happening herself. It was too early to mention Jason. But if she wasn't going to bail on him, she needed an excuse to stay out all night. Marnie foraged Jason's pantry for something to eat. She landed on a bottle of honey and squeezed some straight into her mouth. A quick sugar hit would help her think.

She could say she was spending the night at the hospital with Nanette. She should have been looking after her ex-mother-in-law anyway. Tanya knew her grandmother was accident prone. Something could have happened. But what if she wanted to come and visit? It was unlikely, at least during the night, but could easily blow her cover. She'd have to find a way to put her off.

Marnie swallowed another mouthful of honey and took out her phone.

*Hi, hon. Hope you had fun at the movies. I'm at hospital with Gran, she had a wee fall. She's fine but they'll monitor her overnight, I'll stay here. See you in the morning!*

She took a breath and hit 'send', cringing at the lie. It sounded believable – close to the truth, like all good lies. She was the one who'd had a 'wee fall'. She was the one who needed monitoring.

Leaning on the cool marble of the kitchen island, Marnie waited for her heartrate to settle. She was too rusty and clueless, unprepared for Jason's reaction, the intensity of his touch, his words. He'd been looking for her. He couldn't sleep without her. It made no sense. Even if it was true, being someone's sleeping pill didn't sound like a solid foundation for a relationship. It didn't mean he wanted her for anything else. And what did she want? She'd dreamt of finding someone to grow old with, maybe someone divorced like herself. Whichever way she looked at this – her and Jason – the pieces didn't fit.

Marnie rummaged through the cupboards and made herself a cup of tea. She chose a yellow mug with a chip on it, a dish that didn't seem to fit in with the rest of his matching white china. She took her drink to the dining table where she could see through the bedroom doorway. Jason twitched in his sleep. His head whipped left and right on the pillow, like dodging invisible fists. Marnie held her breath, wishing he wouldn't wake up. After a moment, he seemed to settle again, muttering something on his outbreath. What was torturing him in his sleep? She had a feeling it was the same thing that kept him awake.

Whatever it was, he'd get better. One day, he'd be well again and ready to start a family. Based on everything she'd learned, he'd make an amazing father. He was principled, funny, disarming, someone who could win you over with a few carefully chosen words, make you see things from his perspective. But being gifted and persuasive didn't make him right. Deep down, Marnie knew she wasn't the one. She couldn't force him to be there, to see her struggle with buttons and shoelaces, wake up every morning with swollen fingers, wince at every step she took. That's what you did with your elderly relatives, not with your new girlfriend. Maybe, if she had the disease under control, things would be different. But it was too early to tell how the symptoms would progress. Who in the right mind would want a ticket to this ride? She didn't, for sure.

She would help him, then set him free.

Marnie relaxed, content with her decision. It allowed her to stay a little longer, enjoy his touch, those words that burned into her core. He was that good. Even tired out of his mind, he managed to light up every inch of her, just by talking, touching, being there. Even in his sleep, Jason possessed her. She sat at his dining table as if in trance, unable to go home, unable to take her eyes off him.

Her phone pinged, delivering a reply from Tanya.

*Al gd, c u 2mrw.*

Would it kill her daughter to type a full word every now and then? Marnie smiled, placing the phone back on the table.

The honey reached her blood, making her body buzz and stomach gurgle. Her limbs felt heavy, her whole body suddenly spent.

Marnie finished her tea and snuck back into the bedroom, surveying Jason's sleeping figure under the covers. He looked so vulnerable. Marnie lowered herself on the bed, carefully sliding under the covers. A waft of cool night air drifted in through an open window. In the dark, she couldn't make out the scenery, but based on the layout of the house, the bedroom had a lake view. Marnie closed the window and curled up against Jason's warm body, wondering what the bedroom looked like in daylight. She was ready to find out.

# Chapter 16

Jason sat on the bed, keeping as still as possible. It was morning, but he didn't want to wake Marnie. Instead, he studied the fine lines in the corners of her eyes, the way her skin turned rosy around her cheekbones, translucent under her eyes. Was she really 39? Did her age bother him? It might affect her chances of falling pregnant, but his own mother had been forty-two when he'd been born. Surely, they still had time. She'd told him not to worry about pregnancy, which meant she was probably on the pill. Even if there was another issue, they'd sort it out.

Inhaling the tropical scent of those curls falling on the pillow, Jason tried to imagine his future. Did he want a family? The thought might have been planted by his mother, who called every Sunday for an update on the subject. He knew his parents were proud of his achievements, but the one thing his mum craved was a grandchild. His brothers lived overseas with their families. He was their last chance for a local grandbaby. In their late seventies with failing health, they didn't have many years left. Every time he visited their retirement village in Cambridge, twenty minutes from Hamilton, he braced for those longing looks and carefully worded questions. Was he seeing anyone? Did she come from a small or large family? Was she one of those career women?

His last girlfriend, Amelia, had been one of those, with such a busy schedule that dating her had mostly been an organisational challenge. During his election campaign, their relationship had died a natural death. The guilt of failing as a boyfriend turned into relief at not having to meet her expectations. He'd moved on, confident that everything would work out. Life had been on an upward trajectory. He'd felt invincible.

This morning, he felt connected to that old self, the dreams he'd had, things he'd believed. He would put on his lucky suit and smile at the cameras. Cameras... the thought brought back memories from the night before, along with a cold sweat.

With deep reluctance, Jason reached for his phone charging on the nightstand. He kept it on silent, but the stack of notifications flashing on the screen told him something was up. The news stories. *Please, don't be about Marnie.* He could take the humiliation. He'd laugh along, pretend it didn't bother him. But Marnie seemed like a private person. How would she handle her face being blasted all over national media?

Jason looked at Marnie's sleeping frame, his finger hovering on the phone. As soon as his thumb lowered on the fingerprint scanner, it would suck him in. He wanted one last moment of peace, to dwell on the miracle of finding her, the miracle of sleep. He wanted to postpone everything else – the job, the news. But it was 8:30 a.m. In two hours, he'd have to be at the development site. With force of will, he sat up, lowered his bare feet on the carpet and pressed his thumb on the sensor.

After ten minutes of scrolling and a quick phone call with his assistant, Jason sagged on the couch, his thoughts a verbal hurricane. It must have been a slow news day. They'd run with the story of him, complete with the shaky video the kid had filmed. The clickbait headlines feasted on his public humiliation.

'Selfish lover Jason Hallett begs for 2nd chance'

'Jason Hallett caught on camera with mystery woman'

'Jason Hallett's public late-night confession'

'Jason Hallett in love – who's the mystery woman?'

Jason sighed. He knew what was coming: calls from his colleagues, curiosity veiled in sympathy and well-meaning advice. Opinion pieces in the media analysing the public's reaction to the video, drawing comparisons to similar faux pas and movie scenes. The YouTubers would create remixes and act out the scene, while Twitter would fill with memes. They'd have their fun, and eventually move on. He would get through this, but Marnie… would she run away? Could he protect her from this? Was there any way she could remain the mystery woman? Jason put on his earphones and clicked 'play' on the video embedded in the news article. He cringed at the desperation in his own voice, which at one point hit an uncomfortably high register. It was meme gold, like he was begging for everyone to take the piss.

He'd have to comment quickly, appear open, honest and self-deprecating, while keeping Marnie out of it. It was possible. The kid had been too excited to catch him on camera, only turning in Marnie's direction once, presumably to capture her reaction to his 'bad lover' confession. But the darkness protected her identity. Thank God he hadn't known or used her real name. Now, everyone and their dog would be looking for Beatrice. If they kept out of public spaces and were never seen together… Jason's shoulders sagged, the thought heavier than he wanted to admit. He didn't want to hide. He'd already imagined going out with her, slipping his arm around her as they walked, surprising her with a kiss. But he couldn't do that to her, knowing what she'd have to endure.

A faint sound from the bedroom told him Marnie was

awake. He paused the video, placed the phone on the coffee table, screen down and let his legs carry him towards the woman his entire being craved.

# Chapter 17

Marnie woke to bright light pouring in through the net curtains, filling the room with a dreaminess that perfectly matched her frame of mind. She was still inside the dream, hiding in Jason's cottage, hiding from her real life, family and friends. Nobody knew where she was. Only Jason. Where was he?

Before she got up, he appeared at the doorway, then on top of her.

"Good morning!" He placed a kiss on her neck, lingering there.

His stubble tickled Marnie's skin. "Did you sleep well?"

She didn't really have to ask. She could see the difference

in him, the energy burning behind his eyes. It made him harder to read, more dangerous, someone further out of her league. But as his hand landed on her hip, her body responded far ahead of her mind. Locking eyes with him, she guided his hand under her sweater. As he lifted the hem, she was overcome by a desire to undress. She wiggled out of the loose sweater, then her tight tank top, sighing at the sensation of cool air on her skin. Her nipples stood up obediently, teased by both the temperature and his gaze. The intensity in his eyes made her want to pause. She wanted to take all she could get and enjoy every second of it. His eyes flashed with need as he explored her body.

"God, you're gorgeous." He peeled off his T-shirt, the same one he'd worn the night before, and lowered his mouth onto her body.

Working his way from her nipples down to her belly, he covered her in hot kisses while his hands traced her curves, cupping her breasts and sliding down to where she needed them. Reaching the waistband of her yoga pants, he helped her out of them, leaving only a thin fabric of her underwear between them. Relieved she was wearing a nice, lacy pair, Marnie opened up, her entire body throbbing in anticipation. If he needed to make amends as a lover, she was here for it. He groaned and she felt his hot breath between her legs, driving her wild with need. His touch was light and teasing. Warmth pooled between her thighs, and she grasped a handful of blanket, breathing heavily. How did he turn her on like that, with only a few simple moves? Banishing doubts to the back of her mind, Marnie reached to remove her underwear.

She held her breath as he lowered his mouth to where she needed him, his tongue circling her swollen clit. Pleasure coursed through her like a lightning, making everything else vanish. Where was she? Who was she? Nothing but the pulsing sensation existed, sucking her into its vortex.

"Don't stop," she panted as he circled her again.

"I would never," he rasped, his voice thick like syrup.

Jason took his time, teasing her until she squirmed under his light touch, desperate for him. "More! Please, Jason."

"No problem." She heard the smile in his voice as he dove back between her thighs, applying the pressure she craved, making her whole body throb. His fingers slipped inside and all thoughts vanished from her mind as the delicious sensation built. Higher and higher, almost intolerable in its sweetness. Finally, the low growl rising from his throat sent her over the edge. She came apart, her body convulsing like it wasn't her own. The stars were back, dancing in her vision just like last night, but now from sheer pleasure.

"Your turn," she whispered when she finally found her voice.

Jason appeared next to her. His boxer shorts were stretched out of shape by his hard-on, but his eyes signalled concern. "I want to, you have no idea how much. But there's something I need to tell you about last night. The media..."

He shook his head, eyes filled with regret.

She guessed it. They were all over the news. And he was having second thoughts.

He stared at her exposed flesh, mouth hanging. "Once you see it, you may not want to..."

Marnie closed her eyes, sighing with frustration. Timing! The wretched man was going to ruin this with his overthinking. No wonder he couldn't sleep. Marnie looked up at the ceiling, her body still aching for him. She wanted more. She wasn't going to let him, and whatever was in the papers, snatch this away. Taking a deep breath, Marnie pushed herself up and climbed on top of him. She felt his hard erection against her.

"This might be all we ever have," she whispered. "We should enjoy it."

To her relief, the worry on his face melted as she guided him inside her. She really should have asked for a condom this time, but at her age, with her history, the risk was low. She couldn't be fertile anymore. And he felt so good, filling every inch of her. She let her entire weight rest against him and rocked, deep moans forming somewhere inside her as intense waves of pleasure rose from her core.

He cupped her buttocks, matching her movement, his eyes locked on her, burning her skin. His eyes clouded over. There was nothing more beautiful, more satisfying. She'd lured him away with her, to escape reality. His mouth found her nipple and sucked, sending a sharp tingle down her spine.

"You're so sexy," he rasped, and the thickness of his voice pooled more warmth down her belly.

Discarding her last ounce of shame, she lowered and allowed her breasts to fall on his face, trapping him with her flesh. He groaned with pleasure, nuzzling in-between. She felt invincible. Sexy. And the build-up of another orgasm. Could she really come again? Was her body capable of this? She could hardly believe the fiery sensations coursing through her. She could only submit. Keep moving. Nothing could make her stop.

Her second release almost rivalled the first in its intensity. She cried out as she spasmed against his chest. Her nails dug into his shoulders as her body took over, drawing every drop of him.

She stayed there, unwilling to sober up. The gentle aftershocks travelled through her like a lingering electric current. What felt like minutes later, she finally opened her eyes, as if discovering her surroundings for the first time. What had come over her? She'd never behaved like that.

Rolling off him, snuggled against his warm body, she left her arm on his chest but avoiding his eyes. "Wow. That was..."

"Okay?" His voice carried a cheeky tone.

He turned to face her, placing his forehead so close it was touching hers. His gaze burned her until he found eye contact. It felt raw, more intimate than the pleasure they'd shared.

A burst of joy split her face into a wide smile. "That was amazing. You're definitely redeemed as a lover."

His smile was just as wide. For a moment, the shadows were chased away, replaced by invincible lightness she hadn't witnessed in him before. "I think I need to do that a couple more times, though, just to be sure."

"I'm okay with that."

He inched closer, but soon the light in his eyes dimmed. "I just worry that once you see the headlines, you won't come back."

"Is it that bad?"

"I hope I can keep you out of it. But that means we can't be seen together in public, or... I'm so sorry."

Marnie felt a tight squeeze in her chest. She'd never expected to be seen with him in public. Why would he worry about that? She brushed her thumb across his stubbly cheek, trying to smile reassuringly. "That's fine. We'll be careful. If you want to see me again, just text me, and I'll sneak in here after dark. I'll be your sleep mistress."

"Sleep mistress?" He laughed.

Marnie's cheeks blazed with heat. "Well, not just for sleep, but..."

He placed a kiss on her nose. "Nope. Not a mistress. That sounds like I have another woman somewhere. I would never... and if I heard you were seeing someone else, I'd flip out. Honestly, I'm not good at sharing." The gravity in his voice split her heart wide open.

Marnie nuzzled against his ribs; warm glow engulfing her entire body. "You don't have to worry about that. I'm all yours. We just can't make it public. I'm sorry."

"I understand."

She glanced at the suit he'd hung up on the door. "Don't you have to be somewhere today?"

She knew his schedule and she'd be damned if she let him fail at his job. He'd been given the opportunity of a lifetime, and today's appearance must have been important.

Switching into work mode, Jason jumped out of bed and disappeared into the en-suite. Marnie got up, noting the delicious ache in her core, the sign of being desired, alive. So different from the joint pain. She dressed in her exercise gear and tiptoed into the kitchen. This time, she'd write her number on a huge piece of paper. Or maybe directly into his phone. That way, he wouldn't lose it. She found his phone on the coffee table and turned it over. The lock screen was on, but the notifications caught her off guard. Of course. He was getting messages about last night. She could only see the beginning of each one, and the words gave her a chill.

'Call me!! Now!'

'What the fuck is going...?'

'Shit, Jason! How do you...'

They screamed at him like there was an emergency. Marnie shivered, placing the phone back on the table. A moment's vulnerability from a tired man surely wasn't such a big deal. A PR nightmare, maybe, but no reason to curse into someone's inbox. No reason to—

A shadow fell over the table, making Marnie nearly jump out of her skin as she saw a human shape moved behind the curtains. Someone was out on the deck. She recognised the shape of a camera as they reached a gap between the curtains. A journalist. It had to be. Panicked, Marnie leapt away from window, diving back into the bedroom. She closed the door behind her, leaning against it.

Shit! She was trapped. If she left the house, her face would end up in the papers. She'd be known as the poor woman Jason had fallen asleep on, or something else grotesque. The silly, silly man had publicly branded himself as a bad lover. She hadn't seen the headlines, but instinct told her that was the part they'd focus on. Those words had made her own stomach sink to her feet, begging for him to shut up.

Since her online obsession had taken hold, Marnie had discovered the true extent of Jason's fandom. He wasn't just a politician, he was the voice of Millennials, the go-to commentator on every news story about housing. He was everywhere. Everyone and their cousin would be talking about this.

Shit. Shit. Shit.

Marnie collapsed on the floor, her back against the door. Another shadow appeared, this time in the shape of towel-clad Jason, looming over her in all his glory.

"What's going on? What are you doing there?"

"A journalist. Out on the deck. Taking photos." She could

barely produce words with her throat closing in.

"What the fuck?" Jason yanked at the doorknob, forcing her to scuttle to the side.

"Don't go out there! You're not even dressed."

He didn't listen. The small towel flapping against his thighs, Jason pushed past her and headed to the deck. Marnie risked a peek through the doorframe. The sliding door to the deck was open, the curtains moving in the slight breeze. She caught Jason's tall frame behind the window, hands on his hips. She couldn't make out all the words, but she could tell he was furious, spitting out lines about private property and lawyers.

After a moment, he returned to the bedroom, a smile on his face. "Don't worry, she's gone."

"Did she get a photo of you dressed like that?"

"You mean this?" With a triumphant smile, he held up a small memory card. "I'm sure there are some juicy ones in here if you want a new screensaver."

Marnie scrambled on her feet, her knees nearly buckling. "How can you be so flippant about this? Aren't you worried?"

A smile hovered on his lips. "Sure, but I'm still on a high from… you know. Finding you. Sleeping. Sleeping with you. I'm not going to let anyone take that away."

She caught the blaze behind his eyes, like two flames licking his pupils, drawing her in. Her spine relaxed and she let him pull her in a tight embrace. Pressed against his chest, she felt his steady heartbeat. So good. So right.

"What time is it? Do you have to go soon?" she asked.

"Yes. Will you stay?"

"I wish, but I have to go home to my girl. See that she doesn't burn down the house."

"Is that a figure of speech, or..."

"No, I mean it quite literally. Last week, she put aluminium foil in the microwave. It's my fault. She's the baby, and I always catered to her. Now she needs to learn some basic skills."

Jason chuckled into her hair, then loosened his grip on her to look her in the eye. "Sounds like she needs you as much as I do." His voice held a trace of regret.

"She does. Although she'd never admit it."

"I admit it, if that helps?"

Marnie smiled. He was so gorgeous, so openly into her. When she was with him, she believed it, for moments that stretched in length every time. Her entire body was already on board, craving his touch and that adoring look in his eyes.

"Okay, you have to get ready!" She glanced at the alarm clock, then pointed at the suit hanging off the door handle. "Don't fail your job because of me."

"I won't." He sprang into action, pulling on the pressed pants and the crisp white shirt.

She left him to button the shirt and dry his hair, retreating into the lounge. She could no longer see anyone behind the window. If she ducked out now, she could skip home without being seen and lay low for a few days. Maybe the media attention would eventually blow over just like he'd said.

Marnie opened the kitchen drawers, looking for a pen and a piece of paper. At last, she located a felt pen and a takeaway menu and scribbled her phone number on it. She placed the chipped, yellow mug on it as a paper weight, hoping this note wouldn't get lost. Listening to the sound of Jason's hairdryer, she contemplated just sneaking off. She made it to the door, but something held her back. After what they'd just shared, she owed him a proper goodbye.

She returned to the bedroom and waited for Jason to step out of the bathroom. The sight of him gave her a start. In a suit, his hair styled to perfection, he captured her attention like a work of art. A masterpiece. No wonder the media loved him. His eyes glistened with warmth as he noticed her.

"I just wanted to say goodbye. I left my phone number on your dining table." Marnie waved her hand, taking a step towards the door.

"Okay." Jason closed the distance between them and gathered her in his arms. His mouth crashed on hers, leaving no room for doubt. She opened up, allowing his tongue to invade her and steal her breath away. Heat shot between her thighs again, throbbing away like they had all the time in the world. Her body was not ready to go home. When he finally released her, his eyes burned with passion. "See you soon."

"See you," she whispered back with what was left of her voice, and hurried to the door, not looking back.

# Chapter 18

Marnie jogged down the lakeside path on unsteady feet, hunger gnawing her insides. If she made it home, she'd order something. Something healthy and arthritis-friendly. For the first time since the diagnosis, she really felt like fighting. If there was any way she could be the person Jason believed her to be, she would try. She'd eat once a week. She'd do Pilates and yoga and stand on her head. Whatever it took. She wanted so badly to be with him, to be good enough for him. Even if it was only for a moment.

Deep in thought, Marnie nearly bumped into a tree trying to dodge an early morning jogger. He slowed down to check she was okay, and Marnie responded with a silly grin, brushing her hair and clothes. The man, who was maybe in his fifties, have her a smile and a wink, and she hid her blush, rushing away. What was happening to her? She was behaving more like a teenager than her actual teenage daughter. Had hunger finally driven her mad? It had made her feet light and head woozy, carrying her home on a potent mix of emotions.

I'm a sensible person, she reminded herself as she struggled to fit her home key into the lock with shaky hands. Once inside, she collapsed on the sofa.

Tanya appeared from her room, still in her pyjamas, eyes puffy from sleep. Noticing Marnie, her green eyes sharpened, studying her mother with unnerving intensity. "Did you just get home?"

"Yeah."

"Can you give me a ride to Hailey's?" Her black-painted fingernails fiddled with her spiky haircut that stood to attention, aided by powerful products from the night before.

Marnie gulped, remembering her car, still parked on the other side of the lake. How could she have forgotten?

"I left my car... there. I couldn't drive. Too lightheaded," she lied, her cheeks burning.

Tanya narrowed her eyes. "You look weird. Are you still fasting?"

"Uh-huh."

"You need to eat something." Her daughter crossed the floor with determination. Not waiting for an answer, she pulled a slice of toast from the freezer and popped it in the toaster.

She rummaged through the cupboards and somehow managed to bang the soft-closing doors. Moments later, Marnie accepted the piece of toast slattered in butter and marmalade, delivered on a paper towel. "Thank you."

It wasn't really the healthy food she'd had in mind, but it was a huge step for Tanya, and a lovely gesture. Marnie took a small bite, hoping the calories would restore her wit.

"Is it helping?" Tanya asked, plopping down on the couch next to her. "This fasting I mean. Is it healing the arthritis?"

Marnie stretched out her hands, which were free from pain. She'd fretted about telling her children the diagnosis, but they'd both seemed quite matter of fact, urging her to do something about it. It felt like everyone else believed her chronic illness was treatable, that she'd get over it.

"I don't know," she answered. How much could she tell from momentary absence of pain?

Tanya turned to assess her. "The fasting is working. You look almost skinny."

"Thanks."

"Maybe this arthritis will make you skinny for life. You can start wearing crop tops." She laughed, as if her mother baring her midriff was the most ridiculous thing in the world.

"I need a shower," Marnie announced, stuffing the last piece of toast in her mouth. "After that, I'll go get the car. If you need a ride anywhere, it'll be in the afternoon."

"Afternoon?" Tanya's face contorted as she fiddled with the edge of her crop top, a style she wore most days. Even leaning forward on the seat, a sliver of her white flesh glowed in the morning light. Did her tops get shorter every year, or was Marnie imagining things?

"Yes, afternoon. I'm not your personal chauffeur. I do have a life." She winked at her daughter, gathered herself from the couch and headed to the bathroom.

The look she'd caught on Tanya's face was her reward. Instead of the usual eye-roll, she'd seen suspicion. Shock. Was it such an unfathomable idea that she could have a life outside motherhood? She'd thought she had a full life, between the community house and writing her stories, but she knew Tanya didn't recognise it as such. Teenagers measured with a different stick.

Marnie peeled off her clothes, enjoying the cool air drifting through the cracked bathroom window. She loved her bathroom, a modern oasis she'd customised from the prefab building's blank slate. Harmonious shades of warm grey mixed with white marble, punctuated with golden accents of the flowerpots she'd hung from the ceiling. It wasn't bohemian or colourful like Shasa's space. Her friend was attracted to unusual colour combinations that worked, but only on her, around her. Marnie could never pull off pale purple and mustard with terracotta. She'd always been conservative, soft, predictable.

Except now. She was having an affair with a celebrity, someone who had reporters circling their house. It felt like a dream. Or a nightmare, depending on the moment. Either way, she wasn't as boring as Tanya thought.

Marnie stepped in the shower, letting the gushing water flush off the evidence of her night-time adventure.

Would she see him again? Could she risk it? What if the media came after her? She couldn't handle it like he did. They'd call her out on not being right for him. And she'd crumble. Because it was true.

She'd seen the devotion in his eyes. If she let him, he'd stay with her and risk his career, give up his chance to have a family. He'd waste his time on the wrong woman.

Marnie ran her fingers across her belly, letting the water spill between her legs. The taut skin with faint stretch marks could have belonged to someone younger, someone fertile. But underneath, the timer had buzzed a long time ago. When she and Steve had tried for a third baby, her doctor had told her that she had low ovarian reserve. She'd been running out of eggs in her early thirties. In retrospect, she was relieved it hadn't worked out, seeing how their marriage had ended.

She'd been so focused on the dream of that baby, she'd missed the signs of the impending end; namely Steve upgrading every piece of gear in the house. Marnie had been the last one left, the arm candy that no longer evoked jealous glances, if she ever had. Maybe she could have dressed better or done something to her hair, but she'd resented the people he hung out with, the way they focused on appearances. Almost as an act of rebellion, she'd stepped out of the game and built her identity on who she was rather than what she looked like. A good friend. A good mother. And that had been years ago. Now, at 39, she knew she couldn't be the woman Jason needed by his side.

Could she just enjoy him, have fun and walk away, unharmed? If she let this go on, what would happen to her after the inevitable end? Would she be forgotten and left to live her life with those memories? Or would she be forever changed by the experience, defined by the public fling with a younger man everyone knew by name? Both options filled her with dread.

# Chapter 19

Jason approached the building site trying to control his breathing, his smile unwavering. So far, nobody had mentioned the news story about him, although he'd caught a couple of sideways looks and whispers.

Accepting a glass of water from Tracy, Jason stood aside, letting the photographers get a wide shot of the show home they were about to tour. He liked the Mediterranean flavour of the 3D-printed houses. The technology allowed for more customisation than the typical new builds around New Zealand. The rounded corners and faintly castle-like features were a nice touch. The brand-new suburb still had the empty look of a LEGO village with recently sprouted grass and uniform baby trees. In time, it would turn into a real neighbourhood with berms sporting rubbish bins and illegal parking. If he'd gone down the property investing route, he might have bought something like this. Less boxy, more playful. This is where he could have brought up a family. If he held a nine-to-five job, slept at night and otherwise kept his shit together. So many 'if's.

Rachel, the stocky, unflappable leader of the Labour PR team, approached him and wiped the smile off his face. "Let's keep your visit short, okay? Just a few photos."

She escorted him in front of the show home, where he posed dutifully next to the developers, smiling for the cameras. From the corner of his eye, he recognised one of them, Nick, an old friend he'd lost touch with since running for parliament.

Jason took a step towards him, but Rachel yanked him away. "We better get you out of here. A couple of journos are eyeing you for more comments on whatever the hell you got up to last night."

Dark shadows under the middle-aged woman's eyes matched his own. Rachel had seen it all and couldn't care less about his love life, which Jason found comforting.

He lowered his voice. "How do you think I should play it? You're the expert."

The woman deserved some flattery. She'd clearly been called out here on her day off because of his transgressions.

Rachel stomped her leather boots against the pavement,

rattling a deep sigh. "There's one thing you need to understand, which I'm not sure you do, judging by that display last night..." Her voice lowered, showing a hint of hurt he wasn't expecting.

She glanced over her shoulder to make sure the reporter wasn't too close. The only other person in the vicinity was Tracy, who took an imperceptible step closer, curiosity lighting her face.

Rachel went on. "You're public property, Jason. Kind of like Prince William. As long as you're single, every woman in the country can imagine themselves with you. If you get involved with someone, anyone at all, you break their hearts. They'll want to know everything about this woman, and she better be amazing. Like Kate fucking Middleton."

A layer of cold sweat formed in Jason's hairline, and he belted out a hollow laugh. "I'm not that big of a deal, right?" He glanced at Tracy for confirmation, but only received an apologetic smile.

"I'm not saying it's on the same scale. We don't have the tabloids, but there will be stories, speculation. It's different for you. You won the youth vote. You're their hero, standing up to the boomers, fighting for home ownership for the generation who's been priced out of the market or whatever dreams you sold them."

Pipe dreams. Jason cleared his throat. Ever since stepping inside parliament, he'd been trying to not think about his election promises. Before he'd made it to parliament, he'd believed every word. He wouldn't be a fraud, a liar, like every other politician out there. But it wasn't true. He was a liar, the worst of them.

"And then there are your looks," Rachel continued, giving his body an approving once-over that made him shudder. "You're the sex symbol of the elder millennials, those who haven't fully given up on the dream of home ownership. And you're also the poster boy of younger millennials with daddy-issues, the one bringing a brighter tomorrow for the renters." She punctuated her words with an animated, if a bit disingenuous grin.

Jason's throat-clearing progressed to an honest-to-God coughing fit. Had he inhaled a bug, or just a bit of his own saliva? His lungs hacked away, begging for mercy, as his mind replayed the sickening words. He could never live up to those expectations.

Rachel swatted his back with a force of a semi-professional squash player. "There, there."

Jason straightened his back, which vibrated from being treated as a squash ball, and drew a steadying breath. Two reporters edged closer. He raised his hand in a quick greeting, signalling them he wasn't available. Not yet. The flirty smile worked, and they stepped back, crossing their arms. Waiting.

"So, to answer your question," Rachel continued, lowering her voice, "You have two choices. Out this woman, laugh about the whole thing, have her vouch for you. Or, if she's not keen, lay low for a while. Make sure you're seen by yourself, doing the single guy thing. Act like you're over it, you know the drill. Maybe go out with someone else, get your photo taken. Make it look like you're just out there, looking for love, wearing your heart on your sleeve. Women love that."

"Is that what people think of the video?"

Tracy blushed. "I thought it showed courage and it made me wonder who the woman was. What had happened." Her blush deepened, and she nibbled at her fingernail.

Jason shook his head as if to dispel the image. "Courage? You don't have to pander to me. I know I made an absolute ass of myself. And I wasn't even drunk! It's okay to say it."

Tracy's eyes shone as she hugged her iPad to her chest. "My friend Erin sent me a link to that video last night. I know people are making fun of you, but not everyone..." She flipped the iPad so he could see it and fetched the email she'd received. Jason stared at the row emojis, some of which he'd never seen before. Under the video link, the message screamed with adoration.

*OMG!! Do you know what happened??!! Did he fall asleep on her? I need to know LOL. I can't believe you work for this guy!! Honestly, I can't stop fantasising about him ... He can fall asleep on me any day! Soooo cute!*

Jason thrusted the iPad back to his assistant like it stung his hand. He didn't need to know this. It wasn't healthy. "I have to go."

"Good choice!" Rachel stepped between him and the approaching journalist, giving him the opportunity to exit towards the carpark. Behind his back, she heard him apologising on his behalf.

He was about to walk away when he caught Nick's eye. He raised his hand with a tentative smile, giving him an opening. God, he missed having guy friends! Malcolm was great, but he lived and breathed politics. Jason needed his mates, the ones who didn't call him sexy or cute.

Gathering his courage, he circled the journalist to reach Nick. "Nick! I had no idea this was your project! Amazing work, bro. This is going to be a hit!"

Nick's eyes lit up at the praise, and he shook Jason's hand. The photographer jumped on the opportunity, and they posed together for a quick snap.

"How's it going in the Beehive? You've made quite a name for yourself," Nick said good-naturedly, rubbing his salt-and-pepper beard.

"The media circus is nuts, but the job is interesting." Jason paused for a moment, wondering about how much to share. They used to be so close, playing tennis together every week, going out for beers afterwards. Nick had always left after one drink, to get back to his family, put his kids to bed or help his wife with something. He was a good guy, living a life Jason now envied. "I'm hanging in there. I miss having a life, though. Having time off. The tennis."

Nick nodded, his eyes reflecting a quiet understanding.

Jason turned back to the house. "I love what you're doing here. So, the concrete mixed with recycled fibre. What does that mean?"

Jason had memorised a few lines from the press release and was rewarded with a bright smile on Nick's face. "I know it sounds crazy but yeah, basically, we can mix in a lot of stuff. Recycled plastic. We could reduce the amount that's shipped offshore."

"Brilliant! I'll make sure to drum up some publicity. Are you still playing tennis?"

"Not as much as I used to. Can't you tell?" Nick laughed, patting the padding around his waist. "Too busy."

"Yeah." Jason looked away, wishing he could say he was coming back and wanted to start playing again. His body needed it. His soul needed it. But how could he? The journalist lurched, ever closer, followed by Rachel's imposing figure. These were the shadows that followed him now. Nick stepped back to join his business partner as Jason slunk to his car.

Closing the door of his mint green Prius, he sank into the driver's seat, grateful he'd paid extra for the tinted windows. Everything about him called for jokes, including the car he drove. He'd always taken it in his stride, proud of how secure he was in his masculinity. But this time, words had made their way under the surface, twisting his gut. His newfound happiness was too fragile. What if Marnie couldn't take it? What if she left?

Jason started the car and steered away from the housing site, cursing his distinctive vehicle. He'd have to drive around a bit to lose any tails. He couldn't risk leading any reporters to Marnie's house. And that's where he was going, he already knew it. Well, as soon as he used his connections to confirm her address. With a full name and phone number, it was a piece of cake. The idea of seeing her again pulled him like a beacon at night. Nothing could keep him away. But first, he needed a plan.

# Chapter 20

Marnie placed a salad bowl on the dining table and ignored the loud moan from her daughter.

"Tell me that's not all we're eating."

"That's all I'm eating," Marnie confirmed. "I have to get on top of this illness. It's the only way."

After the fast, her pain hadn't fully returned, and it gave her hope. Maybe the fasting had slowed the progression of the disease. Maybe she could even have this fling with Jason, in secret, if he played his part and avoided public meltdowns. They'd only meet after dark, in private locations. He had her phone number. Once he called, she'd lay out the terms.

"Is he joining us?" Tanya pointed at the lanky figure

moving about in their garden.

Marnie looked out to her deck, squinting at the light reflecting off the dolphin fountain. She'd given up trying to get rid of the fountain and allowed Lando to install the water connection. Everyone would think she was out of her mind – a sentiment Tanya had already expressed – but she didn't care. Nothing could take away the giddiness that had made a home in her chest since the text she'd received from Jason. A single heart. She remembered Tanya telling her the heart emoji was a sign of old age, along with the 'thumbs up' icon, and the thought relaxed her. Jason wasn't too young to embarrass himself with outdated emojis. And more importantly, he now had her phone number. He was busy, but he would call.

Someone knocked on the door, and Marnie stiffened. If Shasa walked in and saw what Lando was doing... she sighed and got up. She'd just have to face it.

She opened the door, and breath caught in her throat. "Jason?"

He smiled his winning smile, out in daylight. Marnie's other neighbours, Sue and John, Mac's parents, looked up from weeding the planter boxes in the community garden. They waved, smiling at Jason as they recognised him. Of course they did.

Alarmed, Marnie pulled the man inside and closed the door. "What are you doing here?"

"I'm kidnapping you." He pulled her closer, his lips

searching for hers.

She fought him for a split second before her body took over, flooded with endorphins. How could she think straight when overpowered by his scent, those long fingers tracing her face, diving into her hair? She couldn't think at all. Instead, white hot fire spread down her spine, taking residence in the pit of her belly. After a whole day without pain, living on salad, this was the perfect icing on the perfect cake, better than any actual dessert. She'd never need food again.

He released her and glanced over her shoulder. They had company. Marnie jerked around, her hands flying to her mouth. Oh, no. Both Tanya and Lando stood at the end of the hallway, jaws hanging like two ventriloquist dummies.

"Mum? Is that...?" Tanya stopped to swallow without blinking.

"Jason Hallett. Lovely to meet you." Jason offered his hand and the practised smile he seemed to be able to pull out of a hat in any situation, although his eyes held an ever-so-slightly dazed look.

Lando switched the wrench he was holding into his other hand and took Jason's in his overly firm grip. "I know you," Lando announced, sticking out his chin. "You're that politician."

Jason nodded. "Yes, I am."

"What are you doing with our Marnie?"

"We're friends," Marnie mumbled, her cheeks burning.

Lando narrowed his eyes. "That looked real friendly."

"Yeah, come on, Mum. Are you… with him?"

Marnie turned to her daughter, her heart beating erratically. Was there any way to salvage this? Any way the reporters weren't already on their way to her home? Any way she didn't have to sell the house and go on a year-long cruise with retirees?

"Tanya, honey, I was going to tell you, but it's all so new." she glanced at Jason, emitting a silent apology.

Jason grimaced. "I'm sorry. I didn't mean to be seen by this many people. I just couldn't wait to see you. The yard looked empty when I arrived. Are your neighbours very nosy?"

Marnie placed a hand on his arm. Her fingertips curled on the inside of his wrist, detecting the rapid pulse under his skin. Her heart matched it, beat for beat. "Sue and John are very discreet, if we just tell them what's going on."

"What *is* going on?" Tanya demanded.

"That's what I'd like to know," Lando echoed. "I'm slaving away in your backyard, connecting your fountain, which I gifted you as a token of my feelings, to be honest."

Marnie cringed, turning around so that Lando couldn't see her reaction. Meeting Jason's confused gaze, she subtly shook her head, her eyes pleading for understanding. "I'm sorry, Lando. I never meant to lead you on," she whispered, casting him a quick look over her shoulder.

The palpable disappointment on Lando's face wound her stomach into a knot. She should have listened to Shasa and told him a firm 'no' to the fountain, as well as everything else. The man was guileless. He didn't deserve this, no matter how terrible his taste in garden ornaments.

"Wait! Are you... Beatrice?" Tanya's voice rose an octave as her eyes widened into cartoon versions of the originals. "Mum, seriously? Is it you?"

"Shhh!" Marnie wasn't sure why she was shushing, as nobody could possibly overhear them. The closest people were John and Sue, all the way in the garden. Holy shit. She had to include them.

Trying to ignore the swirling in her stomach, Marnie hurried out the front door and located her neighbours, busy installing slug traps. "Sue? John? Can I please talk to you? Do you mind coming over for a minute?"

They both looked a little puzzled but followed.

Once they were all inside, Marnie led them into the lounge, urging everyone to take a seat. Sue and John took the couch, while Jason perched on one of the barstools. Lando remained standing next to him, arms folded, back straight, as if to show how much taller he was. Tanya lowered herself into an armchair, never taking her eyes off Jason.

Choosing the barstool next to Jason, Marnie eyed the motley crew in her lounge. "I'm so sorry to spring this on you. But since you've already seen him, I have to ask you to keep this secret with me."

"What secret?" John asked, his voice gentle, clueless.

His arched eyebrows matched his wife's, who was still

holding a dirt-covered spade, trying not to touch any of her furnishings. Marnie took it from her and placed it in the sink.

Jason cleared his throat. "I've been seeing Marnie."

John stared at him, still confused. "And it's a secret because...?"

Sue's mouth formed a perfect O as they all waited for the rest of the sentence.

Tanya let out a frustrated growl. "Because it's Jason Hallett! Have you not seen the news? Everyone's laughing about this video of him talking to some woman about..." It seemed even Tanya didn't have the guts to repeat the lines.

Marnie marvelled the sight of her daughter's mouth soundlessly opening and closing.

"Oh, yes!" Sue blushed, looking away. "Beatrice?"

"That was Mum, apparently," Tanya deadpanned.

Marnie hung her head, wishing to disappear. If it was this painful to tell her family and friends, how could she ever handle the rest of New Zealand knowing?

Jason's hand landed on her shoulder. His voice brimmed with lightness that clashed with every other tone in the room. "Yes, I made a fool of myself. But it's only because I'm head over heels for this woman."

He hopped off his chair and wrapped his arm around her shoulder, making Marnie shiver. She was too scared to look up, to see the horror she imagined on everyone's faces.

"Unfortunately, because of my role in politics, I attract

a lot of media attention. And I don't wish to bring that mayhem on Marnie, so I'd really appreciate it if you could keep this between us?"

"Of course!" Sue agreed, echoed by her husband.

Marnie lifted her chin, risking a look around the room.

Tanya twisted her mouth. "Can I tell Hailey?"

"Please, don't."

Tanya shot her a defiant look, but she could see the silent agreement behind her pout.

Lando harrumphed. "I'll keep quiet, for Marnie's sake. Not yours." He glared at Jason, who acknowledged him with a grateful look.

"Thank you." Jason stood up and raised his volume. "I'm actually glad you're all here."

Marnie tensed. She could almost see the podium in front of him, imagine the political rally. The image made her both hot and cold. How could he turn things around like that? With a few short words, he'd shifted the energy in the room. Even Lando's expression had thawed by a degree.

"I was hoping to steal Marnie away from you for a bit, and I need you onboard. I don't want her family or friends to think she's actually been kidnapped."

Sue and John offered him polite smiles, while Tanya's eyes sharpened. "Where are you taking her?"

Jason glanced at Marnie, his eyes like two beseeching question marks. "If she agrees, I'd like to take her to an undisclosed beach location in Wellington."

"Undisclosed?" Marnie repeated.

"Are you expecting the reporters to torture us for information?" Tanya stared at him pointedly.

Marnie sighed. This was the kind of teenage baggage she came with. She watched Jason's face for discomfort, but he burst into a hearty laugh.

"Honestly, that's what it feels like at times! But no, I'm not expecting them to come after you at all. Not if we can keep this under our hats. I'll give you the address later. I just don't know it off the top of my head, I only just made the booking."

"You've already made a booking?" Marnie tried to lower her voice as Tanya leaned in. She hadn't seen such keen interest behind her daughter's eyes in a long time. Good to know something could break through the facade of perpetual indifference.

Jason's eyes begged for understanding. "I'm sorry, I took a gamble. I just really need to disappear for a bit, and I thought I'd use some leave."

Marnie blinked, trying to rearrange her thoughts, as well as her timeline. "How long are you thinking?"

"Um, two weeks. I understand if you can't get away for that long. I'll take whatever I can get."

"What about Shasa?" Tanya demanded, crossing the floor to get a Diet Coke from the fridge. "She's going to ask about you. Are we going to lie to her and Mac? And Elsie and Earl? They're coming for Sunday lunch at Sue and John's, right?"

Marnie blinked in disbelief. Just last week, Tanya had announced she wouldn't attend any boring lunches at their elderly neighbours' house.

"Am I invited to that?" Lando piped up.

"Of course, more the merrier!" Sue announced.

"Wow. I didn't realise you had so much going on." Jason flashed her an apologetic smile.

Marnie shifted on her seat. "You should have gone with an actual kidnapping." But she couldn't help the warmth in her gut, deeply grateful that he hadn't. She didn't need another Steve in her life, a man who only considered himself. Back in the day, he might have done a similar thing, booking something without discussing it with her, but not out of the desperation she could feel driving Jason, rather to avoid Marnie's opinions or preferences messing with the perfect holiday he had in mind.

"It's okay," Jason said, addressing the whole room, taking charge. "We'll update Shasa and Mac and... who were the others?"

"Elsie and Earl," Sue supplied.

"Thank you. And we'll ask all of them to keep this a secret. I know it gets more complicated, but we'll have to try."

Marnie gave him a quick smile. "Don't worry, they're all very trustworthy. So, when are we leaving?"

Jason's Adam's apple travelled up and down as he gulped. "Now?"

# Chapter 21

"Now it feels like a real kidnapping," Marnie observed, lying flat on the backseat of Jason's rental car, a silver Hyundai, hiding under a throw they'd grabbed off her couch on the way out.

Jason laughed, glancing at her in the rear-view mirror. "I'm so sorry. In ten minutes, we'll be out on the motorway, and you can get up."

"It's okay. I quite like it in here." She curled up sideways to make herself more comfortable. If anyone recognised Jason behind the wheel, at least they wouldn't spot her on the passenger seat.

Marnie had packed in a hurry, and they'd hit the road

in less than half an hour. This was one of the benefits of being low maintenance – she didn't travel with a lot of stuff. As long as she had her phone, wallet and iPad, some fresh underwear and her medication, she was fine.

"Do you want a drink? Snacks? Anything else before we leave town?"

Marnie lifted her head to see his face in the mirror. "Coffee?"

"I'm too nervous about caffeine these days. But you can have one. Smelling it won't mess me up." His mouth curled up in the mirror.

"You slept last night, right?"

"I did! Thanks to you."

Marnie winced. "You make sound like I have superpowers. I don't walk around putting people to sleep with a wave of my hand. At least I hope not! Tanya says I'm the most boring person in the universe, so I don't know."

She felt him slow to a stop and caught the glow of the red traffic light in the corner of the window. His shoulders shook as he laughed. "Your daughter's a riot."

"I worry about her," she confessed. "Or, rather, I worry about us. She despises me. I fear that one day she'll move out and I'll never hear from her again."

Jason's voice was reassuring. "She's a teenager. They're self-absorbed by nature. It usually passes."

Marnie huffed. "I hope so. I feel like I have no part in her life. Other than being a chauffeur, maybe. And the one who hands out money. She doesn't include me in anything."

"Do you include her?"

Marnie lifted her head, taken aback. "What do you mean?"

"I mean, do you ask for her opinion, or help? One thing I learnt about teens in my teacher days is that they want to feel like they're contributing."

"Huh." She'd never thought of that. Maybe her troubles with Tanya were partly her own doing. "I've been trying to teach her to be more self-sufficient, but that just seems to make things worse between us."

"Yeah. Teaching teenagers is hard. Sometimes it's counter intuitive. At best, you can inspire them to learn about something and then let them teach you."

Marnie's mouth curved at the thought. What could Tanya teach her? How to waste hours at the mall? How to walk and text at the same time?

She glanced at the rear-view mirror, and the concern in Jason's eyes made her own well up.

"How is she with her father?" he asked.

Marnie sighed. "She doesn't spend much time with him. His new partner doesn't like having her around, and I just don't have the heart to force it. Steve doesn't care, I think it's just easier for him this way. He never really fought for custody."

"He sounds..." Jason cleared his throat.

"What?" Marnie peered from under the blanket at his side profile, a sick feeling in her stomach. She hated being the one cast aside, the one not deemed good enough. She'd told herself it was Steve, not her. But it was like that message couldn't reach her on a cellular level.

"Well, he sounds like a self-absorbed dick," Jason summed up. "But I'm glad he had the decency to set you free. Some guys will try to have their cake and... you know. Wife, mistress, the works."

Marnie shuddered. She imagined being still married, with Steve hustling other women on the side. That would be worse. She hadn't been happy in their marriage either, tiptoeing around his moods, swallowing his disappointments. He could have stolen the rest of her life.

"I never told him, but I think I wanted out, too," she whispered. "I didn't have a chance to say it, because he was so much further on with his plans."

"I know the feeling," he said, his eyes on the road. "But I hate being the bad guy. It's always easier if the other person pulls the plug and you get to be the aggrieved party with no guilt."

"I suppose. I just felt like I was completely worthless." Her voice choked up and she tried to cover it up by shuffling under the blanket.

The car slowed down and came to a stop. Judging by the shade, they were on a side street, under some mature trees. Marnie sat up, glancing out the window. There were no other cars nearby. Jason turned off the engine and joined her on the backseat, reaching out for her. His glistening eyes took her by surprise. Wasn't he supposed to be hard-boiled, slippery and untouchable, like all politicians?

Marnie peeled off the blanket and let him pull her into his arms.

"I really hope you don't feel like that with me," he said.

Marnie inhaled a lungful of his scent. "No. I mean, it's great that you can sleep when I'm around. That's worth something."

Jason pulled away and his forehead wrinkled. "Is that what you think? Do you think the only reason I like you is that you help me sleep?"

"Well, I get that it's important. If I can help you in any way, I will. But without the sleep thing, would we have anything? Would you still have looked for me? I can't help these thoughts. Sorry."

Jason's fingers gently tugged her hair, turning her to face him. "No, no, no! I hate that you'd think that. I know it sounds that way, but I've been into you from the moment we met. Before I even knew about your superpowers. Sorry, I shouldn't say that. I can't help seeing it that way."

"Why do you think it is, though?" Marnie whispered. She seemed to have lost her voice somewhere deep inside. "Maybe it's my scent, like the shampoo I use, or something like that. If you could get the same effect by sniffing a bottle, wouldn't that be a whole lot easier? You wouldn't have to drag me around and risk media finding out. If they discover my age, my illness, the fact that I'm divorced... It won't be good for either of us. And you have more to lose."

"No! Not true. Without you, I'll lose it anyway." His grim voice took her by surprise. He looked menacing, the shadows growing and changing shape behind his eyes. He wove his fingers through hers, staring at their tangled hands. "I'm so close to quitting. I can't do this without sleep. I'm going to lose it for good."

Tears pooled in his eyes and his hands squeezed hers, like a drowning man holding onto a raft. "I know it's not what you deserve. It's not the beautiful, perfect love affair. I'm broken. I'm a shadow of myself. Sometimes, I hear this buzzing, these faint voices in my head..." He dropped his chin to his chest, swaying his head.

His head touched her shoulder, and Marnie pulled him against her. "It's okay," she said. "I love being with you. It makes me feel alive, like I'm someone else. I shouldn't worry about this not being real. Nothing lasts forever."

His shoulders jerked as cries shook his body. Marnie brushed her thumb across his cheek, gathering tears suspended on his stubble, hardly believing a well-known politician was soaking her chest with real tears. She'd never seen a man cry, not up close. Marnie brought her thumb to her lips and tasted the salty liquid. They were real, even if nothing else was.

Jason lifted his head, flashing her a sad grin. "I'm sorry. This isn't what I had in mind for our romantic getaway."

"Don't apologise. I started it. I find it hard to enjoy the

present and not worry about the future."

"But what if it's great? Our future, I mean."

Marnie smiled, a lump in her throat. He wouldn't get it. She was about to respond when Jason's finger silenced her lips. "Don't say it. Just give us more time, okay? Let me love you and see if you like it?"

Her heartbeat skyrocketed at his words. He couldn't keep dropping bombs like that. "Man, you can really spin those words..."

"Occupational hazard," he smiled, tears still in his eyes.

Marnie tried to draw a breath. She'd never met anyone like him. The man was like a walking contradiction. How could anyone be so charming, persistent and fragile, all at the same time?

Jason opened the door to get back in the driver's seat. "Anyway, before we get out of town, I want to make one stop."

# Chapter 22

Jason parked a few paces away from his cottage, hoping the rental car helped him blend in. With any luck, journalists would have better things to do on a Saturday afternoon than stakeout his home.

"Okay, we're here." He peered over his shoulder at the backseat.

Marnie's curls appeared from under the blanket, and she blinked as she took in the surroundings, her thumb mindlessly playing with her lower lip. At times, she seemed totally unaware of herself, like someone who'd never posed for camera or had to be on guard because other were watching. He found it fascinating.

"This is your street, right?"

"How do you know my street?" He couldn't help teasing her and was rewarded with the sweetest blush.

"I may have walked past a few times, wondering if you were home."

"See! And all the while, I was looking for you, trying to crack that pseudonym you gave me. It was all meant to be!"

She looked out the window, her eyes dreamy, yet sad. "Meant to be, huh?"

Jason held back his frustrated sigh. She could tell Marnie didn't believe they had a future.

"See this house on the left"—Jason pointed at his next door neighbour—"the one with the red mailbox?"

"What about it?"

"It's empty."

Marnie studied the brick house with dark windows and immaculate front lawn. "Why? Is it on the market?"

"No." Jason took a breath, trying to control the anger that always stirred when he approached the subject. "It's been empty for at least three years. A gardening company comes in every two weeks to mow the lawn and tidy up."

His gaze drifted from the lawns to the white-rimmed bay windows. Such a beautiful, solid house. Such a waste.

Marnie's eyes darkened. "An investment property?"

"Yeah. I've been staring at it the whole time I've lived here. I think about it every time I meet people who're struggling with high rents, homelessness, first home buyers trying to get in the market, kids spending weeks in the hospital every winter, fighting respiratory illnesses because their mouldy, crowded homes are killing them… I know we have a supply issue, it's true. But we also allow two hundred thousand houses to sit there, empty."

"Two hundred thousand?" Marnie's voice rose as she glared at him.

"They're not all as nice as this one, obviously. And many are in far-flung locations, holiday homes and such. But for a tiny country in the middle of a housing crisis, that number is too high. It's a disgrace." He paused to look her in the eye. "And I want to change that."

She stared back, her mouth slightly ajar, eyes filled with concern. "How?"

"By taxing the owners."

"Sounds like a great idea."

"It sounds simple, but in reality, it's very complicated. It's particularly hard to determine which houses are actually vacant, and how high the tax needs to be to incentivise the owners to either sell or rent. But even if they don't, the tax we collect can pay for some local housing developments."

Marnie poked her head through the gap between the front seats, her eyes shining. "So, how do you plan to do it? I mean, find out which houses are empty and all that?"

Jason bit his lip. "I don't want to bore you with the details. I mean…" His old mate Nick always laughed and shut him up whenever he sounded too much like a politician.

"No, I want the details," Marnie insisted, checking the street for any movement. It was empty, so she hopped out of the backseat and joined him in the front.

She was such an enigma. Jason couldn't resist reaching for her hand. The contact made him feel better. "I'd start with larger cities with the worst housing shortage, like Auckland, Wellington and Tauranga, using data from water meters. If a dwelling has zero water usage, that's a pretty clear sign of a vacant property."

"But Hamilton doesn't have water meters."

"Not yet. But we're heading that way."

"Who'd collect the tax then? The local council?"

"Yes. Although that's one of the biggest hurdles. The cost of administration would be high. Councils are notoriously slow and difficult to work with, so we're looking at ways to automate parts of the process, especially the data collection and billing." He looked up, expecting to see Marnie's eyes glazed over. Instead, he caught them brighter than ever, golden in the afternoon light.

"I'm sure if you found the right people, a couple of champions from each town who took ownership of the whole thing, that could work. You just need a good team."

"It doesn't happen that easily when something is government-mandated. People tend to look for loopholes and grumble about any new tasks or challenges."

She nodded. "I still love the idea. I hope it works out."

Jason swallowed. "Yeah. I head the working group that's

investigating this, but Kathleen's already decided it's not happening. She asked me to give a statement to that effect next week. Tell everyone that we looked into it, but it won't work."

Marnie's eyes flamed. "Really? Kathleen Rush? How can she do that?"

Jason scratched his chin, trying to smile. "She's the housing minister. It's her call."

"But what if she's not well enough to make these decisions? It's not fair to you or anyone else!" Her eyes burned passion that gave Jason pause. Where was this coming from?

"Did she say something to make you think..."

Marnie nodded, a grave look on her face. "I'm sorry I didn't tell you before. I was scared and tried to forget all about her. And I think you're right, those chocolates got under my skin. But yeah, she sounded a bit odd on the phone. Like she'd suddenly forgotten everything we'd just talked about. She started over and corrected herself. It was weird."

Jason leaned back on the driver's seat, rubbing his temples. It wasn't an isolated incident. It couldn't be. If only they could get the word out there, even just to create suspicion. Maybe he could force Kathleen to take a step back, allow them to investigate the tax for a bit longer. But he couldn't ask Marnie, not anymore. A heavy silence sat between them as Marnie stared out the window, her chin quivering as she chewed on her lip.

Finally, she turned to face him. "I want to do it," she said, pinning him with a fierce look. "I want to talk to those people in your office, or whoever you think should know about Kathleen."

"Are you sure? I know I asked you when we first met, but that was wrong. I shouldn't have. And Kathleen knows you now. She might figure out it was you."

Marnie nodded, her face firm. "I know, but I refuse to be intimidated. What is she going to do? Kill me with a gift basket?"

Jason rested his fingers on the ignition, holding his breath. "What are you saying?"

"I'm saying, let's go. We're already driving to Wellington. We can stop at your office on the way."

# Chapter 23

The highway split into four, then five lanes. After six hours on the road, they finally approached Wellington. The turquoise ocean glistened on one side, steep green hills climbed sky-high on the other, casting a shadow over the road. Marnie's initial nerves had faded during the long drive. She'd loved talking to Jason, hearing more about his parliament reality, as well as what he missed from his old life. So many things she'd taken for granted, like spending a day at the beach, or catching up with a friend with no work agenda.

Marnie had driven most of the way, worried about Jason's fatigue. One good night didn't magically cure months of insomnia. In Lower Hutt, they'd finally switched places so Jason could navigate them to the parliament carpark. Marnie had returned to the backseat, curled under the blanket, and was starting to overheat.

She'd been so sure about their plan, filled with determination, but the closer they got to the capital city, the more out of her element she felt. Her casual top and yoga pants were fine for a secluded beach house, not the parliament. But she couldn't back down, not now. This was too important.

The Beehive looked imposing, the late afternoon sun casting a golden halo over the building. The view was soon replaced by the sickly yellow lighting of the underground carpark. Jason got out of the car and scanned the space. There were only a couple of other cars, no people in sight.

"All clear," he said, opening the door to the backseat.

Marnie climbed out, stretching her aching limbs. Jason had promised to do his best to keep her anonymous, but she accepted the risk. Every nerve vibrating, she followed Jason to the lifts and they ascended to the office floor. Everything looked the same, the maze of long, carpeted hallways. Green and red. portraits of serious, balding men. It was Saturday night, just like last time. But something had shifted. The way Jason touched her lower back, guiding her. She felt his protection, his concern. The warmth of his hand travelled through her, soothing her wobbly stomach. What would it be like to have someone in her corner like this all the time?

He stopped at the office door, his eyes fixed on hers, face drawn. "Are you sure? We don't have to do this. I don't want to risk what we have, that's more important to me."

Marnie's insides flipped at his words, but her mind resisted. "More important than housing thousands of people?"

Jason paused, glancing at the door, the pain evident on his face. "I know it sounds selfish. I'm just scared that you'll regret this."

"Kathleen's not there, is she?" Marnie swallowed.

"On a Saturday night? I shouldn't think so. But I can go in first to check."

Jason reached for the door, but Marnie stepped in front of him. She hadn't come all the way to chicken out at the door. "No, let's just do this, okay? Even if I regret this, I will never blame you, okay?"

At a glance, the room seemed empty. But as they circled around the formation of work stations, Marnie spotted two young guys at their desks, quietly typing away at their laptops. Both looked up, taking note of Jason and Marnie.

"Hi guys! Just showing a friend around the building." Jason walked them closer, and the young men smiled at Marnie.

She fiddled with her necklace, self-conscious about her outfit.

Jason gestured at the pointy-nosed young lad with spiky hair, who shot up from his chair. "This is Kyle. He does research. And here's Ravi. Also research."

"Hi! I'm... Beatrice," Marnie said, offering them a quick smile.

The handsome Indian also stood up, smiling brightly, and shook her hand for a good five-seconds, until Jason steered her away. The guys exchanged a look, both trying to conceal their knowing smiles. Of course they'd watched the video, along with the rest of the nation. She might as well have introduced herself as the 'woman Jason fell asleep on'. Why hadn't she thought of another pseudonym? Marnie grimaced, casting an apologetic look at Jason.

"We'll just get some tea." Jason nudged Marnie towards the staff kitchen. "Can I get you guys anything?"

Kyle trailed behind them like a dog who'd picked up a scent. "I'll have a V. But I'll get it."

He helped himself to a can of energy drink while Jason boiled the jug.

Marnie steered towards the water cooler. "I'll just get a glass of water."

"Private tour, eh?" Kyle winked at her, flicking open the can. "So, how do you know Jason?"

Marnie glanced at Jason, raising her brow. Was this the right guy? Jason gave her the slightest of nods. She took a breath, smiling at Kyle. "It's a funny story, actually! We were both at that art gala a few weeks back. Jason was looking for Kathleen Rush, and he asked me to check the ladies room. I went in and found her on the floor! She was acting a bit strange, forgot my name like a minute after I told her. Must have hit her head real good!" Marnie tapped at her own temple and laughed. Maybe it was a bit much, but she could only hope her tone deaf presentation made her sound completely clueless, someone who had no idea what the information was worth.

She waited for a moment, before turning to Jason, her eyes wide. "Uh oh, should I have not said anything? Sorry, it was just so exciting. Nothing like that ever happens to me."

Jason responded with an animated smile, playing the game. "That's okay. We can trust Kyle."

Kyle nodded with barely controlled enthusiasm. "Absolutely! So, she hit her head? Like, knocked herself out?"

Marnie shrugged, feigning disinterest. "That's what she said. Slipped and fell. Could happen to anyone, right?"

"Right." Kyle's eyes gleamed as he studied her. "Was the floor wet or something?"

Marnie frowned. "No, I don't think so."

"But that's just between us, okay?" Jason repeated, his voice carrying so much weight the air bristled. "Would be terrible if the media found out. If it turns out she's not well and has been hiding it, the PM will be livid. She'll be forced to let her go. That would be terrible."

"Terrible." Kyle's nodding reached bobble-head levels.

"The last thing I want is Beatrice getting mixed up in this. She's done nothing wrong."

Kyle stared at Jason, not blinking. "Of course. I'm sure if there was a story there, a good journalist would find other sources to confirm their suspicions."

"Exactly." Jason gave him a meaningful half-smile.

Kyle opened his mouth to ask something else, but Jason slapped him on the shoulder. "Good talk, Kyle. I'm sorry, we must run. We have a booking."

They left the kitchen and Kyle returned to his desk, his energy drink shaking in his hand. Jason shot Marnie a quick smile and led her out of the office, back into the marble stairway.

"Was that okay?" Marnie asked as the door closed behind them.

Jason brushed a wayward curl off her face. "You're full of surprises, Marnie Browne." He placed a soft kiss on her mouth.

For a moment, she forgot everything. All that existed was Jason, his warm lips on hers in the dimly lit foyer, his spicy scent in her nose, the faint echo of the city somewhere in the distance.

But as he pulled away, she saw sadness lingering in his eyes. "I really hope they don't come after you. Kathleen knows who you are. She might put things together."

Marnie frowned. "I'm sorry I used the same fake name. I just panicked. I couldn't think of anything else. I should have planned something."

Jason shook his head. "Let's not worry about it yet. I'm

pretty sure Kathleen's health is bigger news than my love life. I really hope so."

Marnie's skin prickled. God, she hoped he was right. What if Kathleen came after her? Was she ready for this? From the moment they met, she'd wanted so badly to help Jason. Nothing else mattered. She'd placed her hands on Jason's chest, letting his heartbeat flow through her, settle her.

"I don't regret anything," she whispered. She didn't regret a moment they'd spent together, even though she could sense the inevitable end, somewhere on the horizon. But here, within his gravitational field, she felt incapable of long-term thinking. Unable to save herself. She'd follow him to the ends of the earth and feel this alive, for as long as she could.

A sound of footsteps behind the door made them both look up.

"We better go," Jason whispered.

He guided her down the stairs, through the same endless hallways to the lift they'd taken up from the carpark. His hand rested on her back, then on her arm, never breaking contact. Down at the underground carpark, he unlocked the doors of their rental car, a smile lighting up his face. "I hope you like the Airbnb I booked. It's a bit different."

# Chapter 24

Jason parked outside the Airbnb, excitement making his blood sizzle. He hadn't told Marnie anything about the accommodation. A lighthouse. The only one you could stay at on the entire island. He could have paid more for luxury, but nothing beat a real lighthouse, right?

He shot Marnie a sideways glance. "Are you ready?"

He jumped out of the car, marvelling at how easily his legs carried his weight. The acid build-up that usually tightened his every muscle was gone. The magic of sleep. He circled around to open the door for Marnie.

She rolled her eyes at the chivalry but winced as she stood and stretched her arms over her head.

"Does it hurt?" he asked, ashamed that he'd forgotten about her condition. She hadn't mentioned it again, but every now and then, a shadow crossed her face, making him wonder.

Marnie shook her head. "Not too much. I'm just a bit tingly. And hungry."

"I ordered some food. The fridge should be stocked." Jason led her towards the steps.

She stopped at the foot of the stairs, blinking at the bright white, hexagonal structure rising from the rocky terrain. "A lighthouse?"

"Uh-huh." Jason couldn't help grinning. "You like it?"

Marnie stared in awe. "I love it! But I thought we were supposed to keep a low profile?"

"I know. I thought about that, but I just couldn't help myself. I mean... it's a lighthouse!" He examined her face, holding his breath.

To his relief, the worry melted away and a smile broke through. "It's got very small windows, so that's good. Those bigger ones are up on the top level. So, it's perfect for hiding. As long as the press doesn't find out you're in a lighthouse..."

"Yeah. That wouldn't take them long."

Jason opened the red front door with the key he found in the lock box. Together, they stepped inside. The tiny windows streamed in narrow pillars of daylight, leaving most of the room in shadow. The decor was bare and nautical, not quite as romantic as Jason had hoped.

Marnie skipped around the room, her eyes wide and arms spread. After one loop she took the spiral staircase leading to the upper level. He followed at her heels.

The top floor windows framed a breath-taking panorama across the rocky coastline which levelled into smooth sand before reaching the low-tide waves. The evening sun made everything glow in shades of peach and gold. The beach was empty of people, the road in-between quiet. It was perfect – a secluded fortress at the edge of the world, fifteen minutes from the Beehive. He could make it to the meetings on Tuesday and return here at night. He could sleep and work and not fail. Thanks to Marnie, he had a shot at the housing portfolio. Anything felt possible.

Marnie stood at the window with her back to him.

Jason snuck closer and wrapped his arms around her. "Will you stay here with me?" He cringed at the neediness in his own voice. Like a little boy. Why couldn't he sound solid and dependable? Seductive? He had to improve his game, especially now he'd slept better. Otherwise, she'd never let go of those reservations he felt stewing right under the surface.

"It's beautiful…" Marnie turned around, her eyes clouded. "Let's eat something and go for a walk! Maybe we can spot a blue penguin?"

"Are they common around here?"

"I think so," Marnie chirped, leading the way back

downstairs.

"Remind me to show you the video of Benedict Cumberbatch trying to pronounce the word penguin. It's hilarious."

"Why? Can't he say it?"

Jason chuckled. "Not even close."

She headed to the fridge. Jason held his breath, hoping the host had provided anything and everything under the sun as requested. He'd paid handsomely for the extra trouble.

"Oh, my God!" Moving a stack of yogurts, Marnie pulled out what looked like a tray of readymade turkey sandwiches.

"I told them to go beyond the supermarket and get us something special."

"You paid them to go shopping all over town for us? That must have been expensive!"

Jason couldn't hold back his proud smile. "Don't worry. Totally worth it. Tea?"

He boiled the jug while Marnie unwrapped the sandwiches. They sat down at a small table perched under one of the tiny windows giving to the beach. Jason connected to the wi-fi and found the penguin video.

After laughing at Benedict talking about 'pengwings' and 'penglings', they ate in absent-minded silence, focused on the window. It looked like a painting, a rugged coastal scene from a hundred years ago, with no signs of modern life. Jason wished they could travel back in time, to an era before internet and all the shit that came with it. Those invisible strings, hooked onto his flesh, tugging him with every notification. Without the weight of those demands, without the publicity, everything could be so simple.

Marnie sucked in her lips to catch the falling crumbs and wrinkled her nose. "Why are you looking at me like that?"

Jason's neck felt warm and he wondered if he was blushing. "The light... you look like a painting. I just want to remember this moment."

Her eyes widened in disbelief, and she burst out in laughter, snorting her tea. "What?" She hiccupped through an answer he couldn't make sense of. After a while, her laughter settled and she managed to form words. "I'm sorry! I just can't believe the things you say. It's like I'm watching a movie, and my parents are mouthing those cheesy lines to each other. They used to do that, making faces. When they were still alive."

"Cheesy lines?" He tried to smile. Maybe he deserved it.

"I'm sorry, I didn't mean..." She blushed.

"What happened to your parents?"

Marnie looked out the window, her mood shifting. "Dad died. After that, Mum lost interest in everything. Looking after him was such a big part of her life. I feel like she developed cancer at will, just because she decided it was time. I know that makes no sense, but I always felt like she'd already checked out, and no cure, no treatment could help. You know how people rally their support group and beat cancer? It was never like that."

"So, you swore to never to lose yourself in a relationship

like that?"

Marnie smiled and shook her head. "Never had to worry about that. I was already divorced. It was a rough couple of years."

"When was that?"

"About four years ago." She picked up her spoon and stirred her tea, which was barely steaming. "But I can see Mum in myself. It's terrifying."

"You mean the way you look after me? Yeah, that's terrifying." Jason tried to keep his tone light.

She smiled through a film of tears. "Yeah, I guess that's not the worst part. I love helping you. But I don't want to lose sight of myself completely. Remember that stylist we bumped into, Luna Bella?"

Jason nodded, trying to hide his reaction. Marnie didn't seem to notice, deep in thought.

"She had an impeccable style. You know those people who have firm opinions about everything – what's in, what's out, what you should be doing and eating and drinking..."

Jason raised an eyebrow. "Influencers?"

"Yeah, those people. Well, I'm like an anti-influencer. I'm an absorber, this nebulous blob that will fit themselves around any object to make it comfortable."

Jason couldn't help a cheeky smile spreading across his face. "That's poetic, but maybe you just haven't had anyone around who truly appreciates who you are? I'm not saying me, but... me? I swear I can see a distinct shape in you. I'm not just talking about curves, either. You have character."

Marnie smiled her sad smile. "I wasn't fishing for a compliment but thank you. I should have figured all this out earlier before I... expired." Her voice sounded a little strangled.

"Expired? You mean, like milk or yogurt?"

Marnie gave him a sheepish smile. "Uh, yeah. I mean it's not the best word—"

"No kidding! Didn't know humans had expiry dates. I mean, you're still alive, right? You're not a ghost?" He raised his eyebrows and rounded his eyes in mock horror.

She twisted her mouth. "I know it sounds nuts. I'm just saying it's different for a woman. There's this ticking clock..."

Jason blew out a deep sigh. "Yeah? Let's not waste any time then. Walk?"

She blew a breath, as if to release the dark thoughts. "Okay."

He fetched their luggage from the car. Following his lead, she wrapped up in a hoodie. Jason locked the red door and let her lead the way down the stairs, across the empty road and onto the sand. The wind had picked up, making it feel more like Wellington. Marnie pulled her sleeves down over her knuckles and shivered.

Jason put his arm around her shoulders and pulled her closer. "You know, some of that stuff they put expiry dates on doesn't actually expire? It's just a marketing ploy, to encourage turnover."

"Really? Like what products?"

"Like salt and some oils. My mum used to work at a transfer station and her pet peeve was people doing pantry clear-outs and throwing out perfectly useable stuff."

Marnie chuckled and relaxed against him. Maybe he could get through to her, to show her what she was worth. A gemstone. Priceless. His.

They walked for a moment with the wind on their backs, peering out to the sea. A lonely seagull flew overhead, shrieking into the wind.

"What time are penguins around?" Jason asked. "Or penglings, for that matter?"

Marnie laughed. "I don't really know. Doesn't matter. I love the beach. Especially in the winter when it's empty."

They followed the shoreline around a tight bend. The sand turned into rocks, and they had to lift their feet higher, hopping over puddles left by the retreating tide. Jason felt like a kid with boundless energy, his legs carrying him to new adventures. He hadn't sensed this kind of freedom and ease in months, maybe years. He'd left his phone at the lighthouse. Nobody could reach him here.

He glanced at Marnie. Her hair glowed with an orange halo in the evening light. He wanted to grab a handful of it in his fist and devour her. Could she handle the intensity of his feelings for her? They didn't know each other that well, not yet. But he already knew he wanted this woman, no one else, for the rest of his life. At times, it felt like maybe she wanted it, too. But he didn't want her to go along to please him, to make him comfortable. He wanted her to choose him. Would she? He was a stressed-out mess carrying more baggage than a long-haul plane. How could he ask anyone to get onboard that? He might be her doom, something she regretted for the rest of her life.

"Ouch!"

Deep in his thoughts, Jason didn't see what Marnie stumbled on. He launched forward to catch her in mid-fall, unsuccessfully, and they both landed on the wet, pebble-studded sand. Jason stuck out his arms at the last minute to avoid crushing Marnie with his weight, but still made contact.

Marnie sat up, panting. "Oh, my God."

"Did you break anything?"

She brushed sand off her tights, stretching each limb. "No, I don't think so. You?"

"No. I fell on you." He grinned. "You're nice and soft."

He snaked his arm around her, just in time to stop her from getting up. They'd landed on the perfect spot, a secluded stretch of sand shielded from the wind by larger rocks. Sure, the sand was a bit wet, he could feel the moisture seeping into the fabric of his jeans, but that was a small price to pay for this moment. "Please, stay."

"I'm getting wet."

He raised a hopeful eyebrow and Marnie elbowed him in

the ribs. "Not what I meant."

"That's a shame." He flashed her a wicked smile. "Sit on me. I don't mind getting wet."

He wrestled her into his lap. Marnie laughed, her cheeks flushed. After a moment, she stopped fighting and curled up against his chest, shivering like a frightened bird. He could feel her heart beating under the layers of clothing.

"I'm too heavy," she whispered.

Jason sighed. What would it take to make this woman see what he saw? "I don't know who's told you these lies, but you have to stop believing them."

Marnie twitched in his lap but made a small noise of agreement. "It's just hard."

"I don't think we're meant to do it alone. We're all shaped by other people. We need someone to really *see* us, to point out what's beautiful. We're all blind to ourselves."

"You know you're beautiful."

"I know I'm good looking. I'm constantly told that, so I believe it. But I don't believe it's important."

Marnie hung her head. "I shouldn't care about that. I don't usually. I try to focus on other things, other people. It's better to be a good friend than a beautiful one."

He squeezed her hard. "But you're both! I know you think I'm full of shit and cheesy lines, but you're gorgeous. Like, delicious. I could eat you up." He buried his face into her neck, inhaling the mango scent mixed with something he'd begun to recognise as Marnie, the scent of rest and pleasure.

He kissed her soft skin, unable to stop himself. A wayward moan escaped her, and the primal resonance of it went straight to his core. She had no idea how sexy she was. Jason grabbed her chestnut curls, turning her to face him. The moment their mouths made contact, he was hard. She returned the kiss, hungry in a way that left no room for doubt. Even when her mind floundered, her body responded to him, giving him hope. If only they could stay here, within that bubble of sensation, fire coursing through them as their tongues swirled in a passionate dance that demanded more and more.

As his hand made it under her hoodie, she pulled away, eyes wild. "What if someone sees us?"

"Have you seen one single person out here?" He gestured along the beach out to the vast ocean. "It's like a desert island."

"With my luck, someone will show up. Like an angry security guard. Or the penguins."

"Well, let's give them a good show!"

He shifted under her to make room for his hard-on. With that round ass moulding against his thighs, he couldn't think of much else. He wanted to take her right here, but he wanted her to be fully onboard, to let go of all those doubts. There was something hiding inside her, a wild force stirring under the surface, hiding from everyone, even Marnie herself. He was the only one in the world who could see it, and the thought drove him crazy.

# Chapter 25

Marnie tried to settle her heartrate by inhaling the fresh ocean air. Mixed with Jason's aftershave, it sent her head spinning. She was simultaneously cold and hot. Her ankle ached from the fall, but her lady parts pulsed with need. She felt his hot breath on her neck, his hard length underneath her, reminding her of how he could make her feel. His lips found hers and his fingers dove into her hair, holding her in a tight grip. She couldn't escape, nor did she want to. Instead, she relaxed against his mouth, letting his tongue own her, make her forget everything.

Such a perfect evening, a perfect moment in time, or maybe outside time, in a secret place where real life couldn't reach them. Jason pulled away and they both drew a breath, panting. She saw the desire in his eyes, loud and clear. His hand released her hair and travelled down her body, settling on her hip. More warmth pooled into her core, and she shivered.

"Can I touch you?" Jason breathed in her ear. It tickled, drawing her focus to the sensation.

She nodded before her brain could process the question, and soon it couldn't process much else. He slid his hand underneath the waistband of her tights, his long fingers instantly where she needed them.

"Oh, my God." She rattled out a sigh.

"Do you want me to stop?"

"No."

Closing her eyes, she listened to the white noise of crashing waves. Fine ocean mist built up on her skin, turning into droplets. It was cool, but her insides ran hot, turning into liquid honey as his touch built up her need.

"Don't worry. There's no one around," he rasped, sliding two fingers inside.

She couldn't have asked him to stop. She was too weak, too wet, too much on fire. Her gasps turned into moans that rose over the roar of the ocean and she rocked against his hand. All her reservations washed away with those retreating waves as she surrendered to his touch.

Jason lifted the hem of her hoodie, just enough to reach her lacy bra. The coastal wind pinched her nipples hard, and she trembled as the wind found its way under her layers. Jason closed his mouth on one nipple, sucking as his warm hand enclosed the cold flesh of the other one. His other hand worked its magic between her legs. She might have been able to pull away, to stop the madness, if those fingers hadn't applied just the right amount of pressure, coupled with movement that worked with the rhythm of her breath.

He kept going, responding to her every sound, increasing his pace with her intensifying need, until a sudden release poured through her – a hot wave of pleasure. She gripped his hand, pulsing against it, soaking it. A fleeting thought of shame melted into pleasure. She rode the waves coursing through her as she curled against his hard chest, her bottom digging into the solid wood in his jeans.

Jason groaned, his voice thickest she'd ever heard. "Oh my God. You're so wet.

Marnie smiled, still panting, still riding on the gentle waves, her body refusing to return to earth. She wanted more. She wanted him inside her, right now. On a public beach. Her brain registered the foreign thought as something that didn't belong to her. Soon, she'd wake up and find out it was all a dream. But if it was, she had to make it count. Maybe she could just unzip his jeans, just enough to free that hard-on. It must have been so uncomfortable lodged in his pant leg. Her brain feeling mushy, Marnie scrambled to find the button.

Encouraged by her action, Jason took over and unzipped

his jeans. "You don't have to," he whispered. "We can go back to the house."

Marnie peeled her tights to her knees, then pulled off a shoe to free up one leg. She wanted to straddle him. The crumbled tights hanging off her ankle looked as ridiculous as she felt. But she didn't care. "I've never done anything like this."

Her bare knees sank in the freezing sand, sending a distant signal of pain, but she didn't want stop. This was it. The loose, warm hoodie she'd worn for the walk kept her top half warm and provided some cover. At least her bare bum wasn't hanging out for the penguins.

Here's hoping they really were on a desert island. She inched closer, grabbed his length and guided him inside. All the hot, hard, thick inches of him. She wasn't expecting the build-up of tension in her core. Women were meant to be capable of multiple orgasms. Other women. With Jason, she was one of those women. Her body responded to him with a fervour she didn't recognise. Jason leaned back on the sand, allowing her to ride him with her full weight, with every pound she hadn't lost. His hands explored her skin under the hoodie, sliding down her back, all the way down, between her cheeks. Marnie rocked, discarding all thoughts of their surroundings, only focused on the pleasure that built and intensified, taking over her whole body. Oh, my. Marnie's wobbly cry broke through the ocean rumble as she reached another peak, her muscles clamping down on him.

At the edge of her consciousness, she heard Jason's guttural moan and felt him erupt inside her.

Waves of pleasure travelled through her like little earthquakes, as Marnie pressed her face against Jason's chest, dizzy and shivering. He must have been colder than her, lying against the freezing, wet ground. It was time to go back. But first, she wanted to commit this moment to memory, being one with him on the cold beach, the private moment only witnessed by the rocks.

She opened her eyes, and her gaze fell on a marbled rock the size of a loaf of bread, partly buried in the sand. One end of it was yellow like it had been painted a long time ago. Its light colour stood out against the dark volcanic rocks. "That's a funny looking rock."

Jason followed her gaze and his body tensed. "Oh, my God."

"What?"

He sat up, still half hard inside her, his arm locked around her. But his attention was on the rock as he reached sideways to touch it. He held his hand in place for several beats. "Oh, my God."

"Seriously, what?"

He turned to face her, his grey eyes burning with excitement. "Ambergris."

Marnie blinked. "What's that?"

"The stuff they use to make perfumes. That's a big one. Could be worth ... I don't know, twenty grand?"

Marnie stared at the funny looking rock in disbelief. An old memory surfaced, a news story she'd once read about the substance. "You mean whale vomit? How do you know?"

Jason's eyes sparkled with excitement. "My dad used to take us ambergris hunting. We only ever found two small pieces, but one of them was white like this. It's the mature kind that you get a better price for. He sold that piece for a thousand dollars and used it as a down-payment for a car. And he bought us all ice creams."

He looked away, smiling.

"What an amazing memory!" Marnie marvelled at the wistful delight in his eyes, until her freezing knees reminded her it was time to get up. As she tried to move, sharp pain reminded her of something else. Arthritis. A few weeks ago, it had been the only thing on her mind. With Jason, she kept forgetting about her condition. The doctor had told her to look after herself, avoid cold and draft. She hadn't specifically mentioned sex on a freezing beach, but that was probably on the no-no list.

Marnie pulled back, suddenly hyper aware of her partial nudity, and that she was still hosting him inside her like an awkwardly long, limp handshake.

It felt good to pull her tights back up, to shield herself from the elements. Marnie hopped in place, trying to warm up her legs. The sun had dipped below the horizon, dropping the temperature even further.

Jason hugged her. His fingers snuck under her chin, lifting

it up to make eye contact. "Are you okay?"

"I'm just trying to process what happened. I never thought I'd do something like this."

"Not on your bucket list?" He grinned, victorious.

"No." She offered him a weak smile.

Too many things crowded her mind, the relentless doubts over their future, how good she'd felt, how cold, how loved, how special. A shiver ran through her from head to toe. Jason pulled her tighter against his chest. His heartbeat pounded, calming her wayward thoughts, bringing her back to present. If she could just stay here, they might make this work.

A gust of wind found its way under her shirt, and she trembled.

Jason rubbed her arms. "Let's get you in a hot shower, okay?"

"What about the ambergris?"

Jason knelt to examine the white lump. It was partly buried in the sand, making it hard to determine its true size. He dug into the sand with his fingers, scooping out wet lumps. Marnie joined him, digging on the other side to reveal the entire piece. A strange smell caught her attention and she bent down to take a sniff.

"Isn't it meant to smell like cow dung or something foul?"

"No. This is the good stuff. Look how white it is! This one's cured in the ocean for a long time. The smell changes. I always thought it was sort of pleasant, almost addictive. A bit offensive, but also good."

A sharp pain shot through her finger joints, and Marnie pulled her hands out of the sand. "Maybe we should get a shovel?"

Jason tried to get a hold of the ambergris, to wiggle it free. "What if someone else finds it?"

"Well, I hope it's someone who really needs the money." Marnie pulled her sleeves over her aching fingers and tried to rub them warm.

Jason stared at her with such wonder she felt like hiding inside her hoodie. "You'd give up twenty-thousand dollars if you knew it was going to someone in need?"

She nodded, confused. "Wouldn't you?"

"I guess so. But we found it. Finders keepers, right?"

"You found it," she corrected. "I just thought it was a funny rock."

"No! *We* found it, and we'll split the money. You can give your half to someone in need, and I'll use mine to buy you presents."

On the word 'presents', he dislodged the ambergris and fell on his bottom holding the massive, white lump. It was much larger than she'd first thought, about the size of a new-born baby.

Jason folded the hem of his hoodie to create a makeshift ambergris carrier, grinning from ear to ear. "Let's go."

# Chapter 26

Marnie stepped out of the steaming shower cubicle, relishing the lingering warmth on her body. The bathroom smelled like ocean, but better. Probably some kind of fragrance made with ambergris. Marnie dried herself and dressed, catching a blurry glimpse of herself in the steamed-up mirror. She wiped it with her sleeve to get a proper look. Mascara had run across her cheek, but her face glowed with unmistakable happiness. So, this is what it felt like to fall in love at 39. Her heart had dived in, blind to everything that stood in between.

"Get in here!" The excitement in Jason's voice carried through the door. "I'm about to stick a needle into this thing!"

Wiping her face clean with a fluffy towel, Marnie stepped back into the kitchen. Jason motioned her to join him at the table, where he stood with a fork in one hand, lighter in the other.

"I couldn't find a needle," he said. "But I figured, if we just heat up this fork hot enough, it'll do the trick."

"What does it do?"

"If this is ambergris, the hot metal will melt it. But we don't want to make a big mark on it. That'll lower its value."

"Okay. Sounds like you know what you're doing. I'll just watch." She sat at the table. "Wait! Do you want me to film this?"

"Great idea!"

Marnie grabbed her phone and framed the ambergris, which looked like an odd lump on the camera screen. She took a step back, getting Jason in the frame. Talk about photogenic. He flashed his pearly whites, looking like a celebrity chef about to cut into a thousand-dollar steak.

He spoke to the camera. "We are here, at an undisclosed location, about to test this suspected piece of ambergris we just found on the beach with my partner in crime, Marnie..."

Playing along, Marnie turned the camera on herself and smiled. "That's me!"

Turning back to Jason, she zoomed in on the fork in his hand. "And what is this specialist tool you're holding?"

"It's called a fork." Jason grinned, flicked on the lighter

and began heating the fork with the flame. In a few seconds, the end turned black. Marnie zoomed out, capturing his excited smile. "That should be hot enough. Now, the moment of truth. If it's real ambergris, the surface will melt as soon as I touch it with this."

"And if it's a regular rock?"

"Then, nothing. Hot forks don't melt rocks, right?"

"Right," Marnie repeated, feeling like an idiot. A happy idiot.

"Okay, here we go," Jason announced, giving the fork one last lick of the flame before he lowered it on the surface of the strange rock.

Marnie brought the camera closer, her heart pounding. She wasn't sure why, but the build-up had gotten under her skin. She wanted this to be real. Holding her breath, she watched the dark fork sink into the white substance. A faint hiss. A burning smell with a sweet, strange aroma. And liquid! It was melting into liquid.

On a collective gasp, Jason yanked back the fork and froze, staring at the ambergris. Marnie stepped back, remembering the phone still in her hand. Oh, yes. She was filming this. Why, she had no idea. It wasn't like she wanted anyone else to see this. Well, maybe Tanya and Shasa. Momentous events needed to be recorded. Like the birth of a baby. Marnie shook her head. Why was she thinking about babies?

"It's official!" Jason beamed at the camera. "This is genuine ambergris. Next, we need to weigh this piece to find out what it's worth."

"Any guesses?"

"Honestly, no idea. My experience with ambergris is like two decades old. I don't know if it's still in demand. I googled it earlier, and there's a website we can use to contact potential buyers."

"Wow. Anything else you'd like to add before I turn off the camera?"

To her shock, Jason dropped the fork on the table, grabbed the phone and pulled Marnie into his arms. Turning on the reverse camera, he lowered his stubbly cheek on her shoulder and grinned into the lens. "I just want to add that I've fallen hard for this woman. Look how cute she is!"

Marnie let out a nervous chuckle, trying to hide from the camera, but Jason caught her chin and lifted it up, forcing her to look at the screen. "No! Look. Look how cute you are. Look how cute we are together! I just want you to see it."

Marnie blinked, tears bursting into her eyes. "You're so cute," she said, trying to smile. "I think I'm falling for you, too."

Her admission came from somewhere deep, a confession so flammable a spark could have blown up the whole lighthouse. But she couldn't take it back. She loved this man. Against her better judgment. Against all reason.

Jason turned off the phone, dropped it on the table and pulled her into a hot kiss that tasted of tears. Her tears. He moved from her lips to her neck, closing her into a hug so tight it may have rearranged her internal organs.

"I want to stay here, with you, forever," he whispered. "I'll buy this bloody lighthouse."

"I thought you weren't into property investment," she mumbled against his chest.

"I'll lease it for a hundred years. I don't care. I just want to stay here. Sleep. Eat. Be with you." The desperation in his voice made her shiver.

"What about your work? What about empty homes?"

Jason released her, brushing curls off her face. "I could always pop in every now and then, try to keep things moving until we make some progress. But I wouldn't go for another term. This is it. I could go back to teaching, maybe part time. I could live off my investments. I want to show you..."

He opened his laptop sitting on the wide windowsill and brought up a screen with incomprehensible display of charts, numbers and diagrams. The numbers updated constantly, changing between green and red. "This is what I do when I can't sleep. I trade cryptos."

She stared at the screen, then at him. "What, like Bitcoin?"

"Bitcoin, and the alt coins. I've become pretty good at sensing those trends. It takes a bit of effort, but..." He shrugged, almost apologetic.

"Isn't that risky? You could lose everything."

Jason shook his head. "I play the long game. I don't do leverage bets or anything like that. That's gambling."

"Leverage what?"

"I mean I don't bet on whether something goes up or down. I just invest. Even if it goes down, I still have my coins. I'm not in a hurry, so I wait for the right time. Every now and then, I cash out my gains, put them in gold and silver. I already have seven times what I invested."

Marnie leaned in to study the screen. She couldn't make any sense of it, other than the jagged line going up and down like crazy. She'd heard this was the most volatile market you could possibly get into. "Are you sure this isn't the reason you're not sleeping at night?"

He gave her an uncertain smile. "Pretty sure. I was doing this way before the last election."

"And that's when you stopped sleeping?"

He closed the laptop lid. "Yeah, around that time. This job... everything that we had to do... It's not sitting well with me. That's why I'm working on this. It's my exit strategy."

"Are you really thinking of quitting?" She couldn't believe it.

"I'm not coping. Look. I need to tell you something."

His solemn expression gave Marnie chills.

He grabbed her by the hand and led her upstairs. "It's less gloomy up here." He gestured at the beach panorama behind the windows, the afterglow of the sunset still hanging on the horizon. "Also, I left my charger in here."

He plugged his phone into the charger, and they sat on the navy bed spread. Nausea welled up in Marnie's stomach. She dug her fingers into the blue cotton, focusing her eyes on the small model lighthouse on the windowsill, and his phone, plugged into a charger right next to it. That's as far as she could look.

"I want to be completely honest with you."

# Chapter 27

Jason tried to take Marnie's hand. Why was she squeezing the bed spread with white knuckles? She must have been as nervous as he felt, and he hadn't even said anything yet.

"You know I have this public persona? There's this story out there about me, how I grew up poor, working class family, all that? And then I worked hard, saved up money for a degree, become a teacher and got into local politics..."

"To get the council to fix that deadly intersection. I remember that!" She blushed a little. "Okay, I googled you. But when I did, I remembered the story. It was close to where I lived. I just didn't know it was you."

He smiled for a moment, letting her enthusiasm warm his

heart, then refocused. "It's all true. But just before the last election, Malcolm came to me with a plan. He's a smart guy, a people person, but he'll be the first to admit he's not that charismatic. He knows how to play the game, though. And I think he saw something in me, from the very beginning. He says, every now and then someone comes along who has what it takes. In politics, that popularity, the ability to speak to the media, present a certain image... it's a huge part of it. It sucks, but hey." He shook his head, blowing out a breath. "So, we came up with a plan. Associate minister, then Minister of Housing. I was up against tough competition, though. Teagan Dunn. He has two degrees, including a doctorate. Kathleen wanted him, and we knew they were going to play the degree card. I'd been doing a law degree via distance learning, chipping away at it whenever I could. But when I first got into Parliament, I put that on the back burner. I just didn't have the time or energy to finish it. But we knew it would look good. A double degree. So..."

He glanced at Marnie, begging for her to finish the sentence, but she just stared back, eyes wide. "So?"

"So, we cheated. Malcolm found this ghost writer... to this day I don't know who it was. But they wrote my thesis, and I got my degree, just in time for the election. And you know how that went. A landslide. I made Associate Minister of Housing." He looked at the floor. "But I'm a fraud. Later, I wanted to come clean about it, take it out of my CV. But Malcolm wouldn't let me. That would mean risking everything we've worked for. So, I'm trying to forget and focus on what I can change. What we can achieve."

Jason took another breath, his chest tight as a drum. The truth had been festering inside him for so long, burning a hole into his gut. Releasing it out into the open felt like throwing up. He glanced at Marnie, panic squeezing his windpipe. He'd dumped the burden of his stinky secret on the woman he loved. His own soul felt lighter, but at what cost?

Marnie's laced her fingers with his. Her voice was soft. "It must have been hard when they made such a big deal of that degree. I remember seeing one headline about it."

Jason hung his head. There had been more than one. He'd been celebrated for an achievement that wasn't his, and it tainted every other achievement he wanted to feel good about.

Marnie squeezed his hand. "I can see why you don't sleep."

She was right. He'd wanted to blame the job. Wellington. Malcolm. Everything else. But he always circled back to guilt. Malcolm had told him to lower his standards. Everyone cheated. Those who were smart about it won. He'd thought that achieving his goals would justify everything, help him move on. But what if it didn't? He was moving towards his goals yet falling apart.

He wondered why being close to Marnie helped him relax and sleep. Did her innocence seep into him by osmosis? Her presence also exposed the dirt he'd brushed under the carpet. It was almost a relief, but the shame tightened his gut.

"Well, now you know. I'm a fraud." He kept his head down, eyes closed. Marnie's face would tell him the truth, one glance and he'd know.

His heart in his throat, he turned.

Her eyes met his like two glistening lakes, reflecting his own pain. She blinked, and tears spilled out. "You're not a fraud. You feel guilty, and that's good. It means you haven't lost your compass. And I love that you told me. It means so much."

"I feel better. Tired, but better."

"You look wiped out." Without another word, she pushed him on the bed, helped him undress and get under the covers.

The bed felt heavenly, calling him like an underwater whale song, pulling him down. Jason closed his eyes, waiting for the familiar buzz of nerves right under the surface, but it wasn't there. He felt utterly empty, unimportant, anonymous. Someone just floating on the waves, slowly sinking deeper and deeper. The last thing he felt was a light kiss on his cheek. The last thing he heard was Marnie's whisper. "I love you, Jason. Everything you are. Good and bad. Everything."

# Chapter 28

Marnie took her coffee upstairs, enjoying the way the lighthouse basked in the morning light. Sunday morning. Jason was still asleep, his chest rising and falling. So still. So relaxed. There was no twitching, no frown hovering between his eyebrows. He looked at peace.

Marnie set down her cup and curled up next to him, letting his body heat radiate through her. She loved him so much it was hard to breathe. Maybe she should have been put off by his confession, but she only felt grateful. He'd taken the ultimate risk and told her the truth. It felt almost as good as the confession of his love. He was so eloquent; he could have easily misled her. He could have tweaked the truth, made himself sound better. Somehow, that bare, ugly truth was the most precious evidence of his love she could think of.

Could this really work? Could she stay with him? Marnie pulled in a shaky breath, trying to imagine their life together. What would it be like? How could it work? She felt different. Not the same Marnie she'd been before that Wellington trip. A fire had ignited in her, a tiny flame that gave her courage she didn't know she had, made her take chances she didn't know she could take. She felt her own value, like those green candles climbing the charts on Jason's laptop screen. Would she come crashing down?

A faint buzz on the nightstand drew her attention. Jason's phone, hooked into a charger, crept towards the edge of the wooden surface as it vibrated. If it buzzed again, it might drop on the floor. Marnie stirred gently to avoid waking Jason and reached over him to unplug the phone. It didn't make another sound. She glanced at the screen and froze. It showed a text from an unknown number, but the photo it delivered was instantly recognizable: Luna Bella, naked. She sat on a bed, smiling seductively, her arms toned, her skin perfect. She hugged her knees to her chest, leaving a little gap in between her ankles to show… Dear God. Marnie blinked. Was that her stylist's vagina? It was shadowed by her legs, but she couldn't see any evidence of underwear. Why was Luna Bella's vagina on Jason's phone?

Marnie dropped the phone and leapt out of bed. She

rummaged through her suitcase and yanked on a sweater to cover her skimpy nightgown, as if to negate Luna's nudity by covering her own skin. It made no sense.

"What's going on?" Jason woke and sat on the bed, stretching his arms over his head, a confused look on his face.

Marnie swallowed. "I'm fine. I just... Sorry, I didn't mean to see that." She gestured haplessly at the phone – the tiny, naked Luna lying next to him, exactly where Marnie had been moments ago.

Jason picked it up and a frustrated groan erupted from him. "Shit!"

Feeling like she'd been whacked with a baseball bat, Marnie collapsed on the floor, burying her face in her hands. She didn't want to ask, but she had to know. "Is she... are you...?"

Jason appeared next to her, his voice resonating down her spine. "No! We're nothing. I made the mistake of giving her my number. I was looking for you, and I thought she could help. But she wouldn't give me your number. Instead, she's been asking me out, sending me these..." He growled again. "I'm so sorry you had to see that. I thought she'd given up. I haven't replied. Look."

He handed her the phone with the conversation in full view. Marnie scrolled through the texts, Jason asking for her phone number, then three nude pics from Luna. As she studied it, hope returned to her heart. It was a completely one-sided conversation with no encouragement from Jason. Luna was after him, no question. The thought made her shiver, but she had no reason to doubt him.

She sniffed. "I'm sorry I freaked out."

"It's okay. I would have freaked out too if I saw someone sending you dick pics. Trust me, I would."

Marnie smiled through tears. "It's kind of the same thing, isn't it? I didn't even know women did this kind of thing."

"Oh, they do. Trust me. And it works better than the dick pics, any day."

"So, this works for you?"

Jason let out a nervous laugh. "No! Well, I mean, if I'm completely honest, sure. She's naked. I'm a guy. It's just how we're wired..." His voice faltered. A slight blush broke out on his neck, and it made Marnie's heart squeeze. He wanted to be honest with her, and she loved him for that. "But it doesn't make me want to contact her or anything."

She touched his arm. "I know. It's fine. She looks gorgeous. It'd be really weird if you didn't react to that on any level."

Jason's shoulders relaxed and he pulled her closer. Marnie leaned into his chest, letting all the worry and fear wash away. But even in the sweater, she felt naked. There was so much light, streaming in from every direction, through the windows that at night would once have blasted light outside to guide sailors out at sea. Now, those windows worked in reverse, letting in all the morning light, exposing everything.

Marnie got up, searching for the curtains. She wanted

to get back in bed with him and hide from the world. But when she reached for the navy-blue fabric, his phone buzzed again, this time repeatedly.

Jason picked it up and glanced at her. "It's my mum. I blew her off last weekend. I should really..."

"Of course. Take it. Do you want me to go?"

Marnie stepped towards the door, but Jason guided her back on the bed. "No. I have no secrets from you. Not anymore."

He accepted the call and turned on the speaker phone. "Hi, Mum!"

The voice at the other end trembled from old age but brimmed with delight. "Hi Jason! My lovely boy! Where are you?"

"You won't believe this, but I'm... on holiday."

"Are you now?" His mum sounded surprised. "So, who're you with?"

"Um... a friend. I'll introduce you later."

"Is it Beatrice?" Her voice rose, filled with anticipation.

He tried to laugh. "You saw the video, then? Yeah, sorry about that. I didn't really plan to be filmed."

Jason's mum's voice was warm. "Don't worry, dear. You can't embarrass us. We're too old. But you've found someone? Someone special?"

"Very special."

"That's nice. Is she one of those career women?"

Jason glanced at Marnie, who replied with a confused

smile, shaking her head. “No, Mum. She’s not.”

“More family-focused, then? That’s lovely. We’re waiting for those grandchildren. My eyesight’s getting worse, and I’d really like to be able to see them.”

Marnie stiffened.

Jason stood, turned off the speaker phone, and walked into the ensuite.

Marnie sat on the bed, nausea swirling in her belly. This was it. This is how it would all end. It had been too good to be true. She’d convinced herself they could make it all work, that she didn’t have to give him up. But how could she take this away from him, for his parents? She was a selfish, foolish woman, who’d somehow seduced a younger man and stolen his future.

She didn’t notice Jason until he sat next to her. “I’m sorry. Mum’s a bit funny like that. She doesn’t mean any harm. Ignore her.”

Marnie lifted her chin and stared into his eyes. “Do you want children?”

Jason blinked, his mouth hanging open. “I don’t know,” he finally said. “I thought I did, one day. But lately … I don’t know. I haven’t been sleeping, so I couldn’t really imagine anything like that. Why?”

“What if I can’t?” Her voice wobbled, but she kept her gaze on him, unwavering.

“It doesn’t matter.”

Marnie dropped her gaze back in her lap. “I had trouble in

the past, and I'm so much older now. It might not be possible for me, even with IVF."

Jason groaned. "Neither of us knows the future. Why would we let it ruin what we have now? I told you, I don't even know if I want children. What if I can't handle it? What if I stop sleeping again? I'd be a horrible father."

She swallowed. "But your mum talks about it."

Jason squeezed his eyes shut. "Yeah, she's really hoping I settle down soon. My parents are pretty old. But please don't worry about it. It's their problem, not ours."

Marnie rubbed her fingers. They hurt, reminding her of everything that was wrong. The morning sun outside the windows felt too bright and invading. She gathered her courage. He'd been completely honest with her. She owed him the same.

"What I've experienced with you has been amazing. I think I needed this. I didn't do crazy things in my youth. I got married so young, there was just kids and the mortgage, and the next mortgage, and waiting for things to get better. And then it was all over."

Jason's forehead wrinkled. "Nothing's over yet. You can do whatever you want. What's stopping you?"

"I waited too long to start. If you do crazy stuff at my age, it's called a crisis."

"Crisis is not necessarily a bad thing." He tried to touch her arm, but she pulled it away.

"I don't want to steal your time."

"You're not! What does that even mean?" His hand squeezed her thigh, emphasising the point.

She wanted that touch, she wanted it so badly it scared her stiff. She'd fallen for him, all the way. And now she'd have to make her way out. "There was this story in the paper I read a long time ago, of a girl who lost her new phone in a long-drop toilet."

"Like, in the..."

"Yes, right in there. So, she went in to get it."

Jason made a gagging face. "Is there a point to this story?"

"Well, she passed out. So, her boyfriend went in to save her."

Jason blew a sigh. "Okay, that's a bit extreme, but if you fell in a barrel of shit, I'd fish you out. I promise."

"No! You're not supposed to! He died. He passed out from the shit fumes, and they both drowned."

Jason stared at her, perfectly still, his hand still resting on her thigh. Was he holding his breath to avoid breathing in metaphorical shit fumes?

Marnie wanted to kick herself. Why did she say these things? Falling in love had washed off all her filters. She opened her mouth to apologise, when Jason pulled her in for a tight hug. "You really think you're dragging me into a barrel of shit? What if it's the other way around?"

She breathed in his heady scent and tried to calm her heart.

Jason stroked her hair. "Let's get some breakfast. I'm so

hungry I can't think straight."

# Chapter 29

Marnie searched the cupboards, locating eggs and a can of beans. Her chest felt heavy, every cell in her body ached to the point that she couldn't tell the difference between arthritis and other kind of pain. It was all the same – haywire signals shooting in and out of her fingers and toes, as well as her heart. Hadn't she known this all along? Hadn't she tried to prepare for the end? If only she'd looked ahead, she would have seen this all unfurling in the distance, like a car crash. She could have taken an earlier exit. It hurt so much worse now.

She glanced at Jason. He sat at the dining table, staring at something on his laptop. He seemed to have faith for the both of them, but was it enough? He couldn't change reality. He couldn't make her any younger, even if she felt braver, more alive. Even if she could take the media attention.

As if on cue, her phone rang on the kitchen counter. A blocked number. Marnie set down the bowl she'd used for mixing the eggs and wiped her hands.

"I'll take this upstairs," she told Jason, who responded with a faint nod. There was a hint of disappointment in his eyes. Maybe she should have been as open as he'd been. If it had been Tanya or Shasa, she could have done the same. But this blocked number... she had a bad feeling, one that was confirmed as soon as she accepted the call.

"Marnie?" Kathleen's voice brought with it a familiar chill.

Marnie bristled. "Yes."

"I'm very disappointed."

"Why? What happened?"

Kathleen cleared her throat. "Reporters are at my door, asking questions about my health. Do you think that's fair? Is this what wanted, to take down another woman?"

"No! I mean—"

"I thought we had an understanding"

Marnie rubbed her burning hot neck. What had she done? "I'm sorry. It's not like that—"

"Did you get my chocolates, Marnie?"

The thinly veiled accusation in Kathleen's voice sparked the small flame in Marnie's chest. This is what Jason had talked about. She couldn't let herself be manipulated. She drew a breath, summoning all of her resolve. "I don't owe you anything."

Kathleen sounded taken aback. "That's not what I said."

"And why would you hide your health condition?" Marnie pressed on. "You won't get the help you need, and it will come out sooner or later anyway. Secrets don't stay secret!"

"No, they don't, Marnie." There was a chilling edge to her voice.

"What do you mean?"

"I can tell you're not doing this on your own. You're under Jason's spell. It's very understandable. He's a clever guy. But you know you're not helping his career, right?"

"Why?" Marnie's voice faltered, and she hated the panic that strangled her throat.

"Well. Secrets don't stay secret. You and Jason. A 39-year-old divorcee and the New Zealand's rising political star. I'll find out everything there is to find out about you, and when the time is right, that story will hit national news. I already found the perfect picture to go with it."

Her phone pinged and she knew Kathleen had sent her something. She took the phone off her ear and saw the horrible photo from the community house website. Oh, God. Not that one. Next to Jason's polished headshot, she'd look ten years older, like a deranged con woman who'd bedazzled him for millions of dollars.

Marnie took a deep breath. That fire in her belly, whatever was left of it, she needed it now. She wouldn't go down like this. She wouldn't take Jason down with her. "Jason has nothing to do with this and I'm not in touch with him."

"Are you really expecting me to believe that? I saw a video of Jason and a woman who looked awfully lot like you."

"What can I tell you? It wasn't me and you won't find any evidence to support that story. I don't want to get mixed up with politicians. But if you start releasing rumours about Jason and me, I will have no choice but to go to the media and give an actual statement about what I witnessed in that bathroom, and how your memory failed last time we spoke on the phone. I'm sure they'd be very interested, especially as there seems to be another source already leaking similar stories."

Kathleen's voice betrayed her uncertainty. "Okay, Marnie. I can see you're very determined lady. There's no need to go that far."

"Good."

"If you say you're not in this with Jason, I want to believe you. If it turns out you're lying, I've got my story ready to go. There are consequences, Marnie."

Kathleen ended the call and Marnie slumped on the bed, nausea welling inside. Oh, God. She was really going to be sick. She rushed into the en-suite and kneeled over the toilet bowl. Two painful gags brought up a little stomach acid. She hadn't eaten anything yet. Leaning on the cool edge of the toilet seat, she went through the phone conversation. No. There was no way around it. She had to get out of Jason's life. Otherwise, she'd destroy his career. She'd destroy those dreams she'd tried so hard to help him achieve.

# Chapter 30

Jason stared at the spread of continental breakfast on the small dining table. Marnie had insisted on cooking for him. He loved the gesture but hated the despair that lingered in her eyes. Something had happened, and she wouldn't talk about it. After that phone call, she'd prepared breakfast in silence, her face drawn.

"I'm sorry, I can't do poached eggs, so I always go for scrambled. And they had beans, so..." She handed him a ladle.

Jason filled his plate. Despite the heavy atmosphere, his mouth filled with saliva. "I love scrambled eggs. This looks amazing."

She nodded and watched him eat, hardly touching her own plate.

"Aren't you hungry?"

"I'm not feeling well."

"What was that phone call about? Was it Kathleen?"

She nodded again.

"What is it? Talk to me!"

Her eyes filled with tears, and she dropped her chin, staring at her plate. "I'm so sorry. Kathleen's found out about us and is threatening to go public. I think I sowed enough doubt to make her think it might have been someone else, and told her I could do worse by going to the media and giving a statement. But I don't want to do that. I don't want you tainted by this."

Jason slammed the table. "She's gone too far!"

"Don't worry, she agreed to back down, for now. It's okay. We'll just keep a really low profile."

"No. We can manage this. We can go public on our own terms, if you just trust me. We can—"

Marnie hung her head. "No, we can't. Those stories have been written already, and they're not good."

"No, Marnie. Look at me! We won't let anyone else tell our story!"

Finally, she looked up. There was so much pain and sorrow in her eyes it stole his breath away. "I love you, Jason. But I'm not right for you. I'm sick. I'm old."

A blast of fury filled Jason's chest. "You're not a can of

beans, woman! If you have a fucking expiry date, show it to me! Where is it?"

He sprang up, propelled by the sheer force of his own words. They burned like acid going up his throat, but he couldn't stop, slamming the table for emphasis.

Marnie startled off her seat, her eyes huge. Did she think he was going to hurt her?

Jason launched forward. Too late. She was already on the stairs, running upstairs.

"I'm sorry! Marnie! Where're you going?" He noticed his tight fists and tried to relax his hands. He wanted to follow her, but maybe it was best to give her a minute.

Lugging her suitcase behind her, Marnie stumbled down the spiral staircase, almost slipping on the last step. She had to get away. She'd thought she was helping him, but instead she'd bring him down, she'd ruin his life. First, his career, then his hopes of being a father. He'd played it down, but underneath, the desire for a family remained, an age-old instinct. Once he got his sleeping on track, he'd want it again, and she'd disappoint him. She'd disappoint so many people: him, his mother, the whole country. Even if she could somehow learn to live with his publicity, deal with people like Kathleen and all the strangers who thought they owned a piece of him, she couldn't do this to him. She couldn't be a mistake he'd regret later.

Marnie pushed past Jason, going for the door. Sensing him right behind her, she made it down the stairs, to the small parking bay. Fingers shaking, she tried to locate the Uber app on her phone.

Before she launched it, Jason locked her arm in a tight grip. "Where are you going?"

She hadn't bothered to wipe her tears. "I'm sorry." She almost choked on the words. "It's better that I go."

"No, it's not! I was out of line, and I'm sorry. But please don't leave me here. We can work through this. We'll figure out a way."

"I need to think. Clear my head."

The pain behind his eyes cut to her core. "Why?"

"Because I'm so out of my depth. I'm not right for you. You'll regret this."

"No, I won't," he insisted, still holding her arm. "Please."

She relaxed her arm, planting her feet on the gravel, sighing from desperation. Every moment she spent here, with him, she fell deeper and deeper in love. In shit. In something she couldn't climb out of.

His phone rang, slicing through her thoughts like an alarm.

Jason tried to ignore the phone. Why had he brought the

damn thing? Like a nervous tick, it took so much effort to leave behind.

"Could be important?" Marnie glanced at his ringing pocket.

"It's not," he said, grabbing it anyway. A quick peek at the screen told him it was Malcolm. He never called on a Sunday. Not unless it was urgent. Jason fought the reflex to pick it up. He had to show Marnie she was more important.

She made the decision for him, taking the phone off his hand and swiping the green bubble to answer. "Yes? He's here. Sure, hang on."

She handed the phone to him.

"You found her, then?" Malcolm's cheery voice bellowed in his ear. "The mystery woman?"

"Yes."

"Attaboy! Listen, I hate to cut your weekend short, but I just heard, and you may have not looked at your email, especially if you've been otherwise busy"—he chuckled—"but the time has come! The PM wants to hear the empty homes tax findings next Tuesday. Are you ready?"

Jason drew a sharp breath. That was little over a week. Their working group was a month away from any kind of presentable recommendation. "No, we're not. I thought Kathleen was going to can us this week."

"It seems she's not well. PM has stepped in take some things off her plate."

"Is that right?" Jason glanced at Marnie, his stomach

tightening.

They'd done it.

"Great timing, eh? So if we drop everything and put in the work, we might be able to present this tax. They want to release the results as part of the fiscal strategy report."

"That was never the plan! It's not about saving money, it's about housing people! It's about the principle."

"I know. But if we can show on paper that the new tax will mostly hurt overseas investors and generate enough to, say, pay for one of those new housing developments, like the one you visited in Hamilton, that might sell it. Concrete made from recycled socks. People love that stuff."

"It wasn't all socks—"

"Whatever. It was cheap, right? That means it'll sound impressive. Thousands of families housed by tapping into existing housing stock and thousands more homes built by taxing overseas investors. Everyone will love it!"

"Okay." Jason couldn't help warming up. This was his dream. He'd slept well for two, glorious nights. Was that enough to see him through the week? He glanced at Marnie, who stood in front of him, thumbing her own phone. "Can I call you back? I'm not sure if I can make it today. Maybe tomorrow."

He ended the call and met Marnie's questioning gaze. "We have a chance to present the empty homes tax at the Cabinet meeting next Tuesday. It's too soon, but Malcolm wants to try. And if he's onboard, we have a shot. This might be my only shot."

Marnie's gaze burned with conviction. "You should go. This is important."

"I don't want to leave you like this. I don't want to leave you at all."

Marnie closed her eyes, wiping a tear that fell. "I have to go. Can you just give me time?"

He closed the distance, pulling her in a tight hug. "Promise me it's not the end."

"Let's just put a pin in it, okay?" she whispered. "You go and do your job. I'll see you on the other side."

"If that's the best you can do."

She sniffed against his chest. "It's the best I can do."

# Chapter 31

Jason sank into the backseat of the taxi. He'd dropped Marnie off at the bus station, returned the rental car and called a taxi to Parliament.

The sight of Marnie walking away, disappearing into the crowd at the station haunted him. This wasn't the end. It couldn't be. She needed time, upset over Kathleen's phone call, and he would give her that. The minister was like a virus; she got under your skin and made you sick. He'd heard Marnie gagging in the toilet. He worried about her, so much that it was hard to concentrate on anything else. And he couldn't afford any distractions. Not if he was about to climb this mountain, put this tax together and push it through.

His phone rang. Malcolm again.

"How was the sex-cation? The whole nation is talking about your mystery woman. Rumour has it you've found her and have spent a steamy weekend with her at an undisclosed location."

Jason frowned, frustration growing. "What rumour?"

"Well, I may have released that one. Don't worry, I didn't give any details. But we need some good buzz to keep you in the headlines this week. Nobody's going to write about my love life, that's for sure." Malcolm cackled.

"I'd rather they write about the tax."

"They will. But we needed to do some damage control, after your... umm... outing in Hamilton. There's been talk about you harassing or stalking this woman."

"Stalking? What the hell?"

Malcolm cleared his throat theatrically. "These grand romantic gestures are a bit of a two-edged sword. It all depends on the reception, you know. If she's charmed, then it's romantic. If she's not, it's creepy. On that video, you can't really see her reaction. It's not obvious. And it looks like she ran away, and you ran after her?"

"She ran to my place and stayed with me!"

"Aha. See, that's great. But nobody else knows that. It would really help if you could do at least one public outing with her. Preferably before the Cabinet meeting on Tuesday, or at least before this thing hits the news again. Go for a coffee somewhere, make sure people see you."

Jason looked at the note on his nightstand, his shoulders slumping. "I don't think that's possible. She's gone back to... where she lives."

He couldn't trust Malcolm not to feed more to the press; the man was obsessed with PR, always leaking something to someone to 'keep up the good buzz'. The man had great relationships with reporters, but right now, he needed to back off. Jason couldn't ask Marnie to go public with their relationship. They'd worked so hard to keep her out of the limelight.

"Fine." Malcolm paused, probably calculating their next move. "We'll figure something out. But pack your bags and drag your ass back here. Your team's busy researching and crunching the numbers but we need you. There's a bit of panic in the air because of the deadline."

"I'm on my way."

# Chapter 32

"Choose whatever you want!" Marnie said, holding up Lilla so she could reach the café cabinet.

Lilla's huge blue eyes widened in excitement as she leaned on the glass and coughed, her lungs rattling with phlegm. The poor girl was still battling a chest infection. This was her first outing in a week. Marnie nudged her forward in the queue, hoping she'd make up her mind before they got to the cashier.

"I don't know," the little girl sighed in desperation. "I want the cookie, but I also want the brownie and whipped cream! And I want that"—she pointed at the pink Louise slice, her eyes widening even more—"Can we take them all?"

Marnie laughed. "No. Let's just take one."

"You don't have enough money?" Lilla cast her a look of earnest concern.

Marnie opened her mouth to argue, but her words died on her tongue. She had enough money for all the slices. It wasn't the healthiest choice, but for once, she didn't feel like limiting herself. Oddly, she felt like eating everything in the cabinet. "You're right. I do have enough money. Let's take all the slices!"

Ever since returning home, it had been harder and harder to stick to her healthy diet. From the moment she got out of bed, her appetite raged. At this rate, she'd gain back all the pounds she'd lost. Her sweater already felt tight, and the waistband of her tights dug into her stomach. But what difference did it make? She'd grow old all alone. She could be any size she liked. And right now, she wanted to eat cake.

Feeling a little deranged, Marnie approached the checkout, ready to rattle out a list of overpriced baked goods. After Lilla's three choices, a juice and a fluffy – the cup of foamed milk every cafe sold to its future coffee-drinkers – Marnie added an apple pie, blueberry muffin and a coffee for herself. That oughta do it.

The cashier barely blinked, repeating the order back to her.

"Yes," Marnie confirmed. "Me and the young miss would like all that, thank you!"

Lilla beamed, her curly head peeking over the edge of

the counter. Marnie placed her EFTPOS card on the reader, wondering what had gone into her. This was one of the most overpriced cafes in town. Even her wealthy friend Elsie didn't spend like this on a whim.

"Yippee!" Lilla yelled, skipping across the room.

"Don't tell your mum," Marnie whispered as they took seats by the window overlooking the huge playground. Behind it, the lake glistened in afternoon sun.

She considered herself a sensible person, but recent evidence pointed to the contrary. Maybe she'd run out of self-limiting behaviour that weekend at the lighthouse. Whatever the reason, this was the moment she'd been waiting for, spoiling her friend's nearly-five-year-old.

She could also tell Shasa needed some alone time with her man. Her friend had run around the house trying to locate her daughter's shoes, a harried look in her eyes. Marnie remembered those busy years of motherhood and wondered if she could do it all again.

Throughout the week, Jason had sent her texts, updating her on his progress. He sounded so excited, working so hard, so close to achieving his goals. Marnie had hidden in the bathroom at work, rereading his texts, munching the last of Kathleen's chocolates that the kids didn't seem to like.

At the lighthouse, it had felt like the kinder option to hit pause, to let him focus on the task ahead without worrying about their relationship. But today was Tuesday, the day of the Cabinet meeting. Jason was looking forward to seeing her again, but they couldn't be seen together. She had to end it. That's why she'd sent the letter, dropping it off at the courier on Monday morning. It was done, and now she had to focus on just getting through the day. Walking, talking and eating, obviously. It seemed that had become her new focus.

The moment their treats arrived, she spotted Shasa, standing at the cafe entrance, her eyes scanning the room.

"Oh no!" Lilla gasped, her gaze darting between her mother and the four plates brimming with treats filling up the tiny, round table.

"Don't worry," Marnie reassured her, sipping her coffee. It tasted weird. "Over here!" She waved at Shasa.

"I'm sorry, I forgot the antibiotics!" Shasa lowered herself into a chair, digging into her handbag. "She has to take these three times a day, and I keep forgetting. I missed the morning one and now it's 3:30!"

"Oopsie." Marnie smiled at Lilla, who giggled back. "You better take it now."

Shasa unscrewed the bottle and sucked a dose of sticky liquid into the measuring syringe. As she stuck it into her daughter's mouth, her gaze fell on the spread of sugary goodness. "Looks like you have plenty here to wash off the taste!"

She cast a questioning look at Marnie, who grinned sheepishly. "I'm sorry. We couldn't decide."

"So, you ordered everything on the menu?"

Marnie pulled a face. “YOLO.” She’d never used the term out loud, even ironically.

Shasa narrowed her eyes. “You only live once? What happened in Wellington?”

Marnie’s stomach tightened. “I’m… not sure.”

Shasa leaned forward. “Not sure? What’s going on with you?”

Marnie appreciated the concern in her friend’s voice. Someone had noticed she wasn’t okay. Someone with whom she could discuss the storm that raged inside her with no sign of settling. She hadn’t felt normal since returning from Wellington. Now she was the one not sleeping. Oh, the irony. She didn’t even notice her tears until Shasa handed her a napkin.

“Talk to me. Is it over between you two?”

Marnie wiped her eyes and took a long sip from her coffee, hiding behind the cup. “I think so.”

“Don’t be sad Aunty Marnie.” Lilla hopped off her chair and circled the table to give her a hug.

Bloody child. Marnie couldn’t see the coffee cup from her tears. “I’m so sorry,” she muttered. “I was supposed to just have this… experience.” She sniffed. “This one last hurrah, something to think back to in my rocking chair. And then I’d be all yours and throw you the best bachelorette party and an amazing wedding.” She hiccupped through the words as Shasa’s arms wrapped around her.

Marnie’s phone beeped, delivering a text from Jason.

*It's over! We built a solid case, will find out later if anything comes out of it. I can't believe I'm still functioning. Can't wait to see you. Weekend in Hamilton?*

Shasa cast her a questioning look and she turned the screen so that she could read the text.

Her eyes widened. "That man is in love with you! Why do you think it's over?"

"Because he's going to read the letter."

Shasa blinked in confusion. "Okay, I need to hear the whole story. Let's go for a walk. I'll get a doggy bag for your treats."

A few minutes later, they sat on a bench at the waterfront, away from other people, watching Lilla feed Louise slice to the ducks. A huge waste, bad for the ducks, Marnie registered, but couldn't muster enough energy to react.

"Okay, start from the beginning," Shasa ordered.

Drawing a deep breath, Marnie told her everything. The moments on the beach, the ambergris, the fight. Jason's mum's phone call. Kathleen's phone call. It came out a jumbled mess, with enough detail for Shasa's mouth to drop open as she listened to her story.

"That doesn't have to be the end. He's done that tax thing now, and you said he wants to step down. Why worry about that minister and what she says to the press?"

Marnie wiped her eyes. "Because it will ruin his career. That's why I wrote the letter. To protect him, and to set him free. So that he can have a family with someone younger."

Shasa paused, her eyes flicking away, following the ducks. "What about you? You love him."

Marnie shook her head, dismissing the ache in her heart. She was getting too self-centred for her own good. Turning her attention to her phone, she opened the Pinterest app. "Have you set the date for the wedding yet? I found this amazing flower arrangement we could possibly do ourselves, they had instructions..."

Shasa lifted her finger to her lips. "Shh. Stop. You're allowed to have a life, you know?"

"What do you mean?"

"You're not just my maid of honour, or my babysitter, or someone else's something. You're a woman. You're allowed to fall in love and go nuts."

Marnie shook her head, tears threatening a comeback. They sat in silence for a moment, watching Lilla bounce around, feeding the birds, her high-pitched voice drawing even the aggressive Canadian geese.

Shasa cleared her throat. "Can I ask, how do you know you can't have a baby anymore?"

Marnie stared at her hands as she recalled the painful memory. "It was a long time ago, when Steve and I were still toying with the idea of a third baby. We tried for a while and nothing happened, so I went to get checked..."

"Just you? What about him?"

"He thought it was most likely me. I've always had irregular periods. Anyway, it was me. The doctor said I had a low ovarian reserve. And that was years ago. So, I figured, they'd all have gone by now. Every single egg."

She expected sympathy, but Shasa narrowed her eyes. "That's not a firm diagnosis. Have you had a recent test?"

Marnie shook her head. What difference did it make? But as she prepared to dismiss Shasa's doubts, Lilla jumped into her lap, bumping her head against her chest, and she winced from pain. Were her breasts sensitive? Marnie brought her hand to her side, massaging her left one. Ouch.

"What is it?" Shasa asked.

"Nothing. Just ... weird."

# Chapter 33

**Jason:** I got a letter from you. Snail mail! You must really love me? I hope it's about how you can't stop thinking about me and are on your way to Wellington right now.
- Jason

**Marnie:** (heart emoji)

Jason lay on the bedspread in his condo, listening to the unnatural hum of air conditioning. Almost like ocean waves, yet nothing like it. Monotonic, electric, efficient.

It was Tuesday night, and his head was spinning, like coming down after a week-long bender. They'd slogged it out, pulling together all the missing data, calculating scenarios and double-checking the numbers to make sure they had a solid case.

To his surprise, the past few nights in his flat had gone okay. He'd worked late every night, collapsing on the bed when he could no longer keep his eyes open. Sleep hadn't been long or plentiful, but it had sustained him. By anyone else's standards, it was terrible, but he knew how bad it could get – lying awake all night, heart pounding as waves of sweat pushed through his skin and cooled down, turning into shivers. Three layers of blankets, more shivering, unbelievable tiredness, and then, as he almost drifted out again, it would start from the beginning – the sweats, the heartbeat drumming between his ears, the absolute terror that filled his mind for no apparent reason. So yes, falling asleep and waking up in a state that could be improved by caffeine was a win. Not like the heavenly rest he'd experienced with Marnie in the lighthouse, but a win. Maybe the bliss of the weekend still lingered in his system. He'd felt lighter ever since he'd told Marnie about the fake degree and his desire to quit.

The constant stream of challenges had kept his brain busy for three days, pushing his doubts about Marnie's letter to the background. And now, their presentation was over. They could do nothing but wait as the Minister of Revenue got ready to introduce the bill to Parliament. The government had majority, so technically they could push the bill through in a day. But since they were suggesting a brand-new tax bracket, it would likely go to a consultation by Select Committee. The whole process would take at least six months. He had to be patient.

Marnie's letter had appeared that morning. It sat on his nightstand, unopened, atop a book about lighthouse keepers he'd swiped from the Airbnb. He'd paid for it in form of a hefty tip, and it had served as a decent distraction, quieting his mind before bed. It was better than staring at the crypto market, he had to admit. Maybe Marnie had a point.

Jason stared at the envelope. After how they'd parted, the letter made him nervous. But he couldn't put it off any longer. Jason took a breath and ripped into the envelope. Marnie's handwriting was small and curly, like her hair. He could almost hear her soft voice. Her sweet tropical scent drifted from somewhere, tightening his throat.

*Jason. I've fallen in with love you, which makes this so hard to write. You may think you love me too, but I'm not the one. There's someone out there who's perfect. She'll help you sleep (although I think you may rediscover that skill yourself, once you resolve your guilt, maybe put that laptop away). Anyway, she'll have your babies and carry them with healthy, non-aching fingers. She can handle the life you deserve. She'll be amazing. I'll read about it in the papers, and hate her of course, but I'll be happy for you.*

*I believe in you. You can achieve great things. You can fill those ghost houses with life. I'll be watching from afar. And I know you won't come after me, because you're a good guy, not a creepy stalker. I'm saying this all with a sick feeling. I've felt sick ever since I walked away. It hurts like hell, but I know it's the right thing to do.*

*Thank you for seeing me, touching me, being with me. I've felt more alive than ever before. I haven't felt like me, but in a good way. You've given me more than I thought possible. But I can't take the publicity. The disappointment. I won't pass the test and eventually, you'll see what they see and end up resenting me. And that will taint all the beautiful memories, just like a divorce does. I can't do it to us.*

*Marnie*

Jason stared at the letter, a weight in his stomach, like he'd accidentally swallowed a piece of lead falling from the sky. Apparently, this had happened to an 18th century lighthouse keeper as he'd looked up with his mouth open during a fire. He'd died. Just like Jason would die. Slowly, but surely, with lead in his belly. What was the point of living if he could never feel okay again? Marnie had painted a nice picture, but she was working off a false premise. There was no one else for him.

# Chapter 34

Marnie sat on the toilet, hugging herself. Her period was overdue. For how many days, she wasn't sure. But her breasts had grown a cup size and ached all over. It must have been a cruel, hormonal trick, because she couldn't be pregnant. Shasa had helped her research side effects of her medication and the supplements she was taking. Nothing explained the delayed period, but the DHEA capsules her pharmacist had prescribed as anti-aging, were also used to treat low ovarian reserve. Marnie shivered at the thought. Had she accidentally fixed her fertility and ended up pregnant? Could this really be happening?

Maybe not, but she couldn't muster up the courage to do

the test. She needed support, just in case it was positive. Or negative.

Pocketing the pregnancy test, she pulled her pants up over her tight belly, washed her hands and stepped into the lounge. Darkness had already swallowed the view outside, turning the mammoth fountain into a black, looming monster. The night stretched before her, endless, full of anxiety and circling thoughts. She needed a friend.

"Tanya! I'll be at Shasa's!" She yelled through her daughter's door.

The pop song blasting on the other side lowered in volume, and Tanya replied with an absent-minded, "Okay."

Marnie had never been more grateful to live next door to her best friend.

"Do you want a cup of tea?" Shasa asked, guiding her over the Barbie-covered floor.

"Sure." Marnie sat on the plush, grey couch, removing a sharp plastic toy from under her bottom. The Minion in a miniskirt returned her frown with an obtuse grin.

"That's mine!" Lilla announced, snatching the toy. She ran off to her room, returning five-seconds later with more Minions and a toy unicorn. "Will you play with me?"

Marnie nodded and began mindlessly moving Lilla's Minions and Barbies into a circle. The girl babbled about the villain unicorn the small yellow creatures served. From the corner of her eyes, Marnie saw Mac in the kitchen. He interrupted Shasa's tea-making with a sneaky hug. Their embrace reflected off the glossy splashback and stainless-steel appliances – an exact replica of Marnie's apartment, yet so different. Theirs was full of family life: Lilla's drawings and the preschool term schedule on the fridge, a step for the girl so she could reach the kitchen counter, and of course, Barbie paraphernalia – a scattering of pink plastic and glitter on the floor.

Shasa said something to Mac, who approached Lilla. "Hey! Should we go to bed early tonight and have a slumber party? We can watch funny cat videos." He grinned.

Lilla jumped off the couch and clapped her hands. "Can we have snacks? Strawberry milk? Biscuits?"

Mac cast a quick glance at Shasa, who smiled and pointed at the packet of Scotch Fingers on the counter.

"Yes!" Mac confirmed, and they ran upstairs.

Shasa brought over two steaming teacups and took a seat next to Marnie. "I thought we might need some privacy."

"He's so good with her."

Shasa's face glowed. "I know! They're best friends, always goofing around. This isn't even the first slumber party this week! Not that I'm complaining. It gives me time to take a bath with a book. Some of the videos they watch are a bit iffy, though. Like those funniest home videos where someone always gets hit in the nuts."

"Yikes!" Marnie laughed. "Well, if he gets kicked in the nuts by a fast-learning four-year-old, that's on him."

"Exactly."

Laughing helped, relaxing Marnie's twisted insides. She stared into her teacup, wishing she could extend the escape. But no, the massive lump in her throat returned whenever the conversation came to a lull.

"Have you taken the test yet?" Shasa whispered, taking a sip of her tea.

"No. I'm working up the courage. I thought it might be better if I do it here. Tanya's not great with emotional support."

"Of course. Whenever you're ready." She gestured to the bathroom door.

Marnie tried to get up, but her stomach clenched, paralysing her on the couch.

Shasa smiled. "No hurry. Drink your tea."

"I just need a minute." Marnie tried to smile, but judging by Shasa's puzzled expression, she probably looked like she was in pain.

"Do you want to be pregnant?"

Marnie stiffened. "I don't know. One minute I do, the next I don't. Not with the mess I'm in. And I honestly don't think it's even possible. I'm sick. I never thought this could happen."

"Maybe your body's not quite as old and sick as you think?"

"Maybe."

Shasa smiled. "What if you can give him a family? Wouldn't that be wonderful? You were so worried about it."

Marnie's throat felt sticky. What would Jason say? Would he be happy, or horrified? He'd been so worried about becoming a father. Pregnancy was something she hadn't even contemplated, and the more she thought about it, the less it felt like a solution.

"I told him I couldn't get pregnant. If I am, then I've misled him. I'm a horrible person!"

Shasa gave her a side hug. "You didn't do it on purpose."

"It's still not right. And even if he got over that, there's the publicity. If I had a baby with him, everyone would find out. And people are so mean. You know Jason dated a wellness coach? This amazing, flawless girl who posts incredible pictures on Instagram."

Marnie tapped on her phone to bring up the Instagram feed. Together, they stared at Amelia's smiling face framed by some sort of woody herb she was holding in both hands, radiating youth and good health.

"Look at her! She's flawless, and still people wrote mean comments online when she dated Jason. People called her a gold digger... I thought it didn't make any sense, since Jason's not wealthy. But turns out he is."

Shasa's brow shot up. "Really? I thought he was all principled about not investing in property?"

"His money's not in property. It's in gold and silver and such."

"So, you'd be a literal gold digger?" Shasa erupted in a contagious giggle, taking Marnie down with her.

Her heart momentarily lighter, Marnie sank into the couch, inhaling the herbal aroma rising from her cup. She brushed the phone screen, bringing up more photos. Amelia hugging a dog. Amelia making bliss balls. Amelia in a lavender field, holding the rim of her fedora.

"That's such a cliche!" Shasa laughed, taking over the browsing. "Look at these! Nobody lives like this… 'First thing in the morning, I like to wake up my body with the right balance of protein, brain oil and micronutrients'," she read underneath a picture of Amelia posing with a glass of green sludge. "Nobody looks like that first thing in the morning! There are some serious filters or photoshopping happening. Or maybe it's AI generated."

Marnie sighed. "I wish. She looks amazing even on those gossip sites where someone's just snapped her picture without permission."

Shasa gave her a weighty look. "You have to stop looking at those sites! Stop comparing yourself to other people." She flipped Marnie's phone to hide the image.

"I know. First, I thought that if I could see these other women in his past, if I could convince myself they were only human, just like me, then maybe I could imagine myself in there, next to him. But now I feel worse. I could never be like that."

"What does it matter what those papers write about you?"

Marnie took her phone back. The screen woke up and Amelia reappeared, this time doing a yoga pose that supported her weight on one hand. Granted, she probably weighed little more than a sparrow, but Marnie let out a sigh that turned into a groan. "If they judged *her*, they'll crucify me. I'm way too old for him. Divorced. Single mum. Chronically ill. And I'm either barren, or pregnant and trying to trap him and get my hands on his wealth..."

"You're spiralling. I'm going to call in the big guns." Shasa took out her phone and dialled. "Elsie! Hi! It's Shasa. Are you home? Can we come for a visit with Marnie? She needs some support... Okay... Sounds great. See you in ten!"

Shasa ended the call and flashed her a cheeky smile. "Sorry, but I had to. I'm younger than you so you're never going to take me seriously. Let's go!"

Elsie, 60-something and fabulous, opened the door of her custom-designed house in a silky blouse and tracksuit bottoms fit for a queen. How anyone could dress casually and still look so put together never ceased to amaze Marnie.

"Come on in! Earl will be back from work in an hour, and we're going out for dinner, but let's have a chat before then." Elsie led them to her cosy living room, which had gradually changed since she'd begun dating Earl, the council worker who didn't share her background of wealth or taste for nice things.

Elsie followed Marnie's gaze to the tall rack of records

with an old record player perched on top of a cabinet that didn't quite match the decor. "I know! Earl loves his music, and he's gotten me into these old records, so I thought I'd invite him to keep some here. It's taking all of my willpower to not replace that bloody filing cabinet!"

"It probably makes him feel more at home," Shasa said with a wink. "I've seen those at the council."

Elsie laughed. "That's where he got it from, obviously. They let employees buy the ones they're getting rid of. Thank you for your service. Here's a discounted piece of ugly steel."

Shasa pushed Marnie towards one of the armchairs and took the couch.

"Wine, then?" Elsie fetched glasses from the sideboard and opened a bottle of something red. "I haven't seen you two in ages. How are you?" She directed the question at Marnie, her forehead wrinkling.

Marnie took the wine glass, brought the rim of it to her lips, and froze. "I… probably shouldn't drink."

Shasa took the glass from her and placed it on the coffee table. "It's okay."

"Are you on medication?" Elsie asked. "I can make us some tea."

Marnie waved her hand. "That's okay. We just had tea. But there's a teeny, tiny possibility that I'm pregnant. Probably not, but I shouldn't… you know."

Elsie sat down on the closest empty chair and leaned in.

"Pregnant? I only just found out you were seeing someone."

"So, you know?" Marnie sighed, grateful that she didn't have to explain everything.

"That's all I know. I'm afraid Sue and John are very discreet." Elsie gave her an apologetic smile.

"You should have talked to Tanya!" Marnie rolled her eyes.

"I'd much rather hear it from you, if you're ready to share?"

Marnie dug her heels in the plush carpet and a zing of pain travelled upwards, the perfect reminder of how it all started. The words tumbled out, first heavy and sticky in her throat, describing the diagnosis and the inevitable end of her good years, then followed by the bittersweet moments of her whirlwind affair. Elsie and Shasa listened quietly, captivated by her tale. She caught herself explaining all about Jason's career goals but left out the fake law degree.

After a long silence, Elsie spoke. "What a story. I had no idea. I knew you were seeing someone, and from the way Sue talked, it sounded like he was a public figure. But I didn't know you'd fallen in love."

Marnie shook her head. "It's so complicated. Even if I love him, I have to stay away. I don't know what to do!"

Elsie smiled. "I can understand why you'd feel overwhelmed. It sounds like such a whirlwind romance. A Cinderella story, really."

"You're right!" Shasa echoed, her eyes bulging with excitement. "Marnie's Cinderella!"

"Elderly Cinderella," Marnie corrected.

Shasa held up her hand. "Oh, stop it! Can we move onto the pregnancy test? Elsie has a lovely bathroom, and we're here for you." She gestured at the bathroom, giving her an encouraging smile.

Elsie's brows arched in amazement. "You brought a pregnancy test?"

Marnie pulled the packet out of her handbag.

Elsie studied it like a piece of rock from Mars. "Is this what they look like these days?" She put on her rose gold reading glasses to have a closer look. "You can test on the day of your period? I remember when you had to wait about a month, but I guess the modern woman can't handle such uncertainty."

Marnie smiled. "I've barely survived the last twenty-four hours. And it still might be too early. I should wait until morning. It works better with morning wee I think."

Shasa sank back into her chair. "Fine. Do it in the morning. But, in the meantime, we should work on the way you talk about yourself. Because if you believe you're too old or wrong for him, the relationship will never work out."

Marnie sighed. "That's what I'm saying. It won't work out!"

"Why not?" Elsie asked, sliding her glasses down her nose like an esteemed therapist.

Marnie twisted her mouth, tears stinging in her eyes. "If Kathleen finds out about us, she'll publish this horrible picture of me, she'll tell the press everything about me… how I have arthritis… Maybe I could take the embarrassment, but it'll hurt his career. I can't do that to him."

"But what if you're pregnant?" Shasa asked.

Marnie hung her head. "I don't know. Even if I am, who knows if it works out? Isn't it risky at my age? Can people with arthritis even have babies?"

Elsie pinned her down with a sharp look, a deep frown between her eyes. "Of course they can. People with cancer have babies. It's all about managing your health, learning about your condition and how to live a good life with it. There's not always a cure, but you can usually do something about it. Do you think I'm in perfect health? I'm in my sixties. I have pernicious anaemia and chronically low iron. My thyroid has been removed. I'm on thyroid hormones, I get B12 shots, I take supplements and sometimes an iron infusion. Without modern medicine, I'd be long dead."

Marnie stared at her in awe. She'd always thought of Elsie as someone invincible, a woman who'd somehow sidestepped all the pitfalls and kept her health and youthful appearance into her sixties. "I had no idea. I'm so sorry."

Elsie's gaze was challenging. "Why? I'm not. I'm grateful for every pill and treatment that keeps me alive. It's a bloody miracle."

A glimmer of hope ignited in Marnie's heart as Elsie's confronting words floated in the air between them. Could she be that secure in herself one day? Could she see the world like Elsie did? She'd worked so hard to get in shape. She'd found clothes that were more flattering. Yet, she felt worse about herself than before, when she'd just been walking around in her saggy tunics, completely clueless. It was so much easier to not to put yourself out there at all. As soon as she stepped into the spotlight, every flaw became highlighted.

"Even if I could somehow convince myself that I'm good enough for him, I don't know if I could handle the media, all those ugly comments."

Shasa's voice took on a sharp edge. "I told you, stop reading the comments! That's where brains go to die."

"I have to agree with that," Elsie confirmed, less dramatically. "Do you think members of the public would come at you in the street to voice their jealousy or disapproval? Most people shout their opinions anonymously online, but that's where it ends. They can't steal your happiness, unless you let them."

Marnie sank into the chair, pulling her knees to her chest. Squeezing herself into a tight ball made her breasts ache, but she wanted to disappear. They were right. She'd gone down a rabbit hole and focused on stupid things. Why did she care about the opinions of random keyboard warriors, or even Kathleen Rush? If Jason wanted her, and she wanted him, why was she letting anything stand in the way?

Just when she began to feel better, a little more hopeful, her mind served up the words she'd written in the letter and sent to him. "I think it's too late. I broke up with him. He hasn't called or texted since Tuesday."

"Oh, Marnie." Shasa sighed, her tone softer now. She hopped on the arm of her chair and pulled her into a side hug. "Of course he hasn't. Rejection is hard to take. But if you make it clear you want to try, he might feel differently."

Marnie could only nod, hiccupping through the tears. Maybe she'd find the courage if she just hung out with her friends and absorbed their attitudes. She needed to shift her thoughts. A powerful yawn shook her body. She hadn't slept enough, and it was catching up with her. How did Jason survive on so little sleep?

"Do you want to sleep in the guest room?" Elsie asked. "I'll be here in the morning when you're ready to do the test."

"And I'll come over," Shasa added. "Just text me when you're up, okay?"

Marnie smiled through her tears. "Okay. I'll call Tanya."

# Chapter 35

"We need damage control," Malcolm announced, stepping over empty takeout containers to reach Jason's bed.

"I'm not doing any PR outings," Jason mumbled from under the covers.

He hadn't invited the big guy but wasn't particularly surprised he'd shown up. Jason had skipped the last two casual catchups and was contemplating not showing up to work on Tuesday. Malcolm could smell that kind of shit from a mile away.

"I was thinking something simple to start with. Shower." Malcolm picked up a rolled-up towel from the edge of his bed and threw it on Jason's face.

Jason groaned but did as he was told. After all, it would be harder to hear Malcolm's nagging through a door, over the sound of running water. He could take a really, really long shower. Maybe Mr PR would get tired of waiting and leave.

Malcolm seemed to read his mind. He escorted Jason all the way into the shower cubicle and made no move to leave the bathroom.

"Do you mind?"

"Yes. I need to have a word with you. And I'm going to take a leak while you shower."

Too tired to display his outrage, Jason stepped behind the sliding doors and stripped. Within seconds, the water burned his skin. Always either hot or cold, there seemed to be no middle setting. At least the buzz of it masked the sound of Malcolm's urine hitting the toilet bowl.

"I take it it's over between you and the mystery woman?"

"I suppose."

"She's not keen on your lifestyle?"

"No." He'd give Malcolm what he wanted, with as little information as possible. Malcolm was a nice guy, but right now, Jason couldn't handle anyone.

Anyone but Marnie.

His whole body ached for her, the hole she'd left behind like a crater inside him. The high-pitched ringing behind his eyebrow was back, along with the metallic taste of the sleeping pills his doctor had warned him about. He couldn't even get the prescription renewed anymore. Not legally.

There were other ways, of course. One of them was Malcolm. The giant juggernaut had his fingers in many pies. And as much as it bothered Jason to have him as a bathroom companion, he needed the man.

Jason shampooed his hair and noted the shadow of the bathroom door as it opened and closed. Just as he sighed with relief, the door opened again, the beeping of his phone permeating the shower ambiance.

"Well, isn't she keen?" Malcolm mused.

Was the big guy checking his phone? Miffed, Jason gave his hair one last rinse, turned off the tap and towelled his way out of the shower. Malcolm stood at the bathroom doorway, staring at his phone with an unmistakable gleam in his eyes.

"Are you looking at porn on my phone?"

Malcolm chuckled. "Yes. But only because it was right there. Who's this Luna? She's not the mystery woman, is she?"

"No." Jason grabbed his phone and gasped. Luna had graduated from a naked yoga pose to one that involved no form of exercise and revealed more. Between her bare breasts, she'd pinned one of Jason's campaign flyers. His brightly smiling face against Labour Party red, disappearing into her cleavage. "Where did she even get that flyer? We haven't distributed them in months."

Malcolm nodded appreciatively. "That's no selfie, either. Someone's taken that photo for her. A professional."

Jason shivered. "Creepy."

But Malcolm wasn't listening. He was busy tapping his own phone, muttering something to himself. After a moment, he brought up another image of Luna, this one with clothes, on her Instagram feed. "She's got over two hundred thousand followers."

"Yeah?" Jason couldn't even fake polite enthusiasm as he tied the towel around his waist, pulled another T-shirt over his head and collapsed on the unmade bed. Maybe he'd do a double dose of pills tonight and worry about his dwindling supply later. If he got some deep sleep, he'd be able to deal with all this tomorrow.

"You know what? You could do with an outing with someone like her. The public would eat it up. She's mature, sexy, outspoken... very opinionated. A perfect distraction."

Jason groaned, digging himself under the covers like a crab disappearing in the sand. Malcolm was usually right about these things, but he couldn't jump through these hoops. Not now. "Have some compassion, man! I'm heartbroken. I'm beyond tired. I can't hold it all inside. I want to come clean about the stupid law degree, everything."

"No, you don't," Malcolm replied in a soothing voice. "Why would you do that now when we're so close. Just get the new tax approved and you'll have something to show for yourself. Then you can go smear your reputation all over town. If you still feel like it."

Malcolm sat on the edge of the bed, causing the mattress

springs to shriek. "How's your stash? You out of pills?" He leaned in, a lion sniffing out a gazelle who could no longer run.

Jason nodded. "Almost. The doc says I need to take a break."

"Take a break from what? Sleeping?" Malcolm shook his head in disbelief and his concern warmed Jason.

"I'm gonna die." Jason buried his face in the pillow.

"No, you won't. We'll sort it out. I have connections. But you need to do something for me."

"What?" Jason barked, even though he already knew, the churning in his stomach an excellent guide.

Without a word, Malcolm took Jason's phone from the bed, brought up Luna's text message and turned the screen so that he could see it as he typed a reply.

*Would love to meet. 8pm tonight at Backbencher?*

Jason launched for the phone. Too slow. Malcolm hit the send button and off it went, the world's worst reply to a text message ever.

"Why Backbencher? Everyone's going to be there," he hissed. "I can get media attention anywhere. Why do I have to prance around the Parliament Building for everyone and their dog?"

"Because you haven't shown your face since the Cabinet meeting, and we're losing momentum. You need to get off your bum and act like a winner. These decisions aren't made in a vacuum. Go out and be your charming self. Make sure everyone knows you killed it on Tuesday, and you're confident as hell."

"I can't even stand up straight. My head's all woozy."

"It's happy hour. You'll fit right in!"

"Honestly, I can't—"

"Here." Malcolm unscrewed a small, brown bottle and shook out a tiny, white pill. He handed it over with a grave look on his face.

"What's this?"

"Uppers," Malcolm said vaguely.

Jason's eyes widened in shock. "I want to sleep, not stay up all night!"

"It'll just mask the tiredness, give you some energy. I promise to bring out the big guns and conk you out later. Tomorrow, maybe. I'll check what Brenda has."

Brenda was the Parliament House receptionist and general go-to person with seemingly unlimited supplies of anything one might need – ironic that the lawmakers of the country seemed to operate above the law, doling out prescription drugs from under the counter.

"I thought she only had antibiotics and such?"

"Officially, yes. But she's well connected and very obliging."

"I don't want anything stronger. Just the stuff I'm on now." He pointed at the bottle on the nightstand. "I'm trying to wean myself off."

"Sure, you are." Malcolm gave him a placating smile.

Jason shook his head at the insanity of it all but decided not to argue. He couldn't afford to. Taking a deep breath, he swallowed the small, white pill and washed it down with a glass of stale water on his nightstand. As it travelled down his throat, his phone pinged again.

*It's a date!* Luna exclaimed, this time with no photo. He could only hope she still wore clothes in public.

Jason pulled on chinos, a shirt and a jacket, and checked his outfit in the mirror. One day, he'd have to buy makeup to cover those dark circles around his eyes. Apart from that, he looked the part, even if he didn't feel like it.

"Dapper," Malcolm confirmed, giving him a wink. "Go charm her socks off! Or whatever piece of clothing she has left."

Jason shook his head, noting an ache right behind his eyes and slight dizziness. Great. "Are you going to escort me to the bar? Or can I walk by myself?" He turned his phone onto silent.

Malcolm got up from the bed. "I trust you. Or rather, I have to be somewhere else"—he checked his watch—"half an hour ago. But I'll call you later to make sure you didn't bail."

Malcolm held the door, leading them to the lifts.

Outside, he turned Jason to steer him in the right direction. "Two-hundred metres that way. You can't miss it." The big guy's voice dripped with sarcasm – Jason had only been to that bar about twenty times.

Wandering down the footpath shadowed by tall apartment

buildings, Jason glimpsed the dark sky with remnants of indigo still hanging in the horizon. The blue moment, the fleeting evening light he hadn't seen in months, maybe years. He no longer had enough time to stare at the sky. His life had turned into a to-do list. What if he stopped? What'd be left of him? Who'd be left in his life? His old friends had moved on. If Marnie wouldn't have him, who would?

Did he really believe this other woman had nothing more than a superficial interest in him? The heaviness in his chest spread to his legs, making them stiff and unwilling. Part of him wanted to believe, wanted to keep open that tiny possibility that there was someone out there who really cared and would choose him, warts and all: the baggage of publicity, the guilt, the darkness. What else could he do other than go forth, put one foot ahead of the other and fight to not lose all hope?

# Chapter 36

Jason recognised Luna Bella's cleavage before he recognised her face. The pair of breasts bulging out of her dress matched the ones he'd just seen on his phone screen. This time, there was no flyer. Thank God.

"Great to see you!" She gestured at a chair next to her.

Jason sat across the table. His head felt light and giddy like he was inhabiting someone else's body. The cartoony figurines of politicians decorating the walls seemed to come alive, their eyes following him, creepy smiles widening as he looked up at them. What the hell was in that pill? He was high as a kite.

"I hope you don't mind, I ordered a round of drinks," Luna

murmured as the waitress appeared with a tray of shots.

What was he supposed to say? That he didn't know how whatever he'd taken would mix with vodka? The carefree looseness coursing through his veins carried fragments of panic.

Jason took out his phone and texted Malcolm.

*What was in the pill? What happens if I drink? Heart attack? Anyoureiysm?*

He stared at the last word, vaguely aware of not having spelled it correctly. He added some expressive emojis, hit 'send' and tried to lower his shoulders before looking up at Luna. "Sorry, just have to figure something out."

"No worries."

After a moment, his phone pinged.

*You'll get drunk. And your dick will be fine.*

Jason blinked at the screen, realising that one of his 'sick face' emojis was an eggplant. Oops. Jason shrugged and reached for a shot. Alcohol would probably make an evening with this woman more tolerable. She had a predatory air about her.

On the way in, he'd noticed heads turning. It was time to put on a performance.

Winking at Luna, he downed another shot. "Cheers. I'll get the next round."

"All good," she purred. "How's your week been? I heard about the tax presentation. You're really stirring some trouble out there."

"Trouble?"

She laughed, tilting her head back. "Don't worry, I'm on your side. Those fat cats deserve to be taken down a notch. They think they're untouchable with their portfolios and high yields. I was at an event last weekend and one of those property investor group guys started chatting me up, bad-mouthing you. What a pig." She watched his face for a reaction.

Jason dropped his gaze to his empty shot glass, wishing he had his wits about him. Luna was clearly well-connected and digging for dirt. He cleared his throat, putting on his politician voice. "There are some misconceptions about this law. It's not going to hurt most of them at all. Just a wee incentive to help people make better decisions with their property. Especially overseas investors."

Luna's hand slid across the table and her pale pink nails curled around his hand. "Relax. I told you, I'm with you on this one. Good on you for challenging the status quo. Millennials are cheering you on. You have huge support."

Jason shrugged. "I'm not a Millennial, you know. I'm a geriatric Millennial."

"Geriatric?" Luna's laugh was a little forced. "You're not that old."

"It's just a term I learned recently. And I feel geriatric, so it fits." He looked up, a silent challenge in his eyes.

A pair of carefully painted cat eyes stared back at him, defying age and decay. How old was she? It was hard to tell.

There were no physical signs of ageing. It was weird, just like the halo of colours reflecting off his glass, dancing in the stream of light on Luna's shoulder. Since when did he see colours dancing in the air in a dusty pub? What had Malcolm done to him?

Luna's eyes narrowed as she leaned in, her hand still grasping his. "Let me make you feel young again."

"I just want to sleep." The words burst out. This wasn't what he'd come here to discuss. He must not talk about his issues to this woman. She was not to be trusted.

Luna's eyebrows shot up in animated sympathy. "A rough week, huh?"

"Forget that. I'm okay." Was his speech slurring?

"Honestly, you don't seem okay. Maybe—"

A slick young man approached the table, clapping his hands in exaggerated excitement. Jason recognised him as one of the freelance reporters, the hungry ones always out and about, putting on a gay-routine. "Oh, it's you! Jason Hallett! I haven't seen you for so long I thought you were dead! And who's this gorgeous lady? You haven't settled down, have you?" He pouted in mock-horror. "You'd break my heart!"

Luna straightened her spine, giving him a seductive smile, ready for her photo.

Jason raised his hand to send him packing. The guy had already pulled out his phone.

"Oh, Jason! Just one photo, then I'll leave you alone, I

promise. You'll look great. I'll make my rent. Win-win." His pout was so over-the-top that Jason considered simply handing over cash to cover his rent. No. That would probably look bad.

Jason gripped the edge of the table, trying to think. He was high, or drunk, or both, and the room was spinning. He couldn't risk standing up. Could he risk being photographed?

Luna giggled. "We can't have this guy homeless, can we?" She cast another pleading look at Jason, and he caved.

A faint nod was all Luna needed to scoot closer to Jason, lean into him and pose for the camera. The reporter, whose name was something like Rolo or Rome – Jason's brain offered up useless guesses – gushed about how amazing they looked together. Jason wasn't sure if he smiled. Possibly. His face operated on autopilot, reserving any remaining brain activity for figuring out how to get out of the situation. How to get home. Coming here had been a huge mistake. Doing those shots had been a gigantic mistake.

*Oh, make it stop.*

The reporter left, and Jason sighed with relief. Luna made no move to return to her side of the table. Her hand moved on his thigh, massaging the tight muscle under his trousers. The sensation was too much, cross-firing with every other signal wreaking havoc in his body. "Please, don't," he whispered. "I'm a bit—"

"I know," Luna whispered. "I know you have trouble sleeping, and I want to help you. I'm not expecting anything before we've sorted out this problem of yours."

She gave him a conspiratorial smile, and Jason tensed from head to toe. Who had blabbed about his troubles?

Luna pulled her hand away and rested it on the table. "It's okay. I won't tell anyone." Her beautiful face turned earnest.

Could he really trust her? Did he have a choice? His poor brain had turned into cotton wool. He was at her mercy.

Where was Marnie? Part of him expected her to step in and save her. But she wasn't here. She wasn't coming. She'd broken up with him.

"I have something you might want to try," Luna continued, digging into her purse. "This stuff works. One hundred percent."

She gave him a quick peek at the bottle of pills before hiding it back into the depths of her handbag.

"I don't do drugs." He shook his head, looking away.

"Me, neither." Luna winked at him. "Only when desperate."

Desperate, huh? She'd managed to choose a word that perfectly described the lump of emotion sitting in his gut. He needed Marnie. Right now. He was standing at the edge of a cliff, about to fall. Didn't she see? Didn't she care?

Luna's arm snaked around his and nudged him up. "Let's get you home. Don't worry, I'll take care of you."

# Chapter 37

Marnie stepped closer to Elsie's bathroom window, tilting the white stick towards the light. A pregnancy test was meant to clear up confusion, not add to it, right? Was the faint second line a ghost haunting her vision or a sign of early pregnancy? She wrapped her cardigan around her waist.

A light knock on the door made her jump.

"Are you okay in there?" Shasa had arrived right after breakfast, ready to support her. They were supposed to do this together.

Marnie set the pregnancy test on the windowsill, hoping for the faint line to either disappear or become stronger.

She appreciated her friends, but she needed a moment. This level of anticipation couldn't be healthy. Her stomach was in knots, unable to digest the piece of toast she'd managed at the breakfast table.

Marnie washed her hands and checked the test again. It looked the same. Straightening her back, she took the test and returned to Elsie's dining room. Shasa sat at the table, nibbling on the fresh fruit Elsie had cut up on a plate. The sight of persimmon and mandarin slices made her ravenous and she joined Shasa at the table.

Shasa pried the pregnancy test from her other hand and looked at it. She frowned. "Damn."

"What?" Marnie asked.

"What does it say?" Elsie hurried to look over their shoulders. She placed a cup of barista coffee on the table in front of Marnie. "Here you go. It's not decaf, though. Can you drink coffee when pregnant?"

"Of course," Shasa smiled. "But Marnie's not. Unless it's too early."

"I'm not?" Marnie repeated, wrapping her shaky hands around the coffee cup.

"There's just one line, right?" As Shasa said it, she held up the stick, tilting it in the light just like Marnie had done. "Wait..."

"Let me see!" Elsie took the stick from her and marched to the double doors giving to her balcony. "I can see another line," she announced, bathing the stick in morning light, "but it's quite weak. What does that mean?"

Shasa jumped on her feet and grabbed the test from Elsie. "A faint line is still a line. Doesn't matter how faint, if there's some colour. Mine was faint with Lilla at first." She held the test up again, squinting her eyes. "Not this faint, but Elsie's right. There is a line."

A giggle built up in Marnie's chest at seeing her friends study the stick she'd just peed on. Her whole body shook from the uncontrollable laughter.

The others gave her an odd look, then exchanged a worried glance.

"I don't know why," Marnie said, wiping her eyes. She wasn't sure when the laughter turned into tears, but suddenly she found herself sobbing, holding a tissue Elsie had placed in her hands. "I just never had this level of support before. When I was young and knocked up, I was all alone. My parents were a bit disappointed – they wanted me to study. And Steve… I was just grateful he stepped up and said we could get married. Like that magically solved everything. And that was it. It was all decided. The kids, the house in Glenview, night school…"

"You did so well, though." Shasa sat down next to her. "You got your degree and everything."

"Yeah. Except I don't use it for anything. I don't have a career. I just dabble at things."

"You write books," Shasa reminded her.

"I read the one with the orange cover… the one set on a

cruise ship," Elsie chimed in. "It was exciting!"

Marnie smiled through her tears. She had so few readers that Elsie's support felt like a warm hug. "Thank you."

If she really was pregnant, it would be different this time. She'd have her friends, she'd have her own house. She could organise her life the way she wanted, not around what her parents and Steve's found acceptable. It would work out, somehow. Looking around Elsie's kitchen with its assortment of handmade ceramics and smooth timber, Marnie felt a sense of calm and resolve. As she breathed in and out to settle her wobbly stomach, she felt the slightest hint of something else in her chest. Almost like excitement.

She made her way to the balcony, admiring the pale-yellow morning sky stretching over the lake. The world bathed in sunlight. What a blessing she had right here. Marnie leaned on the railing, amazed at the sudden wave of euphoria. It must have been the hormones, but she didn't want to question it. Down at the water's edge, sunlight bounced off the pitched roofs. Somewhere down there was Jason's cottage. Was he there? Could she just stroll down the hill and knock on his door? Could she confess her mistakes and...? Marnie's stomach lurched, sending a shivery sensation down her limbs. What had terrified her, suddenly felt possible.

She stepped back through the glass doors and found her friends still at the table, their eyes trained on her.

"Are you okay?" Elsie asked.

Marnie nearly walked into the table. "I have to see him."

Shasa threw up her hands. "Thank God. I thought you'd never get there!"

"Do you know where he is?" Elsie asked.

"No." Marnie took the phone off the table. "But his house is just down there. I'll go have a look."

Elsie glanced at Shasa. "Do you want us to come with you?"

She shook her head, slipped her feet into a pair of sneakers and walked out the door. She loved them both, but she needed some time alone. No. Not alone. She wasn't just one person anymore. Getting pregnant was a terrible mistake, until it happened. At that moment, the world turned on its axis. Suddenly, there was no mistake. There was a miracle.

Letting the heavy door close behind her, Marnie hopped down the tiled path to the iron gate. Its swirly shapes made her happy. Her body had surprised her. An egg had released from where there shouldn't have been any, made its way down her shrivelled tube and hung around waiting for a seed. The pure magic of it made her see colours that weren't there, like light splitting through a diamond. No, wait. A teardrop. It broke free and rolled down her cheek. She had to find Jason. She had to tell him.

Carried by lightness and joy she hadn't felt in years, Marnie tumbled down the narrow footpath, across a sweeping lawn, down to the lakeside path. How had she not seen it? He'd tried to tell her. He'd offered her his whole heart, and she'd run away like an idiot. She'd told herself she was protecting his career, saving his future, but she'd only been punishing herself, denying herself what she didn't think she deserved. Until that faint line. A faint idea of a baby. A baby deserved everything. A baby deserved all the love in the world. And if Marnie was willing to give that to the baby, how could she deny it from herself? She had to be the woman worthy of love, for this child, and for her existing children. For herself and for him.

Marnie picked up speed, running along the winding path shielded by silver fern.

*Please be there.*

But when she reached the gate, the house looked empty, the curtains drawn. He was most likely in Wellington. She woke up her phone to dial his number. Maybe it was best to check the government website, to see where he might be. As she opened her browser, three news articles popped up. The first one stole the breath out of her lungs.

Jason with Luna, all bright smiles and closeness she couldn't understand. The stylist leaned on him, her arm draped over his shoulder like she owned him. Marnie stared at the photo, trying to blink it away. Her brain took several seconds to piece together the words next to it. 'Jason Hallett's new beau. Is this Beatrice?'

With a trembling finger, Marnie tapped on the headline. The article was short. They were seen together, looking happy, enjoying Saturday night drinks. Saturday? That was last night. Marnie forced herself to read on. The piece didn't include any direct quotes from Jason or even Luna, but in the middle of the article, the journalist had inserted a post from Luna's Instagram feed. Marnie gasped. She immediately recognised Jason's apartment. She stared at the photos, pain squeezing her gut. Luna had gone home with him. She'd sent him all those nude pics and Jason must have replied. He'd caught the live show.

What did it mean? Had Jason lied to her about Luna, or had the stylist wormed her way into his life, and bed, only last night? She'd certainly expressed her interest in him loud and clear. Afraid of falling, Marnie slipped through the gate and leaned against the fence, sliding down to sit on the dewy lawn. Fury swelled in her chest like a fire ball. How dare that woman steal from her? Her love. Her baby's father. Even her fake name.

No. No. No. Jason was hers.

The rage burnt through her, leaving only ashes. After a few heavy breaths, it was replaced by overwhelming grief. Tears spilled out between dry heaves. Because Jason wasn't hers. She'd pushed him away. She'd broken up with him.

How had she messed up so badly? She could see it clearly now. Those horrible words she'd spoken and believed. He'd tried to reach her through the sludge, but she wouldn't listen. She wouldn't believe anyone telling her she was beautiful, good enough, young enough. Sick or healthy. Fertile or not. She'd rather drown in a barrel of shit.

She'd condemned her body as useless, but it had proven her wrong. Over and over again. This ailing sack of flesh and bones could still deliver incredible pleasure, even create a life. Believe the evidence, it seemed whisper. *You're very much alive.* But what did it matter if she'd lost him? Marnie buried her face in the elbow of her cardigan, gathering the loose ends of it around her like a cloak. With her bottom cold and wet against the grass, her back against his picket fence, she wept.

# Chapter 38

Jason batted his eyelids to clear the blurry film covering his corneas. The day stretched ahead of him, endless, ready to crush him. But at least he'd slept. The pill Luna had slipped him had knocked him out cold, like general anaesthesia. He'd blinked, and it was morning. Jason sat up on his bed, glancing around his apartment. His gaze landed on the woman sleeping next to him, eyes covered by a face mask with a tropical print on it. Annoyance swirled in his gut. Why was she here? Had he asked her to stay the night?

He got up, moving quietly. Maybe he could get dressed and leave without waking her, then dodge her calls until she got the message. Right after he found out the name of that drug. It had left him with a fuzzy head and mild nausea, but he'd managed to skip hours of pain. Without it, he would have endured a sleepless night, and the comedown from the pill Malcolm had given him. Or maybe that was still in store. He leaned over the sink to wash his face, still half asleep, or rather sedated, his arms moving slower than he'd intended, muscles sore and beaten. Weird.

Jason glanced at the mirror and shuddered at the sight of himself. He must have laid like the dead, one side of his face patterned by the wrinkles of his pillowcase. Those pills would be the end of him, but what else could he do? Even if Malcolm secured his usual prescription, could he go back to upping the dosage, hoping for the best, waking up in wee hours of the morning to think about all he'd lost? All he'd done. He didn't want to think at all.

"Jason? Are xyou there?" Luna's purred through the bathroom door.

Jason ignored her, brushed his teeth and finally stepped out, hitting the doorframe on his way out. Since when did he not fit through a doorway? His head pounded, and he threw himself back on the bed, groaning.

"Did you sleep well?" Luna's voice had a seductive edge that made his gut tighten.

He felt her stretching on the bed next to him and buried his face in the pillow. "I think I died for a bit."

"It's great, isn't it? No tossing and turning."

No, he hadn't tossed or turned. Tossing and turning was

a sign of life, one he'd moved past in his transition towards death. He could only hope it was a painless one. "What's in those pills? Do you have more of them?"

"Lots. Don't worry. But you can't up the dose. You'd go into a coma."

Jason sighed. Right now, a coma didn't sound so bad. Wasn't it just a long sleep? From the corner of his eye, he noticed Luna on her phone, typing something. A bad feeling built up in his gut, intensifying the hammering in his head. "You're not posting about… us, are you?"

She tinkled the melodic movie star laugh he remembered from the night before, which brought up another memory. The reporter. He'd taken their photo. It must have been blasted all over the internet by now.

Lying on her stomach, Luna winked at him over her shoulder. "Don't worry! I'd never take a drooling picture of you when you sleep or anything like that! But I have to keep my fans happy. They're dying to find out how our date went."

Jason tensed, turning to look at her. "Date? What did you tell them?"

"I gave it a good spin, don't worry. I'd never make you look bad. I'd never embarrass you." She arched her brow, giving her a meaningful look. "I control the narrative. I know how to woo the public and play the media. I think our relationship can be beneficial to both of us."

Oh, God. The pressure in his head forced him to take deep

breaths. Would he feel like this all day?

"Are you okay? Those pills take a little while to wear off. Just drink some water and take it easy. And we should get some breakfast. Coffee!" She bounced off the bed, clapping her hands. Her purple camisole struggled to keep up with her movements and one nipple escaped the lace, staring him in the eye.

"Oops!" Luna laughed, making no attempt to cover it. She bent over to pick up something off the floor, exposing a lacy thong.

Jason's stir of arousal was so weak he barely felt it. Had he lost his ability to... He really was as good as dead. That horse tranquilliser must have beaten his manhood out of him. Not that he wanted to sleep with Luna. She made him uneasy, like the reporters he had to be careful around. Speaking of which... Jason rolled over and found his phone on the nightstand, still alive, the battery blinking red.

As Luna retreated to the bathroom, he searched for her Instagram account. At first glance, he couldn't see himself in her feed. The last two pictures were pouty selfies. In one, she held a shot glass to her lips and the other... Jason froze, recognising the view in the background – his apartment.

*Jason's crib. A great view of the Beehive, don't you think?*

Jason swiped right to discover more pictures, taken through his window, the Beehive barely visible in the darkness. There was no view to speak of, no reason to share this photo except to advertise her presence in his apartment.

That was it. The story was out there. Malcolm had gotten his wish.

What would Marnie think if she saw it? The thought made him shudder.

As Jason listened to the tap running in the bathroom, he realized he couldn't go on like this. Something had to give. Could he just quit, clear out of here and go home? He didn't have to become like Luna, a calculating climber who used other people as stepping-stones. Ever since he'd voiced the idea of quitting to Marnie, it had grown stronger, burning in his mind like a glowing exit sign.

Could he go back to his old life and become unimportant again? He'd still be a sad, vulnerable wreck, but he'd be free to battle those thoughts without the glossy veneer of public life. He'd no longer carry the deception, that gnawing fear that drove him to google his own name and watch over his shoulder. He wanted to be truly open and honest and known for real, not just to use and be used. He'd shown Marnie his embarrassing, unglamorous self, shared his shameful secret, and she hadn't rejected him for that. Instead, she'd let him closer. Closer than he'd ever been to another person. But she'd rejected the world he lived in, and he couldn't blame her.

He threw his arm over the side of the bed and dropped his phone on the floor, sinking lower into the sheets. Looking at the headlines would do him no good. He stared at the tidy, grey carpet. Since he'd left the room last night, the cleaners had popped in, restoring the room's hotel vibe. The tracks of their industrial vacuum cleaner came within inches of the narrow gap under the bed. As Jason hung his head over the edge, he noticed something yellow, peeking out from underneath. He wiggled his fingers into the gap to pick it up.

His breath hitched. It was the sticky note filled with Marnie's small, curly handwriting.

*Here's my number, just in case you ever want to see me again. Thank you for everything, Beatrice (not my real name, sorry!)*

Next to her phone number, she'd drawn a heart.

Jason's eyes pooled with tears. She'd thanked him, after a night like that.

He read the note again and almost saw the sincere hope in Marnie's eyes as she wrote those words. How had he lost the best thing in his life? His mind circled back to the Beehive, the monster that was slowly sucking the life out of him. He had to get out of here.

Jason pushed himself up and out of bed. He pulled on chinos and a hoodie and found his loafers scattered near the door. Pocketing Marnie's note and his phone, he called through the bathroom door, "I'll get us coffees from downstairs. Be back soon!"

He grabbed his shoulder bag by the door, which had his wallet, laptop and most valuable papers he didn't want Luna to get her hands on. Besides that, he didn't care if she stayed and burned the place.

The bathroom lock clicked. "Wait! I'll join—"

But Jason was faster, out the door and inside the lift before Luna could follow. She probably wasn't dressed to go outside. Watching the sliding door close in front of him, Jason steadied himself on the handrail and hit the button for ground level. Going down, his heart finally picked up speed, pushing through a layer of cold sweat. He breathed slowly, his head throbbing, as he descended to the lobby.

Help. He needed help. Luna was not it. She'd be his doom. Could he just blow her off and disappear? The feeling grew with every step as he wandered out of the building towards the cafe.

Walking around near the Beehive probably wasn't a great idea. He could easily be recognised. His puffy eyes and unfocused gaze would raise questions. Where was the sharp, charming guy dubbed the fresh hope of politics? He wasn't their messiah. He was a failure.

He'd have to leave town and hide somewhere. How long would it take? A year? Ten years? How inflated was his ego that he even worried about that? Jason contemplated pulling his hood up, but that would likely just attract more attention. He wasn't trying to rob the cafe. The sun was already up, heating the pavement, caressing his shoulders with warmth that reminded him of Marnie.

In all fairness, everything reminded him of Marnie. She was all softness and sincerity. Most people had a hard edge that become more pronounced during hard times. Marnie was different. Even as she'd told him she couldn't see him, she'd done it with such tenderness it nearly killed him. Longhand, on proper stationary. Sure, she was scared and deluded, blind to her own worth, but her love was real.

Jason shivered despite the sunshine, trying to swallow the tightness in his throat. Marnie was for real, and she would come through. Maybe he was the deluded one, but he had to hang on to the hope. If he only stayed alive, if he waited, she would find a way back to him. She'd come and save him.

Jason entered the cafe, and the buzz of conversation stilled as people turned to look at him. To escape the attention, he took out his phone. On its last three percent of battery and still on silent from the previous night, it showed three missed calls. As he stared at the screen, a fourth one popped up. Tracy, his assistant. He answered.

Her breathless voice gave him anxiety. "Where are you? Can you get here?"

"The office? It's Sunday."

Tracy let out an exasperated sigh. "I know. They tried to call you, then they ordered me to find you. An emergency meeting in the PM's office. Really hush-hush, by the sound of it."

"Kathleen?"

"That was my first thought, too. I don't know." Tracy's voice was low, others must have been listening in on the call.

"Okay, I'll be there in five."

Jason ended the call and abandoned his place in the

queue, relieved to get away from the prying eyes. His mind ran ahead of him as he rushed down the street towards the Beehive. The building always reminded him of the Colosseum. A ruin.

At the doors, Jason checked his attire. He was way too casual, but it didn't really matter. Not for what he was about to do.

He made his way through security and down the hallways to the meeting room. As he opened the door and slipped inside, five frowning faces greeted him. What happened to smiles and hellos? When had this become his new normal? Malcolm arrived right behind Jason, and they took seats around the oblong table.

Malcolm glared at him. "Nice hoodie."

The PM gave him a sharp look. "We can discuss Jason's outfit later. First, we have to figure out what to do with the housing portfolio."

"Housing? What's happened to Kathleen?" Malcolm asked.

The PM addressed the whole table. "She was hospitalised yesterday. She nearly burned down her house. They suspect dementia. It'll be in the papers tomorrow. If not sooner. We have to make a move, show everyone it's under control."

Malcolm cleared his throat. "We need a bold move, so it doesn't look like we're just putting a plaster on it. Or worse, like we're drowning here."

"Which we are," Rachel confirmed. Her face told everyone

this was a PR nightmare. "Any other portfolio would have been fine, but housing is such a hot potato. If it looks like we've been brushing Kathleen's health concerns under the rug and letting someone who's not well look after housing issues during a housing crisis—"

"Thank you, Rachel. We get the picture. Right now, it's just a house fire. We might be able to keep the health questions out of it for a bit longer." The PM's voice was weary.

Jason saw the dark circles under her eyes from across the table. Was she sleeping okay? He didn't know how she handled the stress she was under.

"I agree with Malcolm," she continued. "An interim solution could be to place someone like Tegan to take over housing, but that will look bad. He has too much on his plate. Like Rachel said, it will look like we don't care. Whereas, if we go for someone new, like an Associate Minister"—she eyeballed Jason—"it'll be seen as risk-taking."

Tegan huffed at the mention of his name, but kept his mouth shut.

Jason swallowed as everyone turned to look at him. Risk-taking indeed. This was the moment he'd been waiting for. His goals and dreams were all on a tray in front of him. And he no longer wanted any of them.

Malcolm's giant hand landed on his shoulder, showing his support. "I'd take that gamble. He's got the youth vote, the Millennials... Jason's the future." The big man had been in his corner from the start. Jason nearly chocked on a sudden wave of remorse.

He stood up, nodding at the Prime Minister. "I appreciate your confidence, but I can't in good conscience even entertain the idea. I've deceived all of you. My law degree is fake. I didn't write my own thesis. It's been eating me up for a while now. I can't sleep. I'm not well."

Five mouths opened simultaneously, a school of aquarium fish at feeding time. The PM was the first to find her voice. "What are you saying? Are you—"

"Please accept my resignation."

A collective gasp travelled across the room.

Jason pulled out the letter he'd carried in his bag for nearly two weeks, one he'd drafted after leaving the lighthouse and later printed in the office. He hadn't been sure if he could actually hand it in but having it there had made him feel better. An exit strategy. Well, not a strategy. He was running away, leaving everyone else to clean up the mess. But damn if his soul didn't feel a whole lot lighter.

The PM's eyebrows shot up as she accepted the envelope. "Thank you, Jason. I appreciate your honesty. However, we might keep the details to ourselves until the news about Kathleen has blown over. Maybe longer. You must understand how badly this reflects on all of us."

"I do." Jason swallowed a huge lump of shame.

Everyone stared at him, mirroring the PM's shock and disappointment. Everyone but Malcolm. His only Parliament friend. His confidante. There was a hint of understanding in his eyes.

Slowly, he stood up and took Jason's hand, turning the handshake into a one-armed bro hug. "Godspeed, Jason."

"Thanks," he rasped, lowering his voice. "I just can't. I have to step away and get better."

"I hope you get her back."

Malcolm's permission was all he needed. After a quick round of apologies and goodbyes, he hurried out. He didn't want to hear their platitudes or face their questions. And he wasn't handing anyone more ammunition than they already had.

Floating on a rush of his newfound freedom, Jason let his shaky legs carry him out through the security, ignoring everyone. Would he miss this place? Maybe. But that was nothing compared to his sense of relief. The secret was out. It no longer held power over him. He'd ruined his reputation, and burned his career, but he was free. There was a way out, somewhere in the distance.

# Chapter 39

"I'm sorry, I don't like the look of these numbers. They're too low."

Marnie shrank in her seat, the doctor's compassionate voice ringing in her ears. Her baby was leaving. The dream that had lifted her from darkness was slipping away.

"What does it mean? A false positive?"

The doctor smiled and shook her head. She had a black bob and an impenetrable shell of professional pleasantness. "No. False positives are very rare. You're most likely pregnant, but either it's very early, or you're miscarrying. You told me you got a faint positive with a home pregnancy test yesterday. Those tests are quite sensitive, but your hCG should be higher by now. So, I'm just saying, given your age, you should prepare for an early miscarriage. Either way, please book another appointment in a couple of days so we can do another test."

She clicked her mouse, bringing up something on the screen. "Now, how're you handling the arthritis? Are the symptoms getting worse?"

Marnie hardly cared about a little joint pain. Maybe she was just getting used to the twinges and swelling. When she didn't focus on how old it made her feel, could handle the illness, for now. She had an inkling the fasting and diet changes helped.

She shrugged. "It's fine. Comes and goes."

"That's good. Look after yourself. Keep those joints warm."

Marnie tucked her hands in her pockets. "So, you think I'll start bleeding soon?"

"If you do, it should be very straight forward, like a heavy period. You can still come and see us, and we'll make sure it's over."

Her heart heavy, Marnie stumbled out of the clinic. She supposed it had been too good to be true for someone like her. Maybe it was for the best.

Her phone beeped, a text from Shasa, asking how she was.

*I'm okay. Probably not pregnant for long, though. Numbers not high enough.*

The three bubbles told her Shasa was busy writing back. Something encouraging, no doubt. The girl believed in true love. She had her sights set on a happy ending, just like for her and Mac. But it wasn't that simple.

Slipping her phone back into her handbag, Marnie focused on walking. All she needed to do was take one step after another, to get her back home. It was best not to think about things she couldn't change. Like this pregnancy. It either was or wasn't. Even if it wasn't, knowing that a piece of Jason's DNA had taken root inside her, forming an embryo that lived long enough to drown her in hormones, made her hopeful. She wasn't dead yet. There was evidence of life, a faint line she would keep forever.

# Chapter 40

The next morning, Marnie woke with a start. She'd dreamt of a baby. A real, tiny human of her own flesh and blood. The delicious new-born smell lingered in her nose, conjured by her imagination. She stretched out on the bed, trying to sink back into the dream, but it slipped away, replaced by the terrible news from the day before.

She sat up and checked her undies. No blood. Not yet. Her breasts ached as she stood up, demanding the support of a bra. What if she just believed in this? Despite the numbers, despite the doctor's words?

Marnie rubbed her belly, whispering to the baby, "Hang in there, okay? It'll all work out. There's a place for you in the world."

She padded downstairs to make herself a cup of tea. Something safe. She wouldn't take any chances. At the foot of the stairs, she froze, taking in the strange scene. Someone was sleeping on her couch. Tiptoeing closer, she recognised Tom. Her son had curled up under a throw rug, looking like an oversized toddler, perfectly positioned under his own artwork on the wall above him.

Tanya appeared from her downstairs bedroom, rubbing her sleepy eyes.

"What's he doing here?" Marnie whispered, quietly circling her son.

"Tom! What are you doing here?" Tanya raised her voice, and her brother jerked awake.

He took a moment to get his bearings, then glared at his sister. "Cheers, Tan. I went to bed like three-thirty."

Tanya shrugged. "Well, Mum was asking what you're doing here."

Marnie shook her head, wrinkling her brow at Tanya. "I didn't want to wake him."

Tanya slipped to the kitchen, and Marnie joined Tom on the couch. "Are you okay? Did something happen?"

"Yeah. The landlord put up the rent, so we moved out."

"Why didn't you tell me? I could have helped, maybe covered the difference."

"No, mum. It's extortion. Nobody should pay that much."

Marnie shuddered. Jason's words about property investing

popped in her head. She missed him so much her heart ached. It hurt more than her swollen morning fingers. How would she ever get over him when every cell in her body called out to the man. Hell, some of the cells in her body were his.

She hugged her son. "You can stay here as long as you like, rent-free."

"I can pay something," Tom mumbled into her hair. "And I won't stay forever. I just need to figure out my next move."

"Of course. What about Hana? Is she still in Wellington?"

"No. Back in Australia. That... didn't work out."

"Oh, dear." Marnie hugged her son a bit tighter.

After a moment, Tom pulled back to give her an assessing look. "Also, I heard about you and Jason Hallett."

Marnie glanced at Tanya, who's face reddened a little as she buttered a piece of toast. "Come on, Mum! I didn't tell Hayley, but Tom's family! How were you going to keep sneaking around without Tom finding out? Since he's moved in and all."

"It's okay," Marnie dropped on the couch. "It's over, anyway."

"Huh?" Tanya's mouth hung open.

Tom gave her a sympathetic frown. "I'm so sorry, Mum. I saw Luna's posts and when Tanya told me, I kind of put it together."

Tanya dropped the butter knife and glared at her brother. "What posts? Who's Luna? You never tell me anything!"

Marnie rubbed her fingers. "I was going to tell you both." She wasn't sure if that was true, but somehow, she felt better now that they knew. Jason and the pregnancy were all she could think about.

She glanced at her children. "As you know, I've been seeing Jason Hallett, but I broke it off. I was scared of the publicity and being too old for him and everyone judging me."

Tanya narrowed her eyes. "That's stupid. You're both old. Why would that matter? You're good enough for him."

She glanced at Tom, who nodded. "Of course you are! I don't know if he's good enough for you."

Marnie shook her head and a sob escaped. "No. He's amazing. But he's moved on already. He's dating that influencer woman now."

"Are you sure?" Tanya asked, straightening her spine.

"Yeah, it's all over the news."

"You should probably check your phone." Tanya gave her a slow nod, her eyes wide.

"Why?"

"Just do it, Mum." She nodded at her phone, charging on the kitchen island.

Marnie got off the couch to pick it up. A text message glowed on the screen.

*I did it. I quit. It'll be in the news soon. I'm not asking you to be part of this mess, but please be there when it's over? That's all I ask. I can't imagine a future without you. – Jason*

Marnie gasped, her ribcage tightening with emotion. Jason

still wanted a future with her. If this was true, she needed nothing else. This was her chance. She wouldn't make the same mistake twice.

Pressing the phone to her chest, Marnie stood in the middle of her kitchen, tears spilling out of her eyes. The kids probably thought she was nuts, but she didn't care. In fact, she was ready to shout it to the world and face the consequences. She was ready to be seen.

"I only saw that pop up on your screen," Tanya said. "I didn't click on it or anything."

"It's fine." Marnie smiled. Squeezing the phone in her hands, she walked over to Tanya. "Can you help me post a video?"

She had to show Jason she wasn't hiding anymore. That she wasn't scared of Kathleen or anyone else. That she was there for him.

Tanya studied her with confusion. "You don't know how to post a video?"

"I do, but how do you make it go viral? How do you make sure journalists will see it, and those who like sharing gossip and other shit like that?"

Tanya's eyes flashed with shock on the word 'shit'. "Mum, are you okay? Your eyes look weird."

Tom smiled. "She's just in love."

Marnie broke into a grin. "You know what? I am! That was Jason. He's quit his job and asked me to wait until this has all blown over. But I don't want to wait. I don't want to be scared anymore. And I remembered that I have this video… How can I make it go public?"

She found the lighthouse video on her phone, the one she'd sworn not to show anyone. And here she was, passing it to her teenager.

Tanya took the phone from her, smiling as she watched. "Wow, mum. This is… wow. If you're sure, I can help you put it on Twitter or something. If you use the right hashtags, it'll go everywhere. Everyone knows Jason Hallett. People will share."

"That's a great idea!" Marnie thought of the advice Jason had given her, asking her daughter to teach her something. "Actually, I might have to add something to it. Like a message? Can you hold the camera and film me?"

Tanya's fingers danced on the phone screen. "Do you mind if I cut off these end frames? You have a bit of a double chin."

"Yes, please!" Marnie ran to the mirror to check her hair. "Do I need makeup?"

"Yes! And do something to your hair," Tanya advised.

After fifteen minutes of styling, Tanya announced Marnie was ready.

Marnie stood in front of the camera, shivering. "I'm so scared I think I might catch on fire."

"I can leave the room, if that helps?" Tom gathered his laptop off the couch and headed upstairs, flashing them a silly grin on the way. "Good luck!"

Tanya waved him off, focused on the screen. “Don’t worry. You look great in this light. Imagine there’s one person watching and not like millions, okay? So you’ll talk normally, like you’d talk to one person.” She looked up from the screen, blushing a little. “I guess you can imagine him?”

Marnie filled her lungs, trying to slow down her pounding heart. “Just push the button, okay?”

# Chapter 41

Jason leaned against his headboard, listening to wood pigeons in his garden. He was home. He hadn't even gone back to his apartment. Luna must have got wind of his resignation through her own channels since she'd messaged him, calling him an idiot and a sinking ship.

So be it. He was happy to sink into his own mattress, in his own home. Jason picked up his laptop to check how the cryptos were doing. Ethereum had rallied last night, and he'd contemplated cashing out. Maybe it was time to get out of the game, for good. If only he had something else to fill his days.

Staring at the green candles climbing higher on the

screen, he wondered about the party trying to keep his resignation on the down low. Jason had his doubts; news like this always got out. If Luna knew about it, rumours were already spreading.

Before he could check the news sites, his phone rang, making his heart leap. Was it Marnie? She hadn't responded to his message yesterday, and each hour that went by added to the sinking feeling in his gut.

Malcolm's name glowed on the screen. Jason answered.

"Great deflection with that Marnie story! Did you plan that together? Boy, you're clever. The press is eating it up."

"What story?" Jason asked, opening the New Zealand Herald home page.

With the first headline, the room started spinning. Marnie. Her doe eyes stared at him from the top of the news site with the heading 'Jason's mystery woman'. She was on front page. Why? Who had blabbed about her? He'd kill that guy.

"I'll call you back," he told Malcolm, ending the call.

Trying to catch his breath, Jason clicked on the link. There was a video. He immediately recognised the freeze frame from the clip they'd filmed in the lighthouse. Had someone stolen Marnie's phone and posted the footage online? Who would do something so diabolical? His finger shaking, he clicked on the 'play' button. Marnie appeared, smiling at the camera. She was in her own house. Someone else held the camera, trying to keep Marnie in frame as she gestured with her hands. She was speaking to him.

"Jason, for the longest time, I was so scared to go public. I was so scared of what people would think of me, that I wasn't good enough for you, that I just wasn't... good enough, full stop. This is me saying I don't care anymore. I want you. I want us. Because you're right. We're good together and I... love you. There." She blushed, turning away for a moment, then facing the camera again.

Jason recognised Tanya's voice yelling, "Go on!" in the background. She must have been holding the camera.

"I'm not hiding anymore. I'm here. I can't wait to see you. And now I'm going to play this video clip. Not because I want the world to see, but because if I don't, nobody will believe me. And I need people to believe and share this, so that it gets to you, and you understand that I'm serious. Okay, here we go."

The video from the lighthouse came on. Jason watched, rapt, hardly breathing. She looked so happy, relaxed, her eyes full of love and adoration. And he... apart from the dark circles under his eyes, he looked happy. He hadn't seen himself like that in a long time. Those happy moments had come and gone, but they'd been real. What he wanted was right there, within his grasp.

Malcolm was right. The press was eating it up. Although full of guesswork and hearsay, the article painted a picture any PR person would have considered a win. They'd found out about his resignation, but the conclusions the reporter had drawn were lovely. Jason Hallett was stepping out of politics to live a 'normal life' with a woman he was in love with. Nothing about his fake degree or drug abuse. He'd mentally prepared for the dirty laundry, but Marnie had distracted everyone with her genuine, heartfelt cuteness. She was so nervous, yet adorable. It was love at first sight, for him and the rest of the country. How would she handle all the attention? The sudden desire to protect her overtook his whole being. He had to get to her.

# Chapter 42

Marnie skipped down the lakeside path, butterflies dancing in her stomach. Jason had asked her to meet him as soon as possible, typing his address to the message. As if she didn't know where he lived. She'd replied with a quick 'On my way' and rushed out the door.

With the path around it finally resurfaced, the playground bustled with the Saturday afternoon crowd. Marnie had left the car at home, too shaky to drive. She'd hoped the walk around the lake would calm her nerves, but her anticipation increased on every step.

A chilly wind blew from the lake, and Marnie pulled her light cardigan over her aching breasts. Part of her missed the comfort of the bulky sweaters she'd used to wear, but she wanted to look her best. Tanya had helped her pick out the outfit– after all the hours she'd spent at the mall, she knew all the shops and quickly found something in Marnie's size. They'd landed on a deep purple wrap dress with a flared hem, showing off more than a hint of cleavage. Marnie hadn't seen her daughter so focused or smiling so much in years.

A couple of passers-by recognised her on the way, smiling and holding up their thumbs. 'It's Marnie!' They'd said, asking if she was on her way to meet Jason. She'd nodded, heartbeat echoing somewhere behind her ears. Her fingers ached slightly, but with the glowing warmth in her chest, other sensations receded to the background. The pain would come and go, but she had something better, something so grand it couldn't be destroyed by anything her body decided to do. Like heavy bleeding, which still hadn't come, although she felt frequent twinges in her abdomen, reminding her of the possibility.

At last, she pushed open the creaky gate and stepped into Jason's garden. Casting a quick glance at the fence where she'd cried not so long ago, she rushed up the steps and onto the deck. The house looked dark and quiet. She knocked on the glass door, but there was no response. Had she misunderstood his message?

Marnie circled the building. His car was parked out front, a mint green Prius she'd seen before. But where was Jason?

"Marnie!"

She turned around and her heart jumped. He stood on the front steps of the house next door. The empty house.

"Over here!" He beckoned her closer. In jeans and a woolly jumper, he was no longer the sleek politician she remembered from their first meeting. He looked relaxed.

In her hurry to get to him, Marnie leapt over the low hedge, landing rather disgracefully on her hands and knees on the lawn. Before she could pick herself up, he was there, hauling her up into a tight embrace. Nothing had ever felt as good. Marnie's whole body shivered as she drew in a lungful of his scent.

"Marnie." His breath warmed the top of her head.

She smiled. "You got my message?"

Jason grabbed her by the shoulders, leaning back to make eye contact. "Oh my God! I nearly fell off the bed. Are you okay? Do you regret it?"

"Not even a little." She shook her head. "I was expecting a horrible fallout, but so far no one's said anything that bad. I mean, the newspaper article was... nice. I haven't been online to read any comments, though. I realised I don't really care what those people think. I care about what you think."

Jason's eyes turned soft. "You were so brave! Let me know if anyone hurts you. I'm always ready to publish an embarrassing video to take the pressure off you. I'll give an interview about my performance issues or something."

Marnie burst out laughing. "You have no performance issues!"

"I don't know. I'm old, expiration date looming… that could be just around the corner." He winked, rubbing his stubbled chin.

"Are you making fun of me?"

"Oh, no! I wouldn't dare." He widened his eyes in mock horror.

Marnie's heart swelled, drumming against her breastbone like it was about to take flight. "I'm sorry about everything. I'm sorry I let Kathleen get to me. I believed my own lies."

"You don't have to worry about Kathleen anymore."

"No?"

"No. She's in hospital. Smoke inhalation. Dementia."

Marnie's heart ached. "Oh, God. I hope she gets some help."

"I'm sure she will, but I really don't care. I just care that you're here now."

She looked around. "Why are we on your neighbour's lawn?"

"This is the address I gave you. It's thirty-nine, not thirty-eight." He nodded at the house. "I wanted to show you something."

He led her up the concrete steps to the tidy, empty deck and unlocked the door.

"You have a key?"

He smiled, his eyes sparkling. He looked better. Almost

healthy. "I just put in an offer on this house. The agent let me borrow the keys."

Marnie froze at the threshold. "What?"

Jason let the door swing open, creaking as it revealed a tiled hallway. His grin had an uncertain edge to it. "We would own it together. I sold the ambergris, so this would be as much yours as it's mine. Fifty-fifty, remember?"

"You ... you're crazy! How much is this? It's by the lake! A million dollars? You can't possibly—"

Jason laughed. "Fine! The ambergris was only thirty grand, but I cashed out my cryptos. It'll still be fifty percent yours. Well, that's my plan anyway, if you..." His gaze searched her face for answers.

Marnie swallowed, heat rising up her neck, making her cheeks blaze. "If I what?"

"If you could imagine sharing it with me? A house? A life? It doesn't have to be this house, but..." His grey eyes, deep and dark like storm clouds, stared straight into her soul.

Marnie could barely speak. "You don't have to buy me a house. I'm yours."

Jason took her hand and escorted her inside. Marnie removed her shoes and walked across marble tiles, onto the soft carpet in the lounge. It had the most intricate fireplace she'd ever seen, with bottle green tiles that looked handmade. It was gorgeous. Forgotten, dusty and unloved, but gorgeous.

Jason approached from behind and caught her in a tight

embrace. His voice was gruff and hot in her ear. "I want to fill this house with life. With you."

Marnie's belly chose that moment to zing with pain that reverberated through her whole body. Was there life inside her? Or impending death? If she lost this possibility, would she be given another one? She could see herself in this house, with Jason, sitting in matching chairs by the fire, reading, eating, talking ... but she had to be honest with him.

Marnie wriggled out of his arms and took a step back, forcing herself to look him in the eye. "Jason, I'm pregnant, but I might be losing the baby." Without warning, tears sprung out of her eyes, and more words flowed through the sobs. "I'm so sorry I didn't tell you. I was ashamed I'd been so careless, that told you I couldn't, when... I honestly never thought it could happen. I was told years ago I was running out of eggs. But it still happened."

Jason stared at her, blinking in confusion. She saw the doubt, worry, then a flicker of excitement sweep across his face like passing clouds. He took her hands into his, his voice thick with emotion. "That's fantastic."

Marnie shook her head. Tears dropped onto the oatmeal carpet and disappeared. "No. The doctor said it might not last. I have to get ready for a... you know."

Jason's fingers lifted her chin until their eyes met. His were full of tears. "Doctors are wrong all the time," he whispered. "And even if it doesn't work out, we have each other. If you want a baby with me, I'm happy to work on that." His lips curved into a lopsided smile.

Marnie smiled through her tears. "I think I do. Maybe. But what if it never happens?"

"Then we still have each other. There are no guarantees in life, even if we were both in our twenties and healthy. So, the only question is, do you want to be with me?"

Marnie nodded, her chest squeezing at the thought. She'd be brave. This time, she wouldn't run away. "I've humiliated myself on national media. I can't go back to my old life."

"Then we better build a new one together." Jason stuck his hand in the pocket of his jeans and fished out a ring, a simple gold band with a tiny stone. "It's nothing flash, sorry. All the money's in the house. But I might get my old teaching job back. Part-time."

Marnie stared at the ring, then at him, forgetting to breathe. After a silence that stretched into the awkward territory, she found her voice. "You don't have to marry me because I got pregnant."

Jason's forehead wrinkled as he studied her. "Do you think I just produced this out of my pocket at will when I heard you were pregnant? I mean, it's not an amazing ring, but I still had to go out and choose it. Or rather, I had my friend Nick do it for me, because I didn't want the story to end up in the news before I spoke to you... which is why it's like this. I told him to pick something simple and boy, did he deliver. We can change it—"

Marnie couldn't help laughing. He was adorable. "It's

not the ring! I don't care what it looks like. I'm not in my twenties, dreaming of a white wedding! I just can't believe you'd want to—"

"Why not? I love you. I wanted to show you I was serious."

"I don't have a great track record with marriage, you know?"

"Me, neither. I've never even tried. People who have a great track record are still married. But I want you, for life, and I've been told this is how it works. By my mum. Repeatedly. She's not just after babies, you know. She'll get a big kick out of seeing me take you down the aisle."

Marnie held her breath as he slid the ring on her finger. To her relief, it was on the loose side. She bent her fingers, cringing at the familiar ache. She'd promised herself, if she ever got another chance, she'd take it. This was it. Was she good enough to be his wife? "You know me, right? You know what you'd be marrying?" Her voice was small, and she hated the echo of her old self that carried through.

"Don't worry about *my* answer. I've made up my mind. What's yours? Do you love me?"

Marnie stared into his eyes, taking in the challenge, the anticipation, the fear. A weight lifted off her shoulders. "Yes! I love you so much!"

Jason closed the distance between them, his mouth meeting hers. Marnie wove her fingers into his hair, desperate for him. She'd felt a fire burning in her belly ever since she'd released that video to the world, boldness that pushed her forward.

Jason's tongue swept into her mouth, claiming her. His arms tightened around her, and he lifted her off the carpet. A pool of tingly warmth gathered between her legs and a moan escaped. The ache for him overtook every other twinge in her body. She needed him, right here, right now.

"When do you need to return the keys?" she asked as they parted to catch their breath.

"No hurry," he replied in a voice so thick that it nearly stuck in his throat. "I love this dress. Can't wait to see you out of it."

His hand slipped in the cleavage, and she gasped. Why had she ever run away from this man and his touch? She must have been mad. He lowered her on the carpet, softly like she was a feather, and undid his belt. The sound of it landing on the floor made her shiver with anticipation.

"You have a condom?" She asked before her mind caught up and she gave him a sheepish smile. "I'm sorry, I mean, I'm already pregnant, so..."

The hunger in his eyes was clouded with concern. "Is it okay? I don't want to risk..."

"No, I don't think it makes any difference. If I start bleeding, then we know. Would that freak you out?"

"I don't faint at the sight of blood or anything." He grinned and unbuttoned her dress down to her waist. He looked at her, his eyes warm and reverent, like admiring a work of art. "I can't believe it. Everything I've dreamed of is right here."

He lowered his lips on her body, kissing his way under her bra, finding her nipples, tugging and teasing until she panted, hot and throbbing for him. He moved onto kissing her neck. "I love you so much. Baby or no baby. I want us, here, forever."

His words travelled through her body like an electric current, burning their message into her spine as she arched her back, ready for him. She'd never been this turned on, this desperate, never felt a desire this intense. She needed him closer, filling all of her. Reaching under the hem of her dress, she peeled off her underwear, tossing it across the empty room. Then he smiled, sliding his hand under the dress, sliding his fingers in. The way he groaned made her chest expand. She wanted to laugh and cry at the same time. His eyes held it all: need, adoration, love.

"I need you," she gasped, unable to stop herself. Her fingers found the button and zip of his jeans.

He didn't need another invitation. Within seconds, he filled her, making all her uncertainty and hollowness disappear, turning her ache into an explosion of pleasure that radiated through her heart. She hardly noticed the moan rising from her throat, until she heard his response, an octave lower but equally out-of-control.

"Oh my God. You're so hot… you have no idea," he growled in her ear, thrusting into her again and again, driving her wild. "I don't know how long I can last." He lifted his face to look at her, his eyes dark and glassy.

She guided him to roll over so she could get on top. That's all she needed. Those dark, grey eyes boring into her soul, worshipping her body, lips apart, his hand roaming down her hips as she straddled him. That's where she found her release, her body pulsing and back arching as waves of pleasure coursed through her.

She wanted to stay here forever, her breasts pressed against his wide chest, their bodies merged. Was this really her, madly in love with a man so sweet and gorgeous? Marnie lifted her head, sneaking a peek of the face she couldn't get enough of. "Are you for real?"

"Are you?" he asked. "Because I'm so relaxed right now, I could fall asleep. It's magic."

She chuckled, no longer bothered by the idea. If it worked, it worked. Why question it? She lowered her head on his chest, listening to his steady heartbeat. "Why don't you? Let's go back to your cottage. I need you to get some sleep so we can do this again. It's probably some weird pregnancy thing, but I'm so turned on it's not funny."

"Oh," he gasped, and hardened a little inside her. "Let's not waste that opportunity."

"After you sleep," she said, reluctantly peeling herself off him.

There was no blood, no sign of anything wrong. She was still scared, but the fear had softer edges, like a dark cloud that might bring a heavy rain, but not a storm. She could cry against his chest. They'd get through it together.

Marnie picked her undies off the floor and smiled. "I think if you do this at an open home, you might have to buy the house."

He chuckled. "Well, I made a good offer. They might take it."

They got dressed and walked over to Jason's house. Marnie followed Jason across the threshold, unable to wipe the grin off her face.

As the door closed behind them, Jason turned around and gathered her in his arms, nuzzling his nose into her hair. "You came back to save me." His voice was gravelly, and Marnie felt hot tears against her scalp as he held her so tightly she could barely breathe. But she knew better than to move. This man needed her, and she'd be here for him for the rest of her days. Yet, she felt like the lucky one. The one who'd been saved and brought back to life. Not expired after all. Like salt.

# 6 months later

The banging on the front door reverberated through the house, making Jason jump off his chair by the fireplace. He'd retreated into the lounge to let the women take over the kitchen. Whatever was going on involved intricate tools he'd never seen before. The air was filled with laughter, music and sugary scents, and the kitchen floor covered in sprinkles that crunched under his feet. Female voices mingled with the clinking of dishes.

"I thought it doesn't start until three?" he asked as he passed the kitchen, catching the sight of Marnie, Tanya, Shasa and Elsie hard at work.

"It doesn't!" Shasa yelled over the kitchen island, which

was packed with cupcakes and general mess. "Is someone at the door?"

Another loud knock echoed through the house. "Can you really not hear that?" Jason laughed, traipsing to the door. Whoever it was, they were determined to get in.

He glanced through the peep hole, an old habit. After the first weeks following his resignation, the press had more or less left him alone. It was probably a neighbour.

Malcolm's rotund figure caught him off guard. What was the big guy doing here? He opened the door, widening his eyes in anticipation. "Malcolm!"

"Jason, my boy, you look good! Married life suits you!" Malcolm invited himself inside, pushing past him into the hallway. "What domestic bliss." He grinned, sniffing the air.

"Um... what are you doing here?"

"You haven't been following the news, have you?"

Jason shrugged. He'd told Malcolm he needed a break from everything. To his own surprise, he'd found it rather easy to stay away from the news sites. If he didn't google his own name, he didn't have to worry about what anyone said about him. The story of his fake degree hadn't broken yet. The party had done their best to keep it out of the news, which he understood. But it didn't matter anymore. If it came out, he'd own it. He'd taken the line out of his CV. The past was past, he couldn't change it. But he could do better from now on.

Marnie met them in the hallway. Her hair had a dusting

of icing sugar, and her cheeks blazed rosy as she shook the neckline of her top to let air in. Jason's gaze dropped from her cleavage to her round belly. He could hardly believe it. The pregnancy that had been given such terrible odds, one that had started so unexpectedly, had prevailed. They were about to fill this house with so much life it would forget all about those years sitting empty, gathering dust.

Malcolm grinned, gathering Marnie into a hug. "Wow, look at you! You're glowing! And you've done something to him," he pointed at Jason, circling his finger at his eye. "I barely recognise him without those dark circles."

She blushed, waving her hand.

"Congratulations on the baby! And the wedding."

"Thank you," she mumbled. "It was a very small affair."

Jason could tell she worried about offending Malcolm; he hadn't been invited. "We eloped," he confirmed. "No press coverage, just a couple of friends."

Malcolm nodded. "Good call." He shifted his weight, dropping the smile. "Look, I wanted to pay a visit since this project was once your baby..." He glanced at Marnie's stomach. "Of sorts. Anyway, they've finally decided to push it through, and I wanted you to hear it from me. I've been chairing the working group since you left. It's not much of a victory, to be honest. The penalties are low. But for as long as the market is stagnant, it'll help a bit."

He pulled a page out of his briefcase and flapped them before Jason's face – a press release with an embargo for the next day. Jason took the copy and skimmed over it. Malcolm was right. The tax rate was pitiful. It wouldn't deter most people from keeping an empty investment property, especially if the prices started rising again.

Malcolm cast him an apologetic look. "If it's any consolation, it's thanks to you that this happened at all. If it weren't for that first meeting—"

Jason held up his hand. "It's fine. It's a step to the right direction."

Malcolm shifted closer, lowering his voice. "You still have support. With a bit of groundwork, you could get through in the next election."

Jason handed the press release back to Malcolm, smiling. "I'll think about it. Legislation isn't the only way to change things."

After returning to teaching teenagers, he'd felt the old passion for discovering talent, for supporting those who struggled. It was hard work, but when you slept at night, anything was possible.

"Very well." Malcolm shrugged, retreating to the door. There was a hint of redness to his cheeks. "For what it's worth, I'm sorry for pushing you in that direction... with the degree. In hindsight, it wasn't the smartest thing to do. I guess I've been in the game for too long. I've become a bit jaded. I didn't foresee what it might do to you, keeping that secret."

Jason stared at him, his mouth hanging open. He'd never

expected to hear these words, and he had no response at the ready.

Marnie stepped in front of him, extending her hand to Malcolm. “Thank you for looking after him in Wellington. I know you’re the one who showed him the ropes, and you even carried out the work after he couldn’t continue. You’re a legend.”

Malcolm’s face melted into a hearty smile, and he gave Marnie another squeeze, before turning to hug Jason. “You found a good woman, Jason. Hold on to her.”

“I will.” Jason coughed, his throat feeling tight. “Thank you for everything.”

Marnie had found the words he should have been able to produce. After posting that video, she’d come more and more out of her shell, and it turned out, had a winning combination of grace and charisma. She could have made a career in politics. Maybe one day, they’d do it together. With Marnie at his side, he could do anything.

Jason smiled at the idea as he opened the door to Malcolm. “I’ll walk you out. I need to show you this insane fountain we got as a wedding gift…”

Marnie returned to the kitchen, chuckling at the thought of Malcolm admiring the shiny, penguin-adorned fountain Lando had installed in the middle of their backyard. Jason had volunteered to put his foot down to keep the ridiculous thing out of their lives, but after seeing Lando's sketch, Marnie had changed her mind. Pregnancy hormones might have messed with her brain, but she found the penguins adorable. She agreed to it on one condition – Lando had to add a lighthouse in the middle. Now, everyone walking on the lakeside track could see the silly thing, and just as Marnie had suspected, the little ones absolutely loved it.

The little ones. Marnie's hands curled around her belly, feeling for kicks. Signs of life. She couldn't get enough of those little movements. The smallest twinges now scared her, and the tiniest kick filled her with happiness. Life was such a rollercoaster. So much had happened since they'd stepped over the threshold of this house.

"Who was it?" Shasa asked, refilling a piping bag with baby blue icing.

Marnie shrugged. "A blast from the past. Just funny timing. I don't think he knew about the baby shower. He'd heard about the wedding, though."

"I can't believe you got married before me!" Shasa said. "Not fair."

"Well, when you forgo the party, it's a lot easier to arrange."

Shasa rolled her eyes. "We should do the same. I'm so over the arrangements." She and Mac had finally set the date, but everything else was still in limbo.

Elsie interjected with a firm smile. "Nonsense! This is your first wedding, Shasa. You should do it right. We will all help."

"Yes, we will!" Marnie assured.

Shasa shook her head, smiling. "With a baby coming? I think you have a full plate."

Marnie lifted a plate of iced cupcakes with golden sprinkles. "I do! But look how pretty!"

She couldn't stop smiling at how different her life was. For years after the divorce, she'd stayed in the family home full of memories. Last year, she'd finally gone out on her own, building that community house with Shasa. She still loved that place, but so did Tom and Tanya. This was Tanya's first taste of freedom, flatting with her big brother instead of living with her mum. And they were only a fifteen-minute walk away, on the other side of the lake.

Initially, Marnie had thought Tom would be the responsible one, watching out for his little sister, but Tanya had surprised her, buying a cookbook and teaching herself one recipe at a time. She was now trying out arthritis-friendly meals and teaching them to Marnie. Maybe the idea of becoming a big sister had nudged her towards independence. Whatever it was, Marnie loved it. She finally knew better than to question the good things in life.

Marnie picked up a wet wipe to clean the dining table. With her swollen fingers, she couldn't do much of the decorating, but she could still hold a wipe. The new drugs helped, and pregnancy had momentarily lessened her other symptoms, replacing them with new, pregnancy-related ones. But she wasn't complaining, at least not very loudly. Her heart was full, life bursting with meaning. She could take the discomfort.

Jason appeared behind her, forcing her to drop the wipe. "You should take a break. Sit down, put your feet up."

"I feel so useless."

"Ha! You're not as useless as me reading a book, occasionally throwing a log in the fire. I was told my job was to stay out of the way."

Marnie chuckled, dropping her head back to relax against his chest. "You're doing an excellent job. What happened to Malcolm? Did he leave?"

"Baby showers aren't really his thing. Plus, we have no VIPs. No networking opportunities. Who's coming, anyway?"

"Sue and Tom. And I'm pretty sure Lando will show up. He has a new girlfriend and I told him to bring her. I've told everyone it's not ladies only. I want an inclusive shower." She smiled. It felt good to voice her own opinions.

"I almost invited Nick but thought better of it. Maybe I'll just take some leftovers to our next tennis game."

After moving back to Hamilton, Jason had reconnected with his old mate. It warmed Marnie's heart to see him take time off work, play tennis, and hang out with old friends.

"Sounds good. There'll be enough leftovers to take to school, too."

"There's never enough for a horde of teenage boys."

"Ha ha. I meant the staff."

Jason guided her to the chair by the fire, forcing her to sit down. "Here. Just a five-minute rest, okay? I don't want you to fall asleep during the party."

"But sleeping is amazing!" she protested, eyelids fluttering as she sank into the soft chair.

"I agree." Jason threw another log in the fire, closed the guard and turned to face her. "I never thought I'd say this, but some things in life are even more amazing than sleep."

Tears sprang into Marnie's eyes. She'd been his sleeping pill, and worried whether there was anything real between them. Now, seeing him healthy, happy, and well rested, looking at her with those deep, grey eyes brimming with love, she knew what they had was real. They'd both found more than a momentary cure, more than either of them had been looking for. She was the luckiest elderly Cinderella in the world.

Ready for book 3 in Love New Zealand series?

## Night and Day

She lives on the other side of the world.
He doesn't go beyond the corner store.

TV producer Mia is torn between her work ambition and passion for songwriting. Facing a huge career choice, she embarks on a round-the-world trip to find answers. Soul searching turns into a nightmare when she's robbed. Stuck in New Zealand with only a guitar on her back, she calls the one local she can think of: an editor she once hired via email.

When Izzy's solitude is crashed by a woman in trouble, he can't resist the call to help. He must show Mia New Zealand is not a crime-infested hellhole. He just has to ignore the instant attraction and creative sparks that fly when they're in the same room, or boat, or... cave. Because she lives on the other side of the planet. It would never work.

**Available wide:** books2read.com/night-and-day-romcom

# About the author

Enni Amanda is a graphic designer moonlighting as a rom-com author, or maybe it's the other way around. In 2006, she and her husband moved from Finland to New Zealand and fell in love with the gorgeous islands and their laid-back people. They spent eight years traveling between the two rather inconveniently located countries, studying filmmaking and running a film festival. Through all the filmmaking, Enni discovered a passion for screenwriting, which eventually led to writing books (a slippery slope). Her heart-warming, funny stories explore real-life issues like identity, found family, and the housing crisis. These days, she lives in the Waikato, close to the rolling hills of the Shire, raising two cute, rambunctious boys while writing away and ignoring housework.

## Books by Enni Amanda

A Tiny House on Wheels (2019)

Coffee on Waihi Beach (2020)

Christmas in July (novella, 2020)

**Love New Zealand series**

Nest or Invest (2021)

Hidden Gem (2021)

Night and Day (2022)

**Love Istanbul series**

My Lucky Star (2023)

My Turkish Fling (TBC)

**Visit enniamanda.com for more information**

# Thank you for reading!

If you enjoyed this book, please tell your friends and leave a review on your favorite retailer website! Referrals and reviews help unknown indie authors like me get discovered.

To find out about my upcoming books, sign up for my newsletter at **enniamanda.com**

www.ingramcontent.com/pod-product-compliance
Lightning Source LLC
Chambersburg PA
CBHW010140030826
48979CB00024B/1065

* 9 7 8 1 9 9 1 1 6 5 0 7 7 *